THE HIDEOUS BOOK OF
HIDDEN HORRORS

EDITED BY

DOUG MURANO

Bad Hand Books
www.badhandbooks.com

For anyone who has ever felt surrounded by monsters.

TABLE OF CONTENTS

FOREWORD

    BY JOSH RUBEN 11

THE PELT

    BY ANNIE NEUGEBAUER 19

WISH WASH

    BY SARAH READ 35

WHEN I CATCH YOU

    BY HAILEY PIPER 55

WHAT'S MISSING

    BY ZOJE STAGE 93

STILL LIFE WITH BONES

    BY ANDY DAVIDSON 105

THE THINGS WE DID, WE DID, WERE ALL FOR REAL

    BY JOHN F. D. TAFF 115

MOONCAKE

    BY LEE MURRAY 139

DUNGEON PUNCHINELLO

    BY JOSH MALERMAN 157

BELOW THE WILDFLOWER HILL

    BY SARA TANTLINGER 187

DON'T OPEN THE CELLAR DOOR

    BY JO KAPLAN..193

ROSES IN THE ATTIC

    BY CYNTHIA PELAYO 211

PERIPHERAL VISION

    BY RICHARD THOMAS 223

HAUNTED INSIDE

    BY GABINO IGLESIAS 243

COUNTING TUNNELS TO BERRY

    BY ALAN BAXTER..257

ANNIE'S HEART IS A HAUNTED HOUSE

    BY TODD KEISLING...279

THEY ARE STILL OUT THERE, YOU JUST CAN'T SEE THEM ANYMORE

    BY JONATHAN LEES 301

ABOUT THE AUTHORS...317

ABOUT THE EDITOR..325

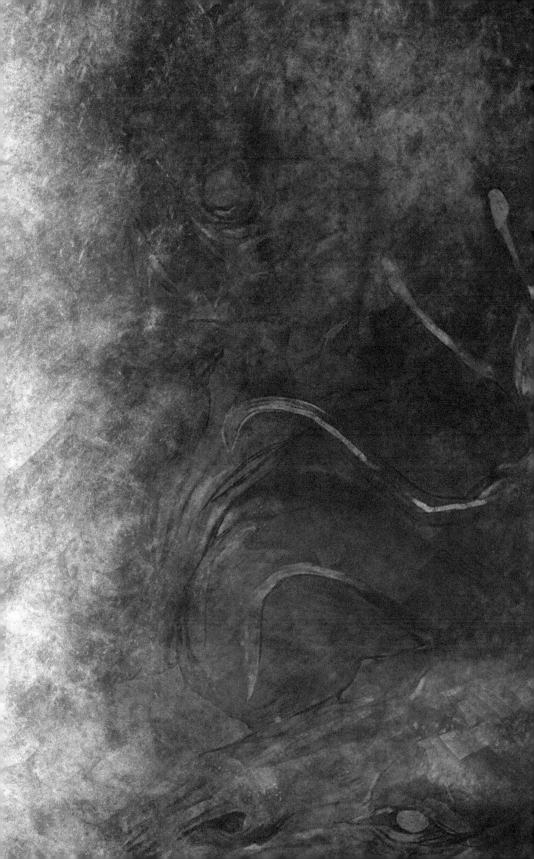

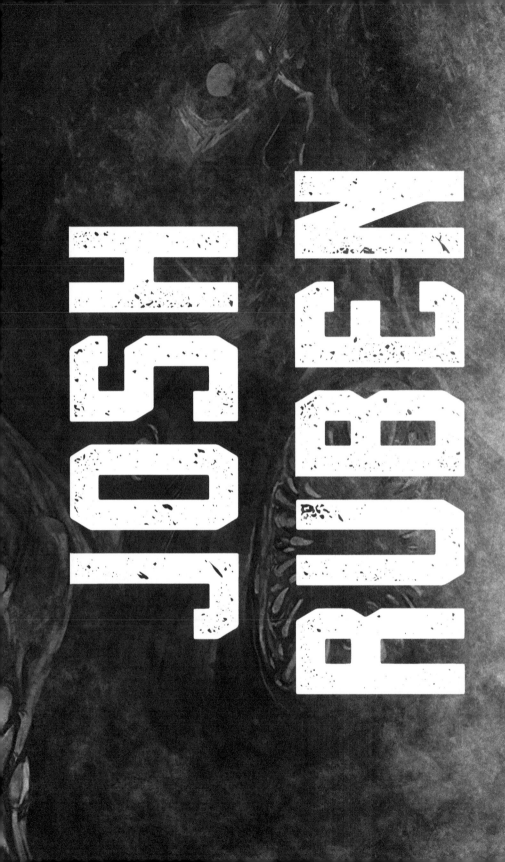

FOREWORD

Well, hello. Welcome. My name is Josh Ruben. I'm a filmmaker, madly in love with this wicked genre that's brought us together, and I'm bloody honored to present *The Hideous Book of Hidden Horrors*.

(Despite what lies ahead for you, readers, I'll be gentle.)

It felt damn good to embark on this "assignment" (and lemme make it clear, reading seventeen stories from this echelon of talented writers felt nothing like homework). I closed this book feeling nothing short of inspired, disturbed, and in numerous instances, *moved* by what you're about to see.

I'm a sucker for chapter reads; a quick *punch-in-the-face* chiller. My obsession, I've found, is devouring stories from various perspectives and historical timelines – how the concept of a *"hidden horror"* is defined by folks unlike me. In some stories, for some writers, these horrors are literal. For others, abstract. I fell for each of them, and, in some cases, found myself comforted by the gore and violence and paranoia; by fish-like creatures and sky-high, paper-thin beings. Life's a horror show, and we absorb scary stories like we do because we don't just like the ride; we *need* the ride. We all gotta touch a little evil sometimes, only to close the book, shut the door, and survive, 'cuz we're creatures who've evolved from threat, and it feels good to survive in this world.

I tend to state the obvious, so, 'scuse my prose, but we're in *a horror boom*. Hell, we're not just in this era of original horror creation, but we've become inadvertent connoisseurs of the stuff. We dually can't get enough of new interpretations in addition to what we've missed along the way. Thank goodness for streaming platforms like Shudder and Screambox and publications like *Fangoria* and destinations like the *Mystic Museum* here in Los Angeles, preserving the "hard media" experience and spotlighting the vintage scaries. There are even independent operations like Terror Vision, releasing soundtracks to flicks like *Chud II, Elves* and *Demon Wind*. Horror fever's here and we welcome the chills.

Why? Well, I'm being regurgitive when I say: we all yearn for the thrill of *"getting through it."* We live in an era where some of us can (and would) pay eighty bucks to get the shit scared out of us at experiential haunted houses just for the thrill of making it out alive. We need to know if monsters exist; we can stare 'em in their reptilian eye and withstand what follows. Movies, books, TV shows, short stories give us the "endorphin buzz" of the aforementioned without getting possessed, mangled, or worse. We love the ride. *We need the ride.*

Though I'm not entirely sure why Doug Murano graciously asked me to write this foreword (there are countless folks in the horror community with a far better grasp of prose than I), but I'd be remiss to not speak to the theme of *"hidden horrors"*, at least, through the lens of my life experience as a (sometimes) scaredy cat.

As freaked as I was by the theoretical thing under my bed, Freddy Krueger manifesting at the end of my childhood home's hallway, I thought a lot about befriending specters, night creatures, and dream demons, asking them why they do what they do: *"Hey, Fred. Why the long claws? What'd I do to deserve this sleepless harassment? I'm seven,"* etc.

I was less terrified by the things of Universal lore and more by what went unseen in waking life. I remember the night my dad took me to see a children's movie called *Hook*. Not much to write home about on the scare-scale, BUT. On the drive home from the theater, there was a wind storm, just like in the beginning of the film. Captain Hook didn't come for me that night through some portal to Neverland, but I sure as shit feared what *might* come for me in the wind, and where that *what* would take me.

When I'd stare out our kitchen window down at the swimming pool in our backyard, the hairs on the back of my neck stood up as I thought about what'd get me while wading in the pool. With water wings snugly affixed to my elbows, I'd imagine a wretched hand pulling me down through the drain at the bottom of the deep end. I'd scare myself ragged thinking about my neighbors, *the Mackenzies*, and what secrets they kept in their boiler room. (Once, I snuck into their house through the basement doggy door and went into their bedroom, only to find a 9mm Luger on the bedside table. I picked it up, examined it, and put it back where I found it. I was six years old). Horrors are hidden everywhere, veiled in a liminal place. Beyond *the known,* is a darker plan waiting to change our lives on a dime. I made it out just fine, that Maryland morning, and I'd bet my life you, too, have made it outta the Bad Plan's way a few times yourself. That's why we devour this stuff.

We don't need to experience terror on a global scale to believe some monstrosity can emerge from hiding at any moment and change everything. We are creatures who've evolved from threat to comfortably being able to read books on the couch, or in the air, or under the safety of the same 'ol quilt, but it's just a matter of *when*. That's what makes life so damn delightfully awfully gleefully, dually, exhilarating and horrid. We all walk the tightrope every day.

If we all had access to plush panic rooms with goose-down sofas, our favorite blankie, our trusted lover and beloved pet, impermeable to exterior threats from the cosmos, *our end comes, eventually*. Your lover may turn on you; your trusty pet may develop a taste for human flesh. Worms might crawl up from beneath the floorboards of your sanctuary... Hell, perhaps *you* might succumb to it, finding yourself a conduit of this "Plan." Then, it's your trusted lover and pet that's only got so much time...

Even if we lived out our days in our safe little bubbles with our comfy surroundings in plush panic rooms with fresh baked chocolate chip cookies and sourdough bread and an endless supply of toilet paper, there's a dead end for us all. *Ain't that some scary shit?* BUT, deep breath! We're here, now, in our special spot with a good something to read. In fact, think of each story ahead as a friendly reminder to stay vigilant of the evils lurking in between the unseen; as a reminder to appreciate air in your lungs and the feeling of planted feet. These fantastic tales are designed to do far more than up your heart rate. Some pose questions of manhood, womanhood, and humanity. Others, the lengths we'll go for a loved one. The circumstances under which we'd kill a fellow human being. The consequences of concavity in our life; the melancholy inkling of a missing piece, and the desire to fill that space at all costs...

Each story begins in a setting familiar to us all, as all hidden horrors do. Behind closed doors, in small towns by railroad tracks. In the graveyard across the quiet country road, on porches and patios, at backyard barbecues, under a crooked copse of pines... Beneath rooftops and plastered walls of suburban Americana are awful perversions and hellish secrets whispered on whiskey breath, about a rotten discovery in the flower bed or a kid's prank gone awfully askew. Existential observations under starry desert skies, under the watch of a supposed greater god. You're bound to read one or more of these hideous horrors and realize you can listen to all the Tom Waits you want when en route to some secret New Mexico mystery, or just out for a hike on the same old trail, after parking your same old van–but you never know what and when that Bad Plan will crop up.

Rest assured, though you'll read about ghosts, immortal entities, zombified abusers and worse, by chapter's end, you'll still be right where you are, with air in your lungs. That's a reminder we all need now more than ever. It's why you're here, reading words from a kid who'd escape reality in the worlds of Elm Street or Midian or Camp Crystal Lake or the schlocky bright blood-red and midnight blue of Hammer lore.

Every day we wake up and gamble. How awful and exciting. That's an inevitability we can't drown out with a heavy metal banger. Sure, it's just a matter of how, why, when for us all. But in the meantime, you've nothing to worry about. You've got a book, your cushy surroundings, your safe routine.

For now.

THE PELT

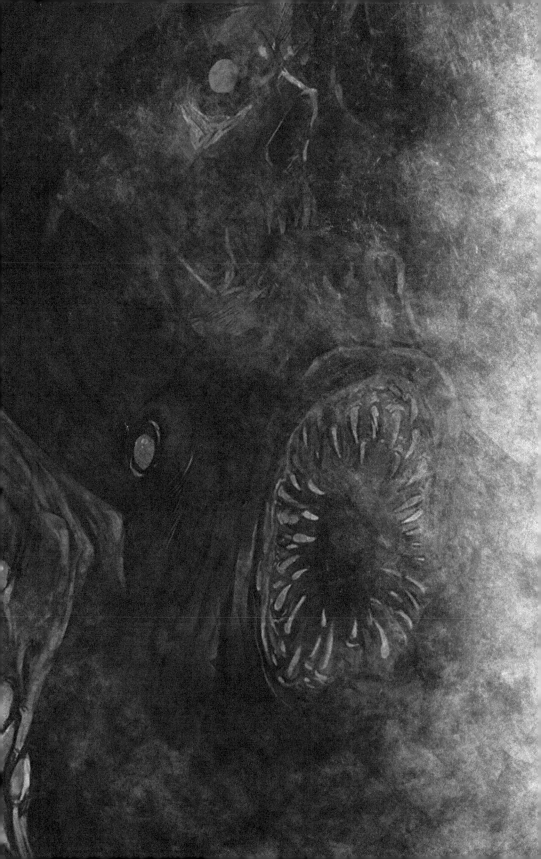

The dogs hadn't barked.

Debra knew because she'd been up all night fuming about the fight she'd had with Mike. Even if she had caught a few minutes of sleep here and there, she still would've woken up. A little whining or whimpering would've done it, but the dogs hadn't made a sniff. As she stared at the strange animal shape on the electric fence, she wondered why.

When she came out to the porch in the predawn dim with a mug of coffee so hot she had to hold it by the handle, she thought at first that a calf had gotten stuck on the fence somehow. It wasn't surprising that the fence's charge was down. They were constantly behind on something, and the fence was as finicky as a housecat in the barn. The place was too big for the two of them. A hundred and thirty acres for two people with no kids was ludicrous, but when the love of your life tells you this is his dream, you make it work. And so they'd bought a gorgeous house on some land in Anderson, Texas—a town so tiny Debra instead called it by the nearest small town's name: Navasota, ten miles southwest and still in the boonies. It was the type of property people called "land," not a ranch or a farm. It was the lifestyle of those wealthy enough to be nostalgic for the good old days they'd never experienced.

They'd stocked it with cattle, a chicken coop, a few horses, two dogs, innumerable cats, and even some fish for the little pond. With two people to maintain everything, and Mike still working as a vet, it was no wonder the fence was dead as often as it was charged.

The dark shape against the fence didn't move. Debra stared, trying to force it into a recognizable form. After a few moments, she began to think it had no head. She went back inside to grab a flashlight, she shucked her flip-flops, got a pair of socks, and shook out her boots before sliding them on.

Grasshoppers vaulted as she walked through the yard. Her flashlight beam caught their movement like the backsides of tiny fleeing ghosts. The most persistent crickets of the night creaked out their cryptograms, and the air was ripe with the scent of sulfuric water but no under-notes of manure. The cattle hadn't been up to the house in a while. So what was this thing without a head?

Her light traced it, and soon she realized it wasn't actually an animal but a pelt draped over the fence. In the off-yellow beam of her flashlight she couldn't determine its color. Something middling, probably, not black or white. It was large but not overwhelmingly so. It was the pelt only. The feet, head, and tail had been detached, so Debra couldn't pose a guess at what type of animal it had come from. Why was it here?

Debra reached out to touch the fur but hesitated. Was it drying, or curing, or whatever the process of preserving an animal hide might need? And if so, why on their property? Neither she nor Mike hunted. Was it a message of some kind? Someone had to have placed it here, which meant that someone had walked over a mile from the road and up to their gated drive. And she'd looked out at this portion of the property last night, from their bedroom's French doors. Wouldn't she have seen it then? Had someone hung it here in the middle of the night?

She saw the random, vivid image of the animal, whatever it might be, still out there running around without its fur or skin. An unidentifiable living hunk of muscle, fat, and veins. A sound escaped her, something she'd intended to be a word that instead came out formless. She felt suddenly worried, threatened, and lifted her light.

The fence looked whole, wooden posts of about chest height holding up the four lengths of wire. She didn't see any obvious downed spots or gaps, but that didn't mean anything. It was obviously off or the pelt would've caught fire. Beyond it the land sloped gently downward to clusters of oaks. As she moved her light to the right, she saw the dark silhouette of the pond, the pale length of the drive, more trees, and then back to the house behind her, sweeping over the concrete portion of the drive and their truck parked there, the garage and its swell into the two stories of the actual house. The kitchen light was on, but the bedroom was dark, quiet. Mike was still asleep.

Should she wake him? He had work today. With their squabble last night, Debra didn't feel like begging any favors. He'd be up soon to feed the horses before driving into town. She left the pelt where it was and went inside.

Debra stared blankly out the window over her kitchen sink. From this spot, she could see the back of their yard from the vegetable garden to the dog runs, but her eyes didn't focus on any of it. She was slumped in contemplation, a swirl of thoughts that didn't connect: the pelt, the fight, the dawn breaking.

"HELLO?"

Debra gasped, whirling. She brought her hand to her chest and forced a laugh, staring at the parrot in his cage next to the dining room table. "Shakes, you scared the crap out of me."

"HELLO?" he squawked again. Then he paused. "Oh, hiiiiiii."

She shook her head hard enough for the tip of her short ponytail to brush her cheek. She walked over to his large wire cage that had its own stand and bent to look at him. Shakespeare danced on his perch, little head bobbing. "I've got the spooks," she told him.

"Okay, talk to you later," he said. "Bye bye now."

"It's that damn pelt."

"What pelt?"

Again, Debra whirled. This time it was Mike standing in the doorway from the living room. He looked all sexy-sleepy with his sweats hanging low on his hips and his dark chest hair ruffled and gleaming. She had a compulsion to say something. Anything. Just enough to dissolve their argument and let them move on today without the cold shoulders. It had been a misunderstanding, that was all. A poor choice of words that had blown out of proportion and left her confused all night.

Instead, she said, "You'll want to put some shoes on."

It looked different in the sunlight. It seemed larger. It hung symmetrically, spine aligned with the top fence wire, and the lowest dip in its belly almost reached the third wire. The ends of the legs, cut before they would become paws or hooves, nearly reached the ground.

"What is it?" Debra asked.

Mike shook his head. He didn't seem surprised or half as concerned as she was.

"Could it be a deer pelt?"

"Nah. The fur's too long."

"A bobcat?"

"Not the right patterning."

"Coyote?"

Mike shook his head. "Too big."

"Mountain lion?"

"Not the right color. Cougars around here are tawny. This is gray, and too patchy."

Debra made a sound of dismay in her throat. He was the vet. Shouldn't he know what animal it came from? "Then what the hell is it? A horse? A buffalo calf? A bear?"

He quirked a smile at the bear option, but still he shook his head. "I don't know what it was."

Neither of them had touched it. The morning sun was already gaining steam, and Mike's lack of emotion over this odd intrusion bothered her. "Well who left it here? Someone had to come onto our property for this."

"It's probably a gift. I'll ask around today at work. Maybe one of my clients thought it would be nice."

Debra restrained a scoff. *Hey, I brought you part of this dead animal,* didn't seem like much of a gift to her. The anonymity of it was baffling. Why wouldn't they leave a note? Why not tell them what it was?

From the corner of her eye, she saw Mike smirk. An unexpected rush of anger spiked through her. "Did you do this? Is this some kind of a joke?" she accused.

"No."

"Really?"

"Yes."

Was he lying? The thought bothered her, especially on the tail of last night's fight. He almost seemed like a stranger, standing there in his work clothes, simpering in the sunlight. She had a strong and sudden urge to slap him into a reaction she could recognize, but the thought shocked her into guilt.

Sugar meowed at them from the corner of the house, where she rubbed against the brick. Debra shook her head, walking toward her. She'd already fed the cats this morning.

Over her shoulder, she said, "I would appreciate if you moved that thing before you leave. And we need to get the fence back up and running soon."

Her only answer was Sugar's erratic little mewings—something wrong that couldn't be told.

In this part of Texas, the sun sank tiredly, slipping below the high points of their land as if relieved. Dusk found Debra pacing the kitchen, circling the large center island countless times, talking to Shakes. By the time Mike got home she had all but convinced herself the pelt came from a wild hog. They were quite the nuisance and could be shot any time as vermin.

Mike walked in from the garage through the short utility hallway that led to both the walk-in pantry and the powder room, and hung his Stetson on the hook in the kitchen. There was a crease around his sweaty forehead from the hat band.

"It's hot as balls out there," he said, grinning.

Half of Debra's anxiety slipped away. He certainly had a way with words. He used "what the crap" so much it had been the parrot's first phrase. Mike had said, "He's a regular Shakespeare, ain't he?" and from then on that had been his name.

Debra felt a return grin tugging at her lips, but she was still mad. She bit her cheek to hold it back and turned toward the island. "Did you find out who left the pelt?"

"Well hello to you, too."

"Wild hog!" Shakespeare screeched. "Wild hog! Itza wild hog!"

Debra turned in time to see Mike raise an eyebrow. Had she said it aloud so often today?

"Could it be?" she asked, voice softened.

"Wildhog!"

Mike shook his head, wiping his eyebrows with the backs of his hands. "It's about the right size for some of the big bastards, but the legs're too long to be a hog."

Debra's stomach clenched. "God, Mike. What is it? Did you find out who put it there?" Why wasn't he as worried about this as she was?

"Wild!"

"If someone had left it as a gift early in the morning, they probably would of called during the day to let me know. I didn't hear from anyone. I asked around a bit, but I just can't figure out what kind of critter it was."

Debra pulled her ponytail down then put it back up.

Shakes began to do the bouncing lurch he sometimes did when he got worked up. His voice could be ear-splittingly loud in their tiled kitchen and dining room. "Wild-wild! Wild-wild!"

"All I can think," Mike continued, "is that it's something not from around here. Maybe a kind of deer or gazelle or something from a colder climate with the longer fur. Or a small moose. A feral dog? I don't know. But whatever it is, it's something boring, not exotic, or we'd recognize the coat pattern. It's probably some sort of herbivore."

"Wwwwwwwwwi-uld!"

"But why was it left on our fence?"

"WwwwwwwI-ULD!"

"I don't know," he said. "But it seems well cured, no gashes or anything. Whoever skinned it must have known what they were doing. Anyway, I'm gonna go hop in the shower."

Debra watched Shakes churn and bob on his perch, pausing occasionally to preen. What would he look like without his skin and feathers? She supposed that underneath, everything pretty much looked like so much meat.

"Wwwwwwww-aiy-o! Why-o!"

Mike slept. How? How could he sleep amidst this? Didn't he have dozens of questions swarming his head like she did? Didn't he care at all?

It had been the same last night. Debra had stayed up in a roil of emotions and he had snored peacefully. He didn't used to snore.

The fight was stupid. She knew this, but it didn't change the reality of her feelings. Her casual, "Ready to watch the show?"—so ordinary, so habitual— had been met instead with, "I don't even *like* that show."

Debra had laughed. His response was so ridiculous that laughter was her only option. Of course he liked it. They'd been watching it almost every week for three years now.

"Come on," she urged. "I know you're tired, but it's only an hour. Forty-five minutes if we fast-forward through the commercials."

"No, I'm serious."

Her smile died, because she could see on his face that he was telling the truth. "What do you mean?"

He'd gone on a tirade about the show and all its flaws.

She was stunned by how badly it hurt her. It wasn't about the show. Debra didn't care about TV, not really. It was the dishonesty. How could he have misled her for so many years? What was the point of sitting on the couch with her week after week to laugh and discuss it if he secretly thought it was crap? Why not just suggest a new show? And if he had some good reason for the deceit, why tell her the truth now?

Perhaps most startlingly, how could she not have known?

The sound of cattle mooing in the distance brought her back to the present. Their calls were low and urgent. Was there something wrong with the cows?

Debra climbed out of bed and padded to the French doors. The cattle weren't near enough to the house to see from here, but nothing appeared to be wrong nearby. The fence where the pelt had hung was empty. She wondered where Mike had put it. What animal had it come from? Were there more of them out there, lurking in the darkness, stalking over their land? Was some mysterious beast upsetting the cattle?

Or was it whoever had brought the pelt? Some*one* on their property?

Debra turned away from the glass to see Mike on his side facing her, still snoring. In the shadows, she couldn't make out his features, the familiar jawline or the dark arches of his brows. He could be anyone, lying there. He could be a complete stranger who vaguely resembled her husband in shape and form.

Could Mike have left the pelt? She'd never known him to hunt or skin an animal, but then again, for three years, she hadn't known he was humoring her by doing something he detested. Maybe Mike didn't go to work some days. Maybe he went out and hunted, field dressing animals before spreading and curing their hides to keep the fur as some sort of trophy. Were his veterinary skills enough to account for that?

How hard was it?

Without looking again at Mike's silhouette, Debra left to turn on the computer in the back office. From there his snoring blurred with the distant lowing until both were indecipherable. She spent the entire night researching how to make a pelt. The whole time she pictured Mike's strong hands doing these things, but she didn't know why.

"Gooooood morning!" Shakespeare sang.

Deborah stood from behind the lower cabinets to see Mike walk into the kitchen, already dressed for work.

"Morning, buddy," he said to the bird. Shakes bobbed his head. Mike turned to her. "You making something?" He eyed the knife drawer which sat on top of the counter.

"Just time for them to be sharpened and oiled."

He moved toward his hat on the hook, so she stopped him with a question.

"Mike, have you ever been hunting?"

He cocked his head at her. "You know I don't hunt."

"But even once? Maybe as a kid?"

He shook his head. "Only quail."

"Quail!" Shakes belted. Debra and Mike both jumped. "Quail!"

"Where'd you put the pelt?"

He squinted at her. "I hung it in the stable."

The answer seemed canned, meaningless, anonymous. It was like he wasn't even Mike at all, just some stranger borrowing his skin.

Shakespeare started to rock back and forth.

"I made you some coffee," Debra said on a whim. She pushed her travel mug, which she had taken earlier to check on the cattle, toward him. All of them were fine.

Mike picked up the mug. "Thanks."

"No problem," Shakes chirped. "Gotta go into town."

"I put some sugar in it this time," she said. "For a nice little change."

Mike paused. He always drank his coffee black. "Oh." How odd, the small disruptions. How unsettling. How would this stranger reply? "Well thanks, I guess."

Debra nodded. It wasn't Mike. She was sure of it.

He took the hat and left.

Shakespeare was silent.

The pelt hung from a nail in the stable the way a robe hangs from a hook on the back of a door. Debra examined it, studying it for clues, but it gave up nothing. It smelled similar to leather, but mustier and sharp enough to taste in the air.

Mysterious, maddening, ineffable. But not meaningless.

Try as she may, she couldn't picture the animal that fit this pelt, exotic or not. The fur was thick, a mixture of soft undercoat and coarse longer hair. The hide on the inside was indeed smooth and free of nicks. She ran one finger along the edge, where the blade had separated the flesh.

The horses whinnied and hooved the ground. Debra fed them, but they did not quiet.

She studied the pelt from every angle.

When he finally woke up, his eyes opened very wide. They roved to look at the restraints holding him to the bed, then stopped on her. "What is this?" he asked. "Did you... slip me something?"

"Slip me something?" she repeated. The shape of the words felt strange in her mouth. "I slipped you something."

He pulled at his arms and legs, but he wouldn't be able to get loose. She'd tied him securely. "Why?"

She sat beside him, on the edge of the bed. He wore only the sweats he went to sleep in. The dark patch of fur on his chest shone dully from the moonlight streaming in the French doors. She wanted to run her fingers through it, but didn't.

"Say something Mike would say," she commanded.

"Say some—huh? Debra, what? I am Mike! What the hell is going on?"

That wasn't what Mike would have said. Mike would have said *what the crap* or *come on baby*. This was someone else. A stranger. Who?

Was it the person who'd left the pelt? Had they taken Mike's skin? Was Mike out there, hideless, wandering around?

And what in God's name had the pelt come from?

The stranger in Mike's skin continued to thrash. "Look, Debra. I know you're mad, but this isn't funny. I don't know what you're trying to prove here, but this is too far."

"This is too far," she echoed. The words didn't even mean anything. There was nothing behind them.

She pulled out the gloves and the butcher knife. It wasn't quite the right kind, but it would have to do.

The person on the bed started to cry.

When she began her process of field dressing, starting with a careful incision near the pelvis, the crying turned to screams. Blathering. Phrases, words, incoherent sentences. Complete gibberish.

Finally, when she got to the ribcage and split it open like she'd learned, the noises stopped and she was able to work in peace.

It was her first time to skin anything, but she thought she did pretty well. She didn't have to worry overmuch about tainting the muscle, since she wasn't going to eat it, nor tearing the hide, since she didn't care to keep it. All she wanted was to see inside—to see what had been wearing her husband's skin.

When she was through, the pelt, organs, head, and extremities sat in a steaming pile on the tarp on the floor. The room smelled raw and metallic. She stood, removing her gloves, and looked down at what remained on the bed.

It was acutely indistinct. Meaty. Still. Not her Mike. She'd been right.

She didn't recognize what was underneath at all.

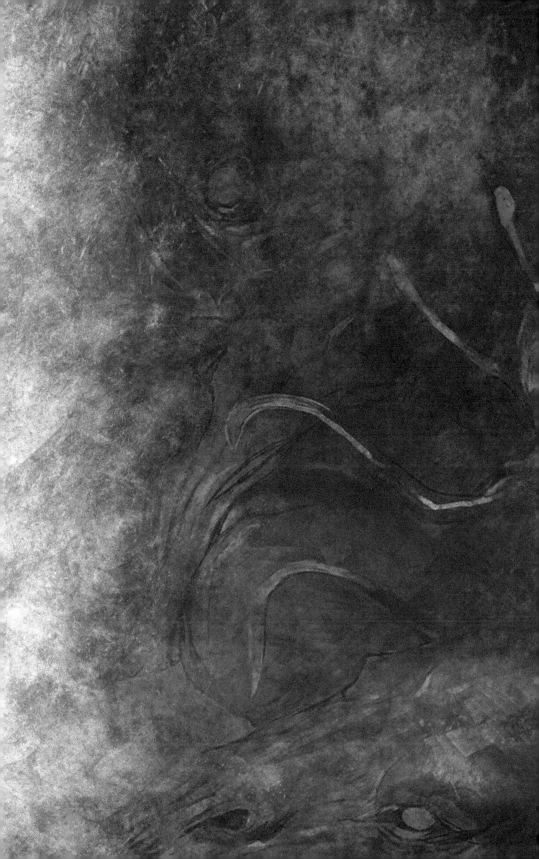

WISH WASH

I could hear my mom's voice inside my head, "You should get better friends," as we walked away from Joey's dad's truck into the woods, Joey swinging his dad's axe, me keeping far enough back.

Thing is, we were never friends, me and Joey. But I thought we could be, if I was cool enough. If I could prove it. Which is how I ended up in the woods alone at night with Joey, his father's stolen axe catching the beam from my flashlight, his father's stolen car disappearing behind the trees.

"I can't even see this trail you're talking about," Joey said.

"It's a deer path. I followed it out here last summer when I got that buck." It was my only claim to fame, that buck. The only thing that got Joey to notice me in any way that wasn't knocking me over or throwing me down by my neck: the twelve-point buck I scored on the first day of break. I'd bagged it right here in these woods. I don't know why I told Joey I'd been poaching, or where I'd found it. I don't know why I told him I only got it because it got its rack all tangled up in the most twisted tree I ever saw. All I know is that while I was talking, Joey was listening, so I didn't stop.

And now it's the first day of summer break again. The sun is set behind the tops of the trees. And Joey's dad's all passed out on his sagging sofa, and unlikely to miss his truck for a few hours. Or his axe. He'd have missed his gun, though, Joey said, even in his sleep, and he didn't dare pick it off his sleeping pa. And for that I've been whispering prayers of thanks to the trees for the past thirty minutes. But as Joey put it, if a buck's all caught up in a tree, a gun's just cheating anyway. My face heated at that. I didn't see how an axe was any more noble, if the animal is trapped. But it made sense to Joey, and I kept my mouth shut. Joey's never been too smart. What he lacked in brains he made up for in force of will.

"Get ahead of me. I'll follow you," he said.

I pushed past him, my feet sinking into undergrowth along the side of the trail. I could feel the axe behind me as much as I could feel Joey. It quickened my pace, and before long, we had stepped into the circle of low growth that surrounded the twisted tree. No saplings had survived in its shadow, though its trunk was not any larger than a man's chest. Its writhing path through the air gave it wide berth.

I swept the flashlight beam over the ground till I found the spot. A few large bones still lay scattered where I had butchered the deer. I couldn't carry much, and I didn't want to get caught, so I'd just taken the rack and choice cuts, left the rest for nature. And they'd taken their chance on most of it. Only the pieces too heavy to drag or too small to bother with remained.

Joey grabbed the light from my hand and swung the beam over the rest of the tree, searching for another prize deer. My heart leapt when we spotted one, its tawny coat hanging slack from its frame, antlers caught up in the tree just as the other had been. This one was already dead, though. And had been a while.

The axe flashed in the beam, and just as I gasped to shout *no*, the forest silence was cut through with a tearing sound and my mouth filled with the taste of rotten game. I bent and heaved all over my own shoes. Between the sounds of my own heaves, I heard Joey coughing, too, and the axe still swinging.

I staggered back from the puddle I'd made and sat hard on the ground. Finally, my gut stopped clenching, and the axe stopped swinging, and the beam of light hit my face like a gunshot. I lifted a hand to block the glow, and saw Joey there, holding his prize up to show me—the rack chopped messily from the dead deer.

"Who else have you told about this old tree?" He set the rack on the ground between us.

I shrugged. I told everyone about the deer, everyone. But I'd said I got it in season. I couldn't remember who else I'd told about the tree, the dirty part of the story, that I'd slaughtered a trapped animal.

"So it's our little secret, yeah?"

I shrugged again, too tired and humiliated to want to feel cool anymore, even to Joey Spencer.

He huffed. "You know what they say about keeping a secret? Two can keep a secret if one of them is dead." He swung the axe at me, playfully. Something wet hit my face.

My stomach cramped again and I folded down over my knees.

Joey laughed and turned back to the tree. "Damn tree keeps killing our deer. Twisted devil thing." He swung the axe again, this time with purpose and a broad stance, and all the power of his ninth-grade varsity swing, and he hit the tree with a thwack like he was bringing all the runners home.

The whole tree shuddered, showering us in dry bark shaken from its dead limbs and twigs dried to tinder.

I pushed myself into a crabwalk and scrambled back from the clearing as the axe hit again and again, and Joey circled the tree taking notches out of its narrow trunk.

Finally he stood back, panting. The tree groaned. It seemed to moan and stretch like a long sleeper, before falling away, taking the nearby pines with it.

Joey picked up the flashlight and shined it over the ruin of the tree. The light disappeared into its hollow center, as if it were the source of all the forest's shadows.

"Whoa." Joey leaned in over the hollow. Then jumped back, just as a hand as twisted as the tree had been, as pale as the scattered deer bones, appeared over the ragged edge of wood.

An old man's face, lined and bearded, followed the hand, then the rest of him as he tumbled out of the tree and onto the forest floor.

The old man's body lay in a shaking heap, a sound as dry as old twigs and hollow as old bones barking from the tangle of limbs and long hair. "You've freed me." The pile of man rearranged itself, untangled its limbs like a fallen marionette pulled upright. His skin was sallow and flaky as birch bark, his beard hanging like Spanish moss.

Joey dropped the axe.

The old man turned to the sound with a crackle of stiff joints. His eyes glittered like black marble through the haze of dust surrounding him. "To repay your kind deed, I offer you abundance." He held his twisted hands open, one toward each of us.

My eyes traced his empty palm, then followed the shaggy sinew of his arm back toward those black eyes.

"A what?" Joey asked.

The old man tilted his head and a clump of hair fell from his skull to the forest floor.

I stood slowly, legs like cold water, and the old man turned to me.

"I can see that you are two gentlemen of distinction. So tell me how it is that two fine benefactors such as yourselves have come to free me from my prison?" The old man reached up to the shattered edge of the tree stump and broke off a handful of splinters, rubbing them between his fingers before bringing them to a grey tongue that darted out of his beard.

"Well, Casey here said he caught himself a big buck at this tree, so we came to see if we could get any more. We figured this tree caught and killed enough deer, and didn't want anyone else learning what an easy pick it was. So I cut it down."

I could still taste the rotten game in my throat, the vomit in the back of my nose. The fallen tree had pummeled the remains of the deer, branches scattering the rot.

The old man's nose twitched above his beard and he grinned. "My little revenge on Artemis, yes," he said. "I remember that buck. You left it here." He looked straight at me, his black eyes flashing the yellow of a wasp's coat.

"It was more than I could carry," I said, looking away from his gaze, staring at my pile of sick.

"And yet you came back?" The old man's eyes squeezed shut like knots on a tree. He ran his fingers through his beard and pulled a twig free, kept pulling till the twig was as long as a walking stick. He leaned on it. "What a fool am I to be freed by fools."

"Excuse me?" Joey's brow twisted and he took a step toward the man. I knew that step. Knew the way he could step into a swing that would probably kill the old man.

"So we're not in trouble?" I asked.

"Not with me," the man said. "And the tree is mine and the land is mine."

"I thought this was county land," Joey said.

"Oh I've been here far longer than the county. Though I've been sleeping so long I suppose I've been forgotten. I think they'll find if they examine the records that this patch of land never quite makes it into the books." He traced a shape in the dirt that it was too dark to see, dragging his stick across the forest floor.

"You were sleeping in the tree?" Joey leaned over the hollow stump and scooped out a fist of rotted wood dust and dry beetles. "That does not look comfortable."

The old man smiled, his mouth a dark hollow like the tree's. "My dear boy, it was not. And that is why you shall both have a reward."

Joey grinned in a way I hadn't seen him do since my older sister Emily's skirt went up in the wind at recess. A manic lust that most reasonable folk took as a warning. The old man didn't heed it. "What kind of a reward?"

"A wish," the man said. "It's the custom. One for each of you."

My shoulders had relaxed some, now that the man seemed happy, and Joey had dropped his axe. I began to hold onto the prospect that we might make it out of the woods after all.

"A wish? For what?" Joey looked to me as if I might have an answer.

"For whatever you want," said the man.

"So we just tell you, and you get it for us?"

"In a manner of speaking, yes." The man tapped his walking stick into the ground as if planting it.

Joey frowned in thought. "You go first, Casey. I have to think."

"I don't know," I said. Five minutes ago, I'd have wished to be back at home, in bed. But if he meant it... If he really would give us anything we wanted... "What do people usually wish for?"

The old man lifted his stick free and drove it into the ground again impatiently. "Gold, usually. Health, long life. Revenge."

Joey looked at me and grinned. My blood went cold. "I know!" he said, nearly catching his foot on the axe blade as he stepped toward me. "I wish for Casey's wish! There. Now I've got two wishes. And he's got none."

The old man and I looked at each other in silence, me in confusion, him with a glint of trouble in his black wasp eyes.

The man leaned on his stick again and turned his gaze on Joey, eyes flashing yellow. "Well, you've just used your wish. So that's still just one."

Joey's face fell, but recovered when he realized he'd at least deprived me of mine. "But none for this loser. It was me who cut your evil old tree down, anyway."

Heat rose in my throat again, not bile but rage. I'd told him my secrets. Led him to the tree. For what? To have him beat me again. Not with his fists, this time, but with his stupid mouth.

The man laughed, a sound like a rain of pine needles. "I'm afraid it's more complicated than that. Casey will still make his wish. But. The product of it will go to Joey."

"What does that even mean?" I asked. I was tired of this strange old man, tired of Joey's meanness, tired of these woods and all the dead deer. Anxious that he had somehow plucked our names out of our own mouths.

"If you wish for riches, Casey, Joey will be made rich."

Joey hooted in triumph, stirring birds from their forest perches.

"*However...*" The man pulled his stick free of the ground and moved toward me, wading through my puddle of sick with his bare, gnarled feet as if it were nothing, till he stopped inches from my face.

He smelled of sawdust and bird feathers, of mildew and lichen, of sugar sap and beetle pepper. His eyes narrowed at my face. His twisted hand rose and traced a dry finger over the crease between my eyebrows, the worry line that Emily said made me look old.

"Be careful, Joey," the old man said. "This child wishes for death. He wishes it every night. Sometimes because of you."

My heart rate stuttered. How could he know?

"And should he wish for death, really wish it, it will fall on you, Joey."

Joey dropped the flashlight and its beam landed right in my eyes.

"How will you know?" My voice was barely more than breath, but the forest had gone silent. "When I wish it, how will you know that it's the time I really mean it?" My eyes burned, maybe from the light, maybe from the secret laid bare, hanging in the rot-seasoned air between me and the old man.

The man reached for my hand, lifted it, and ran his thumb over the rough texture that scoured the back of it. He held it to the beam of light. The scar there shined, its collagen stretched thickly over my veins. Joey had done that. Pushed me off my scooter in the fifth grade, laughed as I slid down the street, abrading away in body and spirit. It had taken weeks to grow the skin back. My spirit stayed raw.

My hand burned again like it did that day. The scar stretched and twisted, bending itself into a vining branch with a knot like a heart at its center. A yelp of pain escaped my lips.

"Press here," the man said, "and make your wish. And I'll know that you mean it."

"How do I reach you? To tell you what I wish?"

"Press here," the man squeezed harder, his thumb shifting the narrow bones of my hand. "And you'll call me. When the mark is gone, you'll know your wish was delivered. Doesn't matter where I am. Doesn't matter where he is." He tilted his shaggy head toward Joey.

He let go, then, and turned to Joey. "It's a pity you've made him so miserable. But maybe it's not too late."

Joey's face had grown so pale that it shone with its own light, visible even over the beam that nearly blinded me. "That's not fair, little man." The edge of threat in his voice was new, even to me.

"I don't make up the rules, son. I must follow them myself." The man began walking away from us, into the shadow of the forest.

Joey turned to me, then. "Come on, Casey, wish for infinity gold and I'll give you half. Or make me king and you can be, like, co-king, or whatever."

"You tried to steal my wish. I should wish for, I don't know, like a hundred bees or something."

Joey flinched.

The old man laughed, this time like a raging crow.

"How long do I have to decide?" I asked the pale expanse of his disappearing back.

"As long as you like," he called back. "I can wait longer than you." He laughed again, the sound fading as the shadows of the forest closed over him.

Joey's face had gone from white to red. He bent and picked up the axe at his feet, choking his grip up close to the gore-flecked head.

I clamped my hand down over my scar.

Joey lowered the axe.

The old man's voice sounded from the dark thickness of trees. "I almost wish I could stay and watch this. Act wisely, fools."

"Where are you going?" I called after him. I didn't want to be alone in the forest with Joey, magic mark or no. I wasn't even sure I believed in it. And it was only a matter of time before Joey realized we'd had no proof that the wishes even worked. That we'd just met a mad old man hiding in a hollow tree and took him at his word.

"Home!" the old man called back. "My wife will be wondering where I've been these past four hundred years."

Joey looked from the darkness of the forest to the even steeper dark of the hollow in the tree. "Four hundred? How did you even get in there?"

"A much cleverer man than you wished me there. Good day, my lads. And thank you again for your service, even if it wasn't kindly meant."

Sound returned to the forest. Bird call and cricket, wind and straining boughs. I hadn't noticed their absence, and yet they all returned like a symphony at full strength.

And I was alone with Joey.

I squeezed my hand over my mark, not daring to let go, hoping that if I believed it long enough, or acted like I did, that he would, too.

I could see him weigh it, his face working. He calculated his odds and came up empty.

"You walk ahead of me. Where I can see you. Let's head back home," I said.

And so we marched out of the woods, away from the hollow tree—the prisoner in front, swinging an axe, and me—hands clasped almost like I was praying.

My mom scrubbed my hand, convinced the mark was dirt, though I told her over again that it was a scab on top of a scar, and that's why I hadn't finished my work in the barn yet. That she should go easy on me.

"Was it that boy again? Joey Spencer?" She shook her head, not waiting for an answer. "You need better friends."

She fell for my excuse, though she wouldn't have, normally. This time there was no lecture on pulling my weight, no implication that I was not part of the family unless I did my part for the family. I started to think maybe the mark was lucky.

Or not. Maybe it was just a scab on a scar, scratched raw by a hermit in the woods. My finger hovered over the knot on the twisted shape.

Do I mean it this time? Really?

I was forgiven for my undone chores. Joey had no such luck. Our adventure had made us late, and the missing truck was noted. He had a shiner to show for it, when he showed up at our farm the next day. I caught him staring at me through a gap in the barn clapboards.

"What are you staring at?" I asked as I hoisted a pitchfork, piling moldy hay into a cart.

Joey slipped around the side of the barn and came in through the wide door. He sat on the edge of the wagon and picked at the hay.

"Guess I can't be mad at you, can I?" he said.

I paused, pitchfork mid-swing. The hair on my neck bristled like a hay bale.

"Was your own doing," I said. "You should be apologizing. Was going to wish for a motorcycle. Would have let you have a go on it."

Joey stood. "Well, go on then, wish it. It's yours, we both know it. You take it and it'll be done. I won't even have a go—won't even touch it, swear. Let's get this over with and I'll leave you alone forever."

I leaned against the pitchfork and mopped my brow with a dusty glove. I peeled both gloves off. I didn't feel comfortable around him without access to the mark. His offer was tempting. But I didn't want to just be left alone. I wanted to be liked. But not by Joey, not anymore. "Figured you'd settle on that eventually."

"Yeah." Joey smiled and held out his hand for a handshake.

"Reckon I'm better off saving it, though."

Joey's smile melted. His fingers curled into his palms. "What do you mean to do, Casey?"

"It's like I've got a second life now, see. Like a cat, but two instead of nine. Seems wise to save it till I need it."

Joey sank back down to sitting. "But then I'd—" He couldn't even say it.

"Yep. It's what you get for stealing anyway, right? You stole my wish."

Joey sat and picked at the hay quietly while I continued to work. Then he jumped from the cart and grabbed the pitchfork from my hands.

I leapt back and grabbed at my mark.

"No! No," he said. "Not like that. Let me do this."

I stared at him, puzzled.

"See, you could get hurt. Way I figure, I can't let that happen. Ever. So. You're stuck with me. Forever. All day, every day, I'll be by your side, protecting you. To protect me. 'Least till you decide you'd rather have that motorcycle."

I don't know if dad ever noticed it wasn't me doing the chores. I sat and watched Joey work, sweat on his brow and blisters on his hands. Bruises on his arms when he didn't have enough time left to do his own work after.

I'd have pitied him. Almost did. But every now and then, if I dozed, I'd wake to catch him watching me—knuckles white around the pitchfork handle, weighing his options. Gauging the distance.

I wanted distance from him, but didn't want him out of my sight. And he neared fits every time he left me, spinning his head around, glancing back, eyes darting from my hands to my eyes.

I wondered how long we could both keep this up. Everything felt stretched tight, ready to snap.

Joey, who had been failing, studied like a fiend to stay in my class. He trained like a thing possessed to join my field team.

Everyone thought we were like brothers. Some even thought we were lovers.

He was in my life and in my face, always, and I hated him. Even when he took the bully's fist to the gut for me, I hated him. Even when he climbed the dead tree to get my model plane back, waded into the swift creek to get my shoe, picked up an angry snake and threw it near across the field, I hated him.

But not as much as he hated me.

We finished school hip-to-hip, him following too close on my heels across the stage to claim our achievement.

And then there would be six hours of every day away from him. Where he'd work his farm and I'd work mine, if I could remember how. If I could even still lift a bale. I'd wasted away under the years of him watching, lifting, doing. I'd grown thin—all sharp angles, like the rack of a prize buck.

"You got to be careful though, Case. You got to watch yourself when I can't." He spoke like he was choking.

I shrugged. "What will be, will be."

I suppose I wanted him worried. Didn't want him to forget his situation. Or why he was in it. His eyes were lit with anxiety. "Don't you want a castle? An island? A Page Two girl on your arm or on your... Don't you want out of here? Out of this town?"

I spun on him, face red, my neck pulsing. "I want you out of here."

He shook his head. "I can't. I have to watch you."

I placed my hand over my mark and he blanched, dropped to his knees, the corded muscles in his arms quaking.

"Get out of town, Joey. Get far away. The next time I see your face, I'll set coyotes to chew it off."

He stared at me, his mouth moving, knees grinding the dirt.

"Go!"

He jumped up and ran across the field toward the trees, head whipping back around, watching me, like always.

I should have known he wouldn't really go. That he would know every way into my house. Know the sound of every floorboard, which ones were silent, and which ones groaned like a felled tree.

It wasn't my life he wanted, not really. He just wanted his own. He wanted my wish. Always had. He had held it in his sights all these years.

He still had the axe, too.

The first blow woke me just in time to see the second coming.

I raised my hands to shield my face, but it wasn't my face he wanted.

My vision pooled black, dark as the forest at night, dark as the center of a tree, a prison where time means nothing.

I woke in starched light, arms bandaged to the elbows.

My sister, Emily, sat at my bedside. Her nails were chewed raw with worry. She stood when she saw me stir.

"Casey. Can you hear me?"

I nodded. My ears were fine. But I stared at the bandages at my wrists, white gauze showing a hint of shadow below, of darkness soaking through.

Emily sniffed, her eyes going as red as her fingertips. "It was that creep, Joey Spencer, wasn't it?"

I nodded, not trusting my voice.

"I'll be right back," she said, patting my bandages.

It didn't hurt. I felt nothing, except a nagging wish, the one I'd always had. An impotent wish. There was no way, now, to tie a knot, pull a trigger.

Emily stepped out of the room. A nurse took her place shortly after, fussing at dressings and tubes, thermometers and sphygmomanometers, tapping buttons to pump me full of numb.

But it was no use.

I wished for death, and I meant it. But there was no way to get it. No one to grant it.

The police caught up with Joey, holed up in a shack in the woods. When they cornered him, he raised not his hands, but mine, and wished aloud for Superman strength.

But either the wishes didn't work that way, or they didn't work at all. Superman can repel bullets, but Joey didn't.

When Emily told me, her raw hands cradling my bandage, my heart clenched.

Was that my wish? I'd meant it, that time. Did my one wish go to Joey, just like the old man said it would? Or with Joey dead, did my wish come back to me now?

"Are you okay?" Emily squeezed where my hand should be.

"I want to go for a walk in the woods."

Emily stopped our truck at the side of the road, where the faint game trail threaded off into the trees. "Here?" She looked at me, worry carved clear across her face. The line between her brows the twin of mine.

"Yeah."

"I think I should go with you."

"No. I'll be fine. It's not far. Just want to pay my respects."

She frowned, but didn't push the matter. Any accommodation, in the name of healing.

I hardly had to think or look to find my way back to the tree. It still lay, twisted and felled, across the clearing. Its hollow had become a den for countless forest creatures, nests and nuts and musk crowding the empty space where once a man had slept. For centuries, maybe, or maybe just after a day of hard drink.

I couldn't smell rot any longer. Just rich soil, as if all had recycled to new freshness.

"Did I make my wish?" I asked the tree. "I can't tell if the mark is gone or not…. Did Joey take my death from me, too? After everything else he's taken?" I choked, then, and wept. I poured out bile as I had on my last visit to the tree, the rot that set it off not so different than last time.

I let it all out over the twisted roots, till I had nothing left.

"I just want my hands back," I whispered to the tree. "If I still have a wish, that's what I want."

I wanted to do the chores I hadn't done for a decade. I wanted to lift and toil, as Joey had done for me since we were fifteen and stupid. I wished I'd never told Joey about the tree, that none of this had ever happened.

I walked back to the truck lighter than I had been in weeks. The look of relief on Emily's face when she saw me exit the woods told me that my darkest wish was maybe not as secret as I'd always thought, that maybe she'd always known.

We made it halfway home before she spoke. "We've hired on help for the farm."

I didn't say anything. What was there to say? Of course they had. I wouldn't be much help, now. I never had been.

The house was quiet, empty, hollow as an old tree. Everyone was out in the fields, working.

"I'm going to lay down," I said.

Emily nodded. "Get some rest. Holler if you need anything."

My room smelled like rotten game, like old death caught in a tree, struggling in vain, wasted away, then split open.

I gagged and wretched. There was still blood on the floor, all over my bed, my sheets stiff with it, and my pillow... My hands lay there, nested in down. Their fingers twisted at angles, like a buck's prize rack. The skin of them greyed and set with putrefaction, but smooth. Scarless. Mark-less. Like I'd never fallen. Like I'd never been pushed.

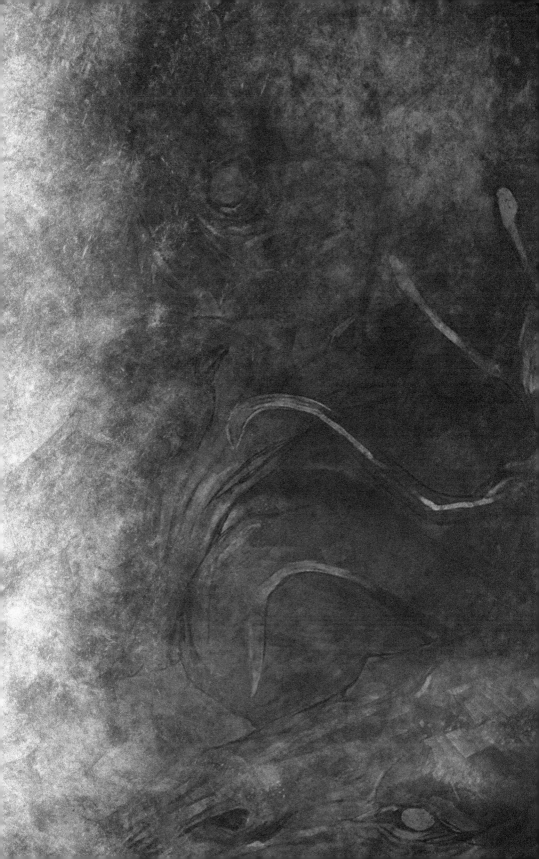

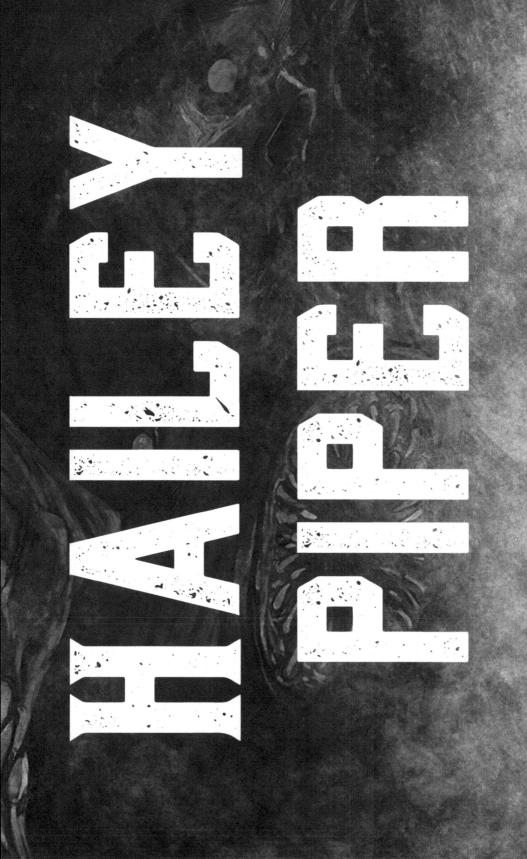

WHEN I
CATCH YOU

The darkness of the bedroom clung silent to May as if it had shut out all sound. No footsteps, no traffic. She was almost afraid to breathe too loud, the way no one wanted to be the first to cough or clear their throat at a eulogy's end.

Sound would be nice right now. Nocturnal noises never bothered May. Living in apartments for the past decade since leaving her parents' house had crushed any fear of footsteps in the night or voices in the walls. Neighbors were busier than mice. Unless Mr. Culbard knocked over his dresser upstairs again and made the ceiling shake, or the Jacques kids raised hell on their video games next door three hours before dawn, May usually slept through the night.

No noise had woken her now; the dark wouldn't let noise into her room. She didn't have to pee, and she wasn't thirsty. Her sheets lay lightly across her, no squeezing or smothering.

But her nerves stirred awake, ready to have her jumping and flailing against the room's thick air. Tension stiffened her spine and limbs, the defensive anxiety of a prey animal whose instincts have suddenly whispered, *You're being watched, and what watches you likes you in a bad way.*

A white curve and a black pupil flashed open in May's head; she shook the memory away. Once her mind had tasted anxiety, her brain would keep feeding, the way it sometimes pawed through the scenes of a scary movie right as she was turning out the lights.

The memory clung, and she thought about every opening in her apartment. Two windows broke the wall to the right of her bed, each blanketed in blackout thermal curtains. A walk-in closet opened the wall to the left, but she left that gaping open at night. She was too old to be scared of a monster in the closet, and the hanging clothes never bothered her. Down the bed, past the footboard, and across the floor stood the bedroom door. She hadn't locked the door, it had no lock, but she'd listened to the metal catch as she pulled the doorknob. The door was shut tight.

Much as it could be, at least. No door or window or covering in an ordinary house could perfectly seal. There would always be a crack between portal and frame, a gap between curtain and wall.

"But not enough to look through," May whispered to herself. "Not enough to see."

She wanted to argue more—it was too dark, and no one else lived with her, and no one could have gotten into the apartment, and if they had, she would hear them, and why would they stand at the door? The bedroom air wouldn't argue back.

She never got that far. It was dark, but not too dark to see. Her eyes must have dilated so much as to push out her gray irises and cover them with her pupils. The room lay veiled in a bluish gloom, the outline of the bedposts, vanity, and dresser becoming clear.

And the doorframe, and the door, and the black rectangle outline. Far away as it stood, she saw through that black line.

To the white of an unblinking eye.

May shut her eyes tight and thrashed one arm to the side, groping until her hand found the bedside lamp and switched it on. Her eyelids' darkness turned golden, and she squinted them open against the bedroom.

Light glared over the sleek door, deepening the gap between door and frame to an impenetrable darkness. Tension clung to May's limbs as she stood off the creaking mattress and made a stiff crossing from bedside to doorknob, twisting and pulling until the door opened to—

Nothing.

Frail patches of light reached past her limbs into the living room, brightening an armchair, the coffee table, and the TV screen near the window. The bathroom stood empty to the left. Her shadow stamped the off-white carpet with a human-shaped stain, but nothing else like it stood in the apartment.

Anxiety melted down her limbs. She must have been more asleep than she'd realized and let herself dream about Ni—

"Stop." No thinking about *her* if it could be helped. The eye had reared up yesterday and now in other dreams and playful memories, the exhaust of an overactive imagination, and none of it was real. There was no predator, and she was no prey.

She slid back from the door, wrapped her fingers around the chilly knob again, and pressed until the door shut with another satisfying metal click. The line between door and frame stood as a benign consequence of separate objects, nothing worse. She turned her back on it and started for the bed.

Tension coiled through her vertebrae and down her limbs, freezing her in place. *What watches you likes you in a bad way.*

She licked her lips. They dried under a quickening breath. She tried to slow it, make it quiet, but noise had never been the trouble at night. There was something else now, and she knew if she turned around again and looked to the bedroom door, she would see the white eye.

Same as she'd seen in the house on Thurston Drive.

Starline was already waiting on the Wheaton Street curb when May emerged from her apartment building's entrance in the early morning. The world was a gray-white haze of faded brick and sunbaked sidewalk and street, with Starline a walking shadow of dark pants, black leather jacket, her face marked with dark rings under the eyes. Her puff of black hair bit at the sky. She seemed underdressed for the cold, but maybe the cigarette between her maroon-nailed fingers kept her warm. Or maybe she thought May was overdressed in her furry boots, thick winter coat, and the pink scarf tucked around her neck beneath red hair.

The exhaustion in Starline's face said she'd left the set of *Night of the Living Ex* hours ago—not happy to be here but showing up. May could only offer coffee in appreciation. Who else could she call for help? Her family lived two states over, and the rest of her exes had less of a *Yes, we can still be friends* disposition.

Smoke whistled out from between Starline's lips. "Didn't get a wink's sleep, did you?"

May had hardly looked in the mirror before leaving her apartment. She had to be wearing dark circles under her eyes to match Starline's. Probably deeper and darker against her pale skin.

Cars slithered by, blowing chilly February air against May's leggings. She should have worn pants over them—not so overdressed after all. The walk would give some warmth, and foot traffic seemed thankfully light. An elderly couple neared, and a woman carrying a trash bag crossed the street a few paces away, where a clean-shaven man in a green beanie and coat puffed a trail of smoke, as if the universe had offered Starline a partner in nicotine before May met up with her.

"I got up early for this, Mayday," Starline said, taking another drag. "No wasting time on skittish nerves." She started up Wheaton Street and then glanced over her shoulder. "Sorry, I don't mean to bully. We're okay; my shift's not until noon."

May would be meeting clients before then. Not where they were headed, that had been yesterday's business, but other houses. Would they judge her tiredness? She would get her make-up situated before then.

But the house on Thurston Drive came first, and she hadn't wanted to go alone.

"It means a lot," May said, white mist sliding through her lips as if she'd bummed Starline's cigarette. She hurried to catch up and then walked at Starline's side. "You're going to think I'm silly."

"Already do." Starline nudged an elbow into May's arm. May skirted away, and then Starline pulled her into a walking half-hug.

Flashes of high school lit May's thoughts. They had walked this close in those days. May could fully sink into the memory and let Starline be their guide if she knew the way, and if May weren't so nervous.

If there hadn't been others in their orbit back in high school. Those had been good days. If only Nica hadn't tainted them.

But she'd always been about what might come. *Bigger things ahead*, she'd written on too many of those fucking yellow notes.

A damp mist clouded the sun as it sank and peeked over flat rooftop corners and through skeletal tree limbs. The area only seemed to grow grayer as one block led to another. A white food truck rumbled by, its logo peeling in unreadable narrow patches, and its pained engine echoed up the street. A man in a flat cap and jacket hurried down a concrete landing and steps, headed for May and Starline, and then passed them by. His footsteps faded in the cold as another set of footsteps clacked on the sidewalk. May glanced back.

Maybe twenty steps back walked the man in the green beanie and coat, the same she'd seen smoking across the street from her apartment. Coincidence? Had he been watching Starline, or waiting for someone else?

Except he walked this way now.

"I think someone's following us," May whispered.

Starline raised a thick eyebrow, fished into her jacket's pocket, and plucked out her smartphone. The top peeked over her shoulder and made a subtle *click*. The man froze in the phone's screen, same as May had seen, only a little blurrier and unmoving. If only he would stay motionless.

"I think someone just might," Starline said. She grinned around the remaining half of her cigarette. "Does he like us?"

He might. And he might've taken photos on his phone or misread some behavior on May's or Starline's part, a façade at invitation, pretended depth, the kinds of benign gestures and speech that Nica would cling to and suck at like an emotional tick until May watched her every word and action not to risk Nica's attention.

She nestled deeper into her winter coat, invaded by a fresh chill.

"Stirring up Nica memories, huh?" Starline asked. All grins and mirth vanished from her face as she eyed May's pink scarf. "Okay." She inhaled through her cigarette again, turned around at the curb's edge, and stared at the man through a plume of smoke.

May stopped and turned with her as the man jerked toward the street and hurried across. His cigarette tumbled loose halfway and spat ashes onto the faded yellow line marking the asphalt. May looked away when he reached the far corner and turned off Wheaton Street.

Starline kept watching. "See? Glare them down, and they skitter off."

May forced a nod Starline probably couldn't see. To watch the watcher used to work on Nica. Anytime May spotted that pinkish face through a window, around a corner, through a half-open door, Nica would dash away as if May had no object permanence and to lose sight of Nica would erase her from memory.

If only.

Starline's stare had turned May's way. Concern beat back the exhaustion in her eyes. Did she understand yet why May had texted flustered in the night? Did she already know the eye had echoed Nica? That this might be bigger than the house on Thurston Drive?

Apartments gave way to townhouses a block from the turn onto Thurston Drive, as if preparing a traveler for a rise in affluence the farther they walked from May's apartment. These homes had lawns and driveways, basements and attics.

The house May had visited yesterday wore canary yellow paint beneath a black-shingled roof. A vibrant green sign hung from the mailbox, advertising For Sale with ReaFresh beside an old photo of May in a gray suit dress, with numbers and information below. Dark curtains sprang open from the picture window, baring the family room to the meek sunshine, and when May brought clients through, she would emphasize the benefits of natural light like the sun wouldn't glare off a TV screen no matter where the new owners set it. She'd tell them the basement made for a creative space, up for anything they could imagine, and there were plenty of bedrooms for the kids. Not that the clients would necessarily have or want kids, but ReaFresh made a big deal about homes for the American family, and they had a specific idea what that looked like.

At least for today, May didn't need to lie. She led Starline up the broad stone steps to the stoop, entered her key code into the black box hanging from the front door's knob, and plucked out the keys she needed to let herself and Starline into the foyer.

Market houses never smelled right. May noticed paint, cleaning products, a dampness from the basement usually masked by human odors, but the house never smelled like people.

Starline slid her boots off and set rainbow-colored socks on the tan carpet. "How's it feel to sell places you'll never afford?"

"You sound like my father," May said, shutting the door. It wasn't true, but the comparison might steer Starline off track.

Starline pressed her foot against the carpet and then watched the fibers reform as she lifted it. "I think about it sometimes. How much cash slides through a hand versus how much the hand makes an hour handling that cash. Wally's makes more in a day than I'll see in a year. But you get commission, right?"

May shucked off her boots, coat, and scarf. "I don't want to talk money right now."

"No one does," Starline said, shrugging. "But everyone's up for a ghost story."

May opened her mouth to say it wasn't a ghost, but how would she know? She only knew what she'd seen. A ghost didn't comfort her any better than guilty hallucinations or waking dreams, but at least then the problem would be outside her head.

"Do you really think it's that?" May asked.

"Not really," Starline said. "If I believed any of this, I'd already be out the door. Empty houses have a weird feel."

May didn't get that sense, but maybe she was used to them.

Starline wandered through the empty family room space and into the kitchen, where refrigerator, oven, and sink at least pretended at some semblance of human life. If she kept going, she would find the door to the basement. Out the other side of the living room, she would find the back door to the patio, a side room, a bathroom, and the stairs to the second floor. More rooms, another bathroom, plus a pull-down ladder to the attic.

"Which way to the ghouls?" Starline asked. She tested the kitchen sink for water and snapped her hand away from the stream. It had to be cold; no one had turned the water heater on. "What were you up to yesterday?"

"Nothing." May flopped defeated hands at the cream-colored walls. "Making sure everything was ready for the clients. Sometimes animals get into these places and I have to clean up the droppings."

"Any worse haunts than mice and rats? Maybe a murder?" Starline eased toward the far side of the kitchen, where she stared at a shut steel door. "Someone buried in one of the basement walls? Ritualistic human sacrifice?"

"How should I know?" May asked.

"You're a real estate agent. Don't you have to know everything?"

"It isn't like in movies. It's notoriously hard to find out a house's history, especially if it predates online listings."

"But ReaFresh would have paper files, right?" Starline asked. "You can't access their records?"

"We'd need records to access," May said. Her collar itched, and she clawed beneath her sweater's neckline. "If this house ever saw any blood and guts, it's not like the address would end up in the newspaper. There would have to be a landmark nearby to get close. And even if there was evidence, my bosses want to sell the house, not scare potential buyers. If there's anything hidden on one of our client properties, it stays that way until it's forgotten."

Starline scoffed. "Almost makes me glad I rent. At least if there's a goblin in the walls, it's management's problem." She reached past May's sight, and a metal rattle said she'd twisted the doorknob to the basement.

May drifted through the family room. She wouldn't warn Starline about trouble lurking beneath the house; far as ReaFresh was concerned, the house was vermin-proof. Maybe ghost-proof, too, at least downstairs.

Up here was a different story. May found herself at the bathroom door, where a marble countertop grasped a stainless steel faucet and knobs above a clean white basin. The mirror was clean, as was the toilet, towel rack, and what she'd seen of the shower beyond a decorative turquoise curtain the owners had hung to make the bathroom more appealing. Whatever they'd used when they lived here had found its destiny in the garbage before May had ever set foot here.

She wondered if the old shower curtain might have protected her from what had happened yesterday. People had splashed it with hot water, soap suds, shampoo, bodily fluids. They'd given it a lived-with feel.

This turquoise blanket was cold. Maybe it invited cold things.

She had stood in this same bathroom around noon yesterday, her bag popped open to the right of the sink. Her makeup had needed a touch-up of blush and lipstick, and she hadn't been completely happy with her eyes. There was time. That she'd stood here so fearless—not in a brave way, but in an empty, lacking way—seemed ludicrous now, but she couldn't blame herself.

She'd been tracing her eyelid with a pencil when her gaze flickered across the mirror. Past her pale cheek and a stray red lock, beyond her shoulder, stood the shadowy line where the fresh shower curtain parted from the tile wall. No two surfaces could every entirely fuse, but the gap had to be less than an inch wide. She shouldn't have noticed it.

She shouldn't have spotted the reflection of a white eye staring from the dark.

Her makeup pencil had clattered in the sink, and she'd spun around, hands grasping the counter's edge, mouth crying out, *Who's there?*

No one had answered. The eye stared on, sending a jolt through May's arms, and she'd snapped up the wastebasket and chucked it at the shower curtain. Her feet had twisted, about to run, but the wastebasket struck the shower curtain rod and tore it off the wall, baring the tile wall, showerhead, and tub to the rest of the bathroom.

There was no one. Clean and empty, not even an errant bar of soap or bottle of conditioner.

May had felt silly and cleaned up, adjusting wastebasket and shower curtain rod minutes before the clients arrived. She'd had to smudge her makeup with the heel of her hand and hope none of them noticed a stray scratch of incomplete eyeliner over her left eye. She might have forgotten the moment, chalked it up to her brain playing tricks on her, if the eye hadn't found her in the apartment last night.

A presence filled the air, and another jolt sent May jerking to one side—Starline stood in the bathroom doorway. No ghost, no eye except the ones in her face, ringed with darkness same as May's.

"This one?" Starline asked. She either hadn't noticed she'd made May jump or pretended for her sake. "Not the bathroom upstairs?"

"This one," May said. Her voice came out in a squeak.

Starline drew the shower curtain all the way open and then shut it again. Or at least, shut it as much as possible. There was always a gap, however small.

"Leave it open." May tried to smile. "Please."

Starline pushed the curtain halfway and turned to the mirror. "So now what?" she asked. "Light a candle, call Bloody Mary? Candyman? The Pied Piper?" She stared into her own reflection. Her mouth opened again, tongue's tip between her teeth, and then she pursed her lips. She'd been about to offer another name, one much closer to their lives than any fictional monster.

"I didn't say anything before," May said. Had Starline stuck with Bloody Mary and the like, she might've seemed to be taking this for a laugh. If she'd been about to mention Nica, did that mean the blame fell to Mary? "If I said anything, I was just muttering to myself about my makeup."

Starline peered closer and ran a fingertip down one dark-circled eye. "At the mirror?"

May nodded at their reflections.

Starline tucked gentle fingers beneath May's jaw. Her grip was warm. "Can you blame a ghost for looking?"

"I don't want to be watched by—" May couldn't make the words come out. To acknowledge the otherworldly was an invitation, no different than calling to them through reflective glass. She glanced to the floor, a sleek sheen of seamless circular patterning. Standing here felt dangerous, but at least there were no tiles. No cracks for an eye to peer through. "I don't want to be watched by anyone."

Starline scanned the mirror. "Maybe my eyes aren't so good as yours, but I don't see anything."

Neither did May. Only memories of yesterday.

"Could be this isn't about the house?" Starline leaned close. "Out with it. That guy didn't have you freaked over just himself. You already had Nica on the brain. You're still wearing her scarf."

"It was a gift," May said, laying a protective hand at her neck where the scarf had coiled before they stepped into the house. "That makes it mine."

"But it's still wrapped up in her." Starline stroked two fingers down the back of May's neck. "Don't you still think about her when you put it on?"

"It's been a year," May said.

"Already?" Starline whistled sharply. "Just now?"

"The other day." May's mouth felt dry, but she didn't want to slurp from this bathroom's faucet, especially if a ghost had wandered through as of yesterday. "I didn't want to commemorate or anything."

"Why would you?" Starline asked. "After how bad it got." Her high-pitched whistle made May's ear ache. "Remember her weird love rituals back in high school? She'd saved up all that money for white roses and then lined them in a circle. Valentine's Day, right?"

May gave another nod.

Starline nudged May's arm. "Want me to stay over tonight? I can grab a bag after work. Girls' night, like when we were together. Not in a Nica *let's get back together* way, but pizza, pedicure, horror movies—"

"Not that last one," May said, but she said it through a smile. Starline had followed here where the eye first emerged, but there was no sign of it. If she followed to May's apartment, the same might be true. Starline could dispel any ghost through hard attitude alone. With time, maybe it would have all been in May's head.

Except the part where Nica was gone. Starline couldn't change that. No one could.

If Starline was the Living Ex, then Nica was the dead.

May let that thought haunt her head when she met clients at the ReaFresh office, where she kept her car for the free office parking, and followed them to or met them at houses of interest. For months before and after their breakup a year and four months ago, Nica would haunt May herself, waiting at ReaFresh houses where May was the listing agent or stalking the parking lot.

She'd always had an eccentric streak. May remembered that junior year's Valentine's Day ritual with the rose petals and cries for love, but Starline had used their ancient history as a blanket to hide a more recent past. Nica's high school-age rituals might have been weird but innocent, sure. Years later, when hers and May's relationship had soured, they'd become wet, grim ceremonies.

She had stumbled onto the last one by mistake a year and four months ago. She and Nica had argued that morning about something May couldn't remember anymore, one in a mountain of arguments about responsibility and money and boundaries. Guilt had gnawed at her through the day, and she'd headed for Nica's without warning, hoping the upstairs presence of the family whose basement Nica rented from would keep them both on their best behavior.

May's footsteps had gone quiet down concrete steps, as if she'd known she was sneaking up on Nica. As if she'd known what she would find might claw icicles down her spine.

The basement hadn't helped. A damp cool place, poorly heated in the autumn and worse in the coming winter. Nica had pushed her desk and seat toward the wall by the bed and rolled up the red-and-gold rug to sit at the center of the stone floor. White candles drooled wax in a circle around her. Nearer lay white rose petals. Each lay on the floor like a white eye staring at the ceiling. A crimson pupil dotted each petal and glistened in the candlelight.

The drops had been squeezed from Nica's pricked fingertips.

May couldn't remember what she'd squawked out at that moment. *For God's sake, Nica* was possible, or *What the fuck, Nica?* She had definitely screeched out Nica's name, made her jerk and turn and knock one candle on the floor, igniting a rose petal before its flame spattered to smoke over stone.

"It's a love spell," Nica had said. "To heal us." A wounded hand waved over small flames. "I'm doing this for us!"

There had been a lot of shouting then, and May hadn't given a shit if the family upstairs heard every word. This was the end. There was no walking back from bloodshed.

Nica had stayed on her knees the entire time, candlelight flashing in her pale hair, white eyes, and tearstained cheeks.

"Don't do this," she'd said, hands clasped. The pressure squeezed out another few drops of blood, and they trickled down her wrists as if desperate to escape. "Please don't leave me. I'm here. I'm here for you, and that's it. I'll worship you."

"What the hell does that mean?" May had asked. "I'm not one of your spirits. I'm a person; do you understand? Worship won't take care of me when I'm sick, or help me decorate for Christmas. Worship won't understand me. Do you get it? I don't want worship. I want a stable relationship, and that can't be you."

Nica had shuddered back, almost knocking over another candle. "But I love you. I thought you loved me."

"I thought so, too," May had said. "But now I think I was just used to you, after all these years, and that isn't fair to either of us."

She had stepped out then and not looked back. She'd never been the one to break off a relationship before, hadn't perfected any technique. Nica was the first and the last.

But Nica hadn't let go.

Office and house hauntings went from once or twice a week to a daily occurrence. Nica had wanted to fuse her solitary form into a relationship that might save her from herself before, but the desire turned desperate in those four post-breakup months. In line outside a restaurant, stepping into the ReaFresh offices, and even at home, May would glance over her shoulder, and spot Nica in a dark hoodie, fists clutching the sleeves like they could hide her body.

And maybe it worked. She shrank in glimpses and moments to a foot poking from behind a building corner, a breath in a lonely room, an eye peering through a crack beneath a door or a gap where curtains didn't entirely meet over a window. May had never known when she was being watched, but she knew Nica could never see the full picture. She only saw what she wanted to see.

Sometimes she left what she wanted, too. Blood-tipped rose petals as evidence of ritual. Promising yellow notebook pages and Post-it Notes explaining how Nica wasn't trying to get back together with May, only wanted to be sure she was okay.

Don't fret, pet, she'd write. *Bigger things ahead.*

May hadn't been okay. She'd needed a court order to crawl even halfway toward okay.

For all the good it did. Shortly after, Nica vanished.

In the first few weeks, May had imagined Nica might pop up anywhere. A ladies' room, a street corner, May's office, her bedroom. The disappearance seemed less like Nica had gone anywhere, more like she'd perfected her stalking, starving herself to the kind of slender shadow that slips through walls and lives.

But her absence became a hole. There was no body, but Starline, old roommates, and eventually May had accepted that Nica wouldn't have gone away like this if she were planning to come back. Weeks passed in vile fantasies—a kidnapper, a murderer, a suicide, an accident, an impossibility— before May let Nica slip away again.

One last goodbye.

The day drifted toward its end as May parked her car in the ReaFresh lot again, used the employee restroom, and then started her walk home. A couple more solid sales and maybe she could think about affording a down payment on a house before her landlord hiked the rent as he had every spring the past three years. She could see herself in a pretty house with a lawn and driveway, an attic and basement, much like the house on Thurston Drive.

Minus the ghost.

Except that her apartment wasn't the problem. Neither was the Thurston Drive house. To return there with Starline this morning might have felt dangerous, but if so, May faced the same danger at home. That unblinking white eye had stared at her through the line between door and doorframe sure as through the gap between shower curtain and tile wall, a voyeur caught on the wrong side of the solid world.

If it were a ghost, it had traveled five blocks from the Thurston Drive house to May's apartment. Weren't ghosts stuck in the place where they'd died? That had to depend on whether the ghost was an entity of someone dead or a footprint of past events. It depended on whether she decided to believe in them.

And whether she had acknowledged and invited a ghost into her life. If a ghost had found her and wanted her, she had a pretty good idea of who it might be. But when had she acknowledged or invited? The scarf didn't count. It had been a gift; that made it hers, not Nica's. May hadn't spoken Nica's name in several months.

On purpose, at least. What if May had muttered something that sounded like *Nica* under her breath yesterday? What if she'd called out for Nica in her sleep?

She might as well have said, *Come on in, make yourself at home* in both locations.

Her apartment building stared beneath the dimming February sky. Windows glowed in patchwork across its face until it reached the bottom floor, where curtains hid the lowest apartments. One of them was May's.

If she stared long enough, would she find an eye between those curtains, staring back?

She reached into her bag and drew out her phone. Her thumb tapped out a text: *Can it be your place?*

The text screen to Starline hung unmoving for a moment, and then dots said Starline was typing. *Sure. Roomie might bring gf tho, and then a soundtrack.*

May smirked and lowered her phone. That was fine. Noises at night had never been her problem.

Whether they were May's problem or not, the sounds in Starline's apartment were strange past midnight. Laughter filled the walls instead of rowdy kids glued to an X-box, and a hoarse-voiced couple shouted overhead instead of knocking over their furniture. Nothing wrong with the sounds; they were only new enough to unsettle May from sleep.

She and Starline had polished off most of their pizza and then sat bloated and greasy-fingered through *The Wind in the Willows*, the most innocent movie she could find that Starline would stomach. Even then, she remembered how some Disney VHS or DVD from her past had packaged some scene from the story alongside a telling of *The Legend of Sleepy Hollow*.

No escaping ghosts, she guessed. Everyone carried them, imagined or real.

There were no pedicures either, and hardly any conversation. May was tired, Starline was tired, and they'd let a silence follow them that now slipped out of the dark and away from Starline's bed, letting the outer noises in.

She had a firmer mattress than May's; maybe newer. It didn't creak when May slid to the floor in fluffy winter pajamas and crept toward the bathroom. Starline's roommate and girlfriend hadn't come home as far as May could hear, but she kept quiet as she shut Starline's bedroom door and headed for the bathroom.

Something about the caution felt like old times, sleeping over at each other's houses, holding hands in the dark. Would the ghostly eye be jealous?

"Don't think about it," May whispered. She shut the bathroom door and flipped the wall switch.

Merciful yellow light showed an ordinary bathroom, the same she'd seen a hundred times. Sink, toilet, bath. Chilly tile flooring bit at May's feet. She avoided the mirror and her reflection, sat down to pee, and then washed her hands.

The water was cold, even with the hot water nozzle turned all the way. It reminded May of the Thurston Drive house's faucets, its bathroom and mirror, its—

"Stop."

She glanced to the mirror as water helped her fingers wipe the soap away, half-expecting frost to coat her face, and the bathroom's reflection opened around her. Its ceiling warped in the high glass where a blow must have bent one corner of the medical cabinet underneath. Creamy paint slid down the walls, around dirty towels and a rack of toiletries, and paused where a deep maroon shower curtain hit the opposite side of the bathroom.

Most of it. Ripples of mildew coated the bottom where water must have splashed from the tub, painting dark finger-like stains. They paused at the curtain's edge, where it almost met the shower wall but stopped in the way all things stopped, leaving a slender black gap.

Around an unblinking white eye.

Sudden sharp heat snapped at May's fingers, and she tore them back from the steaming water. She jerked the hot water off, the cold water on, and made herself busy soothing her scalded fingertips, an excuse to avoid the eye.

What had Starline said this morning when that man had followed them? To glare them down, and they'd skitter off.

May left the water running hard. The drain protested in a steady gulp, working the water past hair and soil. It seemed to synchronize with her heartbeat, one wet thud to another, as she turned around and stared at the gap between shower curtain and wall. At the eye.

She saw it clearer now without the reflection, in the stark bathroom light. A layer of dew glistened around its dark pupil. The iris was too thin from here to make out its color.

The watcher didn't skitter off. It lingered, waiting, wanting, reaching across the cold bathroom into May's skin as if the eye had fingers formed of its wet white jelly. Starline's advice might have worked on the living, but whatever watched wasn't alive. Maybe never had been. Maybe had died in heartache.

May could imagine other things in that gap of darkness. Nica's pale hair. A yellow note tagged to the shower's innards, making promises and declarations of love, as if May should appreciate an unwanted gaze, always uninvited. She had been mostly alone this year, sometimes guilty, sometimes haunted, and now what? Nica expected her to find comfort in this ghostly voyeuristic lullaby. *At least someone is happy to see you*, she might have written on the note. *At least someone wants you around.* Even if that someone had to be Nica, eager to see May, capture her, worship her.

"I never wanted that, Nica!" May shouted, charging for the maroon curtain and thrashing it open. "I never wanted y—"

She bit hard on her lip. No one stood in the shower; no one lay in the tub. She'd expected that and had hoped she might find the yellow note she'd imagined, but nothing clung to the tile wall but soap scum.

Her teeth eased from her lower lip as a copper taste hit the end of her tongue. Biting back the words would do no good. She had already said Nica's name. There, an acknowledgment and invitation. No need for a ghostly eye to spy through gaps in curtains or cracks in doors—Nica could step into the open if she was really a ghost and have her chance to see May again. This might be what they'd needed from the beginning. No shouting, no silly rituals, only an emotional exhalation to air out every breath of unfinished business left hanging in the atmosphere since Nica's disappearance.

The sink drain went on gurgling in time with May's heart. The tension and cold only squeezed harder. May shook herself away from the tub and turned to the sink to shut off the water.

Her eyes settled on the mirror. The shower curtain hung open in the reflection, same as out here in the real world, but to the side of the mirror stretched a black line where the glass formed a door to the medicine cabinet.

A wet white orb glistened within the meager gap.

May stormed to the sink and yanked the medicine cabinet open. Only pill bottles, cotton swabs, and everything else she might expect, but no eye. No ghost.

But now the line crept up the inside of the cabinet, where the mirror-door opened on its hinges. Another black line stood where the bathroom door shut against its doorframe, keeping out the rest of Starline's dark apartment. Black creases separated the tiles along the floor, the toiletry rack cast a narrow shadow against the wall, and even the faucet's foundation and the sink's drain left dark spaces where a glistening eye stared at May.

It could watch her from anywhere. Everywhere.

"Stop," she said again. Her feet dragged back across the tiles, feeling each line, and then she crumpled onto her knees and threw her hands over her eyes. "I'm sorry. Please, don't look at me anymore."

Scant light slid between the cracks where her fingers couldn't meet, and she lifted her hands an inch before an eye might appear through the gap.

Even that wasn't enough. There were cracks in her palms, too, the kinds of lines a fortune teller might read. If one traced a fingernail down May's palm now, she might prod an eye and leak a white puddle across May's skin.

May jerked her head to one side and shut her eyes. Her heart hammered in her ears too fast for the gurgling sink drain to keep up. She couldn't see anything now, and that would have to be enough to pretend nothing could see her.

Light pressed against thin skin. An eyelid couldn't shut flush into her face unless melted into one seamless cover, sealing May's eyes away forever.

And in the gap beneath her trembling eyelashes, she saw the ever-staring eye.

"How many eyes do you have?" she snapped. She shook her head from side to side and pounded her fists against the bathroom tiles. "You can't look everywhere! You can't. I can't."

Metal jangled as a doorknob turned, and May's eyes flashed open as Starline filled the bathroom doorway. A black tank top hung over her thick pajama bottoms. Her eyes were tired slits over dark circles.

"You okay?" she asked, her voice a creaky hinge. "What happened to you?" She pursed her lips and waited.

May splayed her palms over the tiles—no, the lines, she couldn't look—and turned to Starline, jaw opening and shutting. How to explain the million cracks in the world through which Nica might look?

Even between lips. They couldn't fuse any better than an eyelid, only meet and form a black line, where another white eye stared from inside Starline.

May wheeled around in a screeching turn. She aimed her knees at the wall and stared into its painted texture.

"Look at me," Starline said.

May wouldn't look back. She would stick with the wall. There were dots here, uneven strokes here, but no creases or lines for an eye to peer through. May could sit here, unblinking, unturning, for the rest of her life, and she would never see another ghostly eye.

Firm fingers grasped the underside of May's jaw and jerked her head to one side, coming face to face with Starline. She tried to turn away, but the fingers squeezed. They would leave a bruise if May kept fighting.

"Is it her?" Starline asked. No need to say Nica. But then, May had already said the name. Acknowledged, invited. A little attention could send Nica a long way.

Or draw her close.

"I think—" May started, swallowed, tried again. "I think she did something before she disappeared a year ago. She always had those rituals, and you don't know how bad they got. Flowers and fire. And blood, too."

"You think she did something in life to open a door back?" Starline's fingers slid from May's jaw. "Like what? You think she took her own life?"

"I don't know," May said. She used to think she would never know, but now everything had changed. Like Nica wanted her to know, couldn't rest until everyone knew.

"So, what?" Starline asked. "We go to Nica's?"

May rubbed her jaw. "There is no Nica's. The family who owned the house cleared her stuff out of their basement a couple weeks after she disappeared."

Starline stood up straight as if stricken. "How would you know?"

May let her mouth hang open, let the question dangle.

Starline cursed under her breath: "You went looking."

"I was worried when she—when I didn't see her," May said.

"When she quit stalking you," Starline said.

"She wasn't well."

May let the tile floor's chill snake up her fingers, hands, forearms, all the way to her chest. She watched Starline's eyes open wider by the moment, adjusting to the light and too-early wakefulness. The lines throughout the room seemed neutral now, as if the eye behind the world had no interest in seeing anyone but May.

"What if you sent the wrong message?" Starline asked. "You'd been avoiding her for four months by that February, but to go looking, she might have thought you wanted to see her."

"I didn't." May sounded groggy now. "And how would she know?"

"Same as she knew things when she was alive." Starline tugged the lower lid from one eye. "She watched."

"But I didn't mean it like that," May said.

"Since when did Nica ever take anything from you as less than a grand gesture?" Starline asked. "And now she's come to make good on that interest.

Maybe that house you're selling has nothing to do with it. It's about you, and where you were when—" She swallowed against the rest of the thought.

But May understood. "She's really dead, then. And we know when. A year as of the other day, huh?" An anniversary unobserved and uncelebrated, unknown and unloved.

"It tracks." Starline glanced to the open shower, its maroon curtain folded against the wall to one side. "It's like she's stalking you again, leaving those creepy notes about your future and the bigger things ahead, waiting for the slightest hint you want her back. But she'd run when you'd confront her."

"Skitter off," May muttered.

"Like she can't stand to watch out in the open," Starline said. "You need to make a clear statement. Correct whatever suggestion you made by checking on her."

As if May's concern had been a mistake. "I already broke up with her. I shouldn't have to do some counter ritual to hers to make that clear."

"Nica was complicated." Starline's hands waved in front of her, drawing indiscernible shapes in the air. "But sure, a counter ritual, we could do that. Get something of hers, use it to talk at her, make your statement."

May sighed hard. "I told you, her place is gone."

"But you got something of hers, right?" Starline asked.

May was about to protest when she realized. Her thoughts drifted out of the bathroom to Starline's coat closet, where pink fabric wound around May's coat by the collar.

"That scarf is mine," May said, rubbing her neck.

"But you got it from her." Starline waved a hand. "And the place doesn't matter. We can do it at your apartment. Or better yet, that house you took me to today. That's where you saw her first, right?"

May hadn't seen an eye before then. She realized the eye might have been following her all that day, outside her notice until she happened to spy it in an unlucky reflection. That might have made the Thurston Drive house a point of new significance in hers and Nica's relationship, the kind of touchstone Nica would appreciate.

"I thought you'd run if you thought this was real," May said.

"I would," Starline said, shrugging. "I don't exactly believe in ghosts, Mayday, but I think you've put yourself through something. And if there's a ghost? It's Nica. And there's nothing Nica can do."

May supposed that was true. Nica had never been the violent type except against herself, at least while she was alive.

"Star?" May took a rattling breath and stared hard into Starline's eyes. "I never told you everything about the breakup. I made it sound like I saw the blood and stormed out that night, but we fought first. I said things I didn't mean. I was cruel. Maybe that changes things with her now."

"Maybe, Mayday." Starline reached down to May and took a forearm in one hand, her waist in the other arm, and pulled her to her feet. "And maybe you need clarity too, huh? Lay you both bare, see each other head-on, eye to eye. And then you send her the clear message she could never seem to get in the past, but she'll get it now."

"Telling her what?" May asked.

"To move on," Starline said. "In every conceivable way."

May carried a plastic bag out of Starline's apartment, where she and Starline started off. They would pass May's apartment first, and then they would carry on toward Thurston Drive, about a seven-block stroll. Icy air chewed at May's face where her scarf—Nica's scarf—might have covered before. This dark February three hours before dawn, it lay in the bag with a few of Starline's roommate's candles.

Starline clutched a cigarette in one hand and tucked the other in her jacket's pocket, where she told May she kept a canister of mace.

This time, despite the dark and the cold, May wasn't afraid anyone would accost them. Now that they'd chosen to face Nica, there was a sense of unreality wrapped around and protecting them, as if the world knew that to allow the existence of ghosts meant to allow anything, even walking safely at night.

Even a strange secular exorcism of the heart.

The Thurston Drive house seemed no more ominous lit by streetlight than by pale sunshine. May fetched the key and led Starline inside, hoping the neighbors would be too asleep to notice lights in the empty house. If anyone called the police, May doubted they would believe she was showing the house to Starline, but being a ReaFresh employee might at least get them out of legal trouble. Spiritual trouble was another story.

"The basement," Starline said once May flicked on the kitchen light. "Like Nica's place. Underground to underground."

And to wherever Nica might be buried, May kept herself from saying. This visit was morbid enough without wondering what had become of Nica's body. Or how she'd died.

"If there's no spirit, what then?" May asked.

"Let's say there's enough spirit for you to feel guilty," Starline said, leading toward the basement door. "And you're going to put her out. Like a candle."

Dim light reached up the basement steps when Starline flipped the switch. The owners must have installed a low-wattage bulb, or the kind that's luminance faded the longer it burned. Starline's boots clomped down firm wooden planks, a little over a dozen from kitchen doorway to concrete floor.

The owners hadn't dressed up the house's underside. No furnishings, no creative decorations, and they hadn't remodeled wood panel walls in favor of a modern feel. They had chosen to leave the basement's future appearance and purpose to potential buyers' imaginations.

May's imagination could run wild here. Every dark gap between panels offered an opening for a ghostly eye. She would never know where Nica might peer through from some otherworldly secret place.

"It's perfect," Starline said. "Plenty of space, like Nica's. This'll be a snap." As if she'd done this a hundred times. May could see her doing something of the kind, some Valentine's Day burn barrel to exes of the immediate past. Whatever forces someone believed in the universe, everyone had their personal rituals and comforts.

Even a gifted scarf. The plastic bag crinkled as May drew out the looping pink fabric and offered it to Starline.

"No way, Mayday. That part's your show." Starline whipped a matchbook from her jacket. "I'll take candle duty."

She groped for the plastic bag and began to set candles in a wide circle. They were glass cups filled with scented wax, and they made a tinkling sound as their bottoms tapped the concrete floor. Labels gave them names like Autumn Harvest and Windy Beach, and May hoped they would be appropriate for a ritual like this. She and Starline might be making it up as they went along, but Nica had used nameless white columns of wax, the kind May expected to see perched on a candelabra in some period piece movie.

Flawed as she used to be, Nica had not been entirely understanding of human imperfection.

"I feel useless," May said. She dropped the empty plastic bag by the stairs and approached the candle circle with her scarf.

"You'll be busy in a minute," Starline said. She crouched to the floor and struck a match. White heat flared over its top. "Shut off that light and come sit with me. It's cold, but we'll get through it."

May let darkness overtake the basement and then sat on her knees and let the concrete chill nip through her leggings. Cold, yes, but no worse than the water in Starline's bathroom, or the frost of an eye piercing May's skin.

Starline reached past May to light another candle, and then another, until seven wicks burned competing calming scents against the damp basement. Their meager light reminded May of Nica's basement; doubtless part of Starline's plan. With the walls hidden in shadow, the spaces between wood panels seemed wider. That, too, had to be part of Starline's plan. Wider openings, let Nica come through, bare herself entirely.

Starline let her match die on the floor and then grasped May's hand. "Showtime, Mayday."

May clutched the scarf in one hand, squeezed Starline's hand a little tighter, and looked over the dancing candle flames. "Nica?"

"A little more conviction," Starline whispered, like she didn't want anyone to know she was here.

May cleared her throat and tried again. "Nica. I'm calling to you. Are you here?"

"Don't ask." Starline's grip tightened. "Demand. Put your back into it."

"I don't know how." May felt herself shrinking in the candlelight. The same shadows that ate the basement walls would devour her too.

"How many times did she cross the line with you?" Starline asked through her teeth. "The notes were everywhere. She got into your place. Into your office."

"Nica, we need to talk," May snapped.

Starline's teeth shone with firelight. "There, that's more like it. Call her out like you did when you were pissed. Reach past the guilt and remember how shitty she made your life for months on end."

May drifted over a year back, into the worst dregs of the post-breakup. Her sense of self had merged with the air, a public thing, all privacy broken by Nica's prying eye, not spectral or imagined but real and demanding. There was never a chance to feel at peace when May couldn't be certain she was alone.

But before the breakup, had it been any better? Within the final two months came the worst assumptions about May's punctuation marks in text messages, the dip in tone for a mid-word syllable, the movement of her eyes and lips in every face-to-face interaction. May's life had become a constant eggshell walk around Nica's paranoia to keep any semblance of peace.

High school-age Nica had been intense, but adult Nica? Girlfriend Nica? She was worse. And now ghost Nica carried on the unhappy tradition.

How dare she act like May should take the blame? She'd had every right to be cruel when they broke up. Everything she'd said in that basement that night had been true.

May straightened her back and clutched Starline's hand a little tighter. "Nica, the truth is, we never should have happened. Maybe if we'd stayed friends instead of trying out a relationship, I could've helped you."

"Yes, keep going," Starline whispered. "Remember why you ended it. And end it again."

"I can't help you now," May went on. "All I can do is the same as I did the last time we were in a basement together, understand? I'm here to look you in the eye and tell you it's over. This is goodbye."

Goodbye.

The walls' shadows deepened to tarry darkness as the whisper slipped past May's ear. Had she not been tensing her back so hard, she might have trembled against Starline, but instead she held stiff, as if she'd heard nothing.

Starline jerked May's hand. "Tell her again."

May swallowed against a cry. Starline didn't seem to have heard anything. There might have been no sound at all. They had never bothered May at night anyway.

"This is goodbye," she said, a tremble in her voice. "This is goodbye, this is goodbye, this is goodbye."

She kept saying it, a mantra to join and overpower the cold basement and whatever might watch through gaps in its candlelit wooden panels. Nica might be creeping within these walls, as desperate in death to lose herself in May as she'd been while alive.

But her paranoia had built a false May. Peering through a slit in a door, or a keyhole, or a gap in curtains, there was never a way to see the full picture. That was Nica even before the worst of the stalking. She had only captured fragments of May and filled out the rest for herself, only seeing what she wanted to see. Any love between them had grown too large for real life, to picturesque for any flesh-and-blood woman to compare.

Nica was never going to be happy, and putting her right had never been May's job. Tonight would be Nica's last chance to understand.

Another "goodbye" slipped out May's lips as every candle flame bent toward one dark wall. The scarf hadn't ruffled; neither had Starline's hair, as if there'd been no gust through the basement.

But Starline must have noticed the flames. Her head twitched like she'd caught something out the corner of her eye, where May watched her turn in slow inches over one shoulder.

Her grip turned vicelike. "I see it," Starline said, half-gasping.

May didn't want to look. She'd had enough of eyes in the bathroom an hour or so ago.

But if she didn't turn to face Nica, why had they come out here tonight? How many times had May repeated *This is goodbye*, and didn't she mean it?

She had to look.

Her fingers ached in Starline's grip. Not Starline's fault; she hadn't seen the eye in the bathroom upstairs, in the bathroom at her apartment, in May's apartment. Maybe they would have been safer holding this bizarre ritual in the second floor bathroom, somewhere with a mirror, and not this echo of the underworld where Nica used to live, but too late now. They had called her, and here she was.

May twisted her stiff neck, inch by gentle inch, until she looked past her shoulder, and Starline's shoulder, into the mounting black gap that swallowed the Thurston Drive basement.

A pale flower petal hung in the darkness as if floating on a black pond. Dark blood dotted its center—the pupil of a watchful eye. Always staring.

White rose petals slipped through the darkness and drifted past the circle of candles. Another drop of blood dotted each one's center.

A rain of eyes.

Breath hissed through Starline's teeth, and only now did May notice Starline had a mantra of her own running almost below hearing: "It's just Nica, it's just Nica, it's just Nica."

A louder whisper rushed wind-like past May's ears. *Eye*, it said.

May swallowed again. She felt a scream forming a hard bubble in her throat. "We should stop," she said, almost a croak. "I want to stop."

Starline's mantra melted down her lips. "Can we?"

May had no answer. She'd never done anything like this before. Playing with made-up ceremonies built on raw feelings seemed more Nica's business than anyone else's. They were in her territory now.

Eye, said the breath in the walls, and another rain of blood-dotted petals danced through the basement.

May tasted the air's chill. She sucked greedily at it, eager to freeze her lungs and everything else inside. Maybe then she would be sturdy enough to do this.

"Nica," she said, barely above a whisper. "I don't know if you can understand me, but I'm going to try." She felt Starline press close to her side; that would have to be her strength now. "We're not together anymore. We can't be, and I wouldn't want to be. We broke up. And you—I don't think you're alive anymore."

Eye? The whisper came out questioning.

May shuffled toward the edge of the candlelit circle. The eye in the shadows no longer resembled a flower petal, but the wet orb she'd spotted before. She wasn't going to let that stop her this time. She kept glaring into it and hoped this time it would skitter off forever.

"It's time you move on from me," May said. "From everything."

A settled breath eased from the darkness. *Eye*, the voice said again.

Was that right? Was it talking body parts? Or was it saying *I*? Did it mean the self?

"Yes, you," May said, and a surprising smile broke through her lips. "I never hated you, but we didn't work, and we shouldn't have been, and now you have something else. It's like you used to write, remember? There are bigger things ahead. There have to be. If you can come back, there has to be a *there* to go to."

The whisper breathed a new answer. *I am.*

May held up the rumpled pink scarf. "I bet there's a whole big afterlife. Maybe lots of them. Or there's something like reincarnation. Or maybe it's some kind of infinity I can't think of because I'm not gone yet, but you're going to find out. You're going to get there."

I am, the voice said again.

May beamed. "You are."

The voice creaked through every wall. *I am not Nica.*

A new eye glistened above the other, at first a dotted petal and then glaring with pale flesh. Another eye opened to its side, and then another above and beneath that. White petals surfaced along the walls' watery darkness, spreading in a sea of eyes.

Starline wheezed out a muffled shriek. Her hand jittered loose from May's, and she scuttled backward, knocking over one of the candles. Wet wax splashed and hissed over the concrete floor, an echo of a fallen candle in another basement over a year ago.

But these weren't Nica's candles, and those petals in the walls weren't Nica's eyes. There was nothing much she could do—Starline had been right about that—but she'd been wrong in other ways. She'd been the first to say the word *ghost* in this house. May had almost echoed her to say it wasn't a ghost, but she hadn't known for sure.

She hadn't known she was right.

May began to tremble. "Nica, this isn't funny." Denial seemed safest.

The eyes filled the basement. *She showed me*, the voice whispered through the walls. *You let me.*

May shuddered. An acknowledgment. An invitation. "Who are you?" she asked.

The basement groaned around her. The house had become a black blanket stitched with more eyes than she could count, as many eyes as it needed to see her. It would always see her here, and maybe anywhere. Starline muttered something. The basement shrouded and muffled her.

May tried to stand, but her legs had gone to sleep beneath her, and she toppled onto the concrete floor again.

Its hard surface had gone as soupy as melted wax. Once-firm concrete buckled under her knees, the toe of her boot, the press of her palm. There was no floor in the darkness anymore, only the arms of a tremendous embrace. The shadows drank May into their throat, and she watched a vast underworld of roots spread beneath the world she knew. It reached beneath streets and into houses and apartment, up office floors, elevators, parking garages. Nowhere, but everywhere, some great voyeur always peering through gaps and cracks in the world.

A bright world.

May wasn't sure how the candles had seemed so dim and frail before when sitting encircled by them on the basement floor. They danced with sharp light now, illuminating every wood-paneled corner, every ripple in the unyielding concrete floor, and every crease in Starline's jacket.

She sat hugging herself at the circle's edge, her mouth hanging open, icy clouds puffing from her face. With each breath, the tension melted from her limbs. She uncurled shaking hands from her trunk and then reached them elsewhere in the candle's circle.

What was she doing? May could only see fragments through the slender line of light. *Starline*, she wanted to call.

Starline slid out of sight, leaving only candles in May's view.

May followed along a hard surface until another breach in the darkness opened for her. Starline crouched there, pawing at the floor. Her hands lifted a familiar pink garment to her chest, and she stood glancing every which way, as if she'd lost her keys.

Or something more precious. "Mayday?" Starline called.

Here, May tried to say. Nothing came out. Her forehead slammed against the inner wall, but the darkness bowed beneath her blow, no firmer than a puddle. She tried to squeeze her face through the gap of light, but there wasn't room. No sound could break through, no body.

Only sight.

"Mayday?" Starline turned in a circle, her boot knocking one candle aside. "Where'd you go? May?"

Here, May tried again, but her voice seemed caught inside her. *Starline, here.*

Starline's glancing froze as she turned to face the slender line of light. Clouds slid faster through her lips, and she shuddered back. One hand covered her face.

Starline! It's me!

The pink scarf fluttered out of Starline's grasp as she bolted for the stairs. Her boot tripped on the lowest wooden plank, and she nearly slammed her teeth into a higher step, but she caught herself on her hands and dashed out of the basement. Only the candles remained, dancing against the walls. They seemed dimmer now, darker, as if Starline's heart and breath had kept them bright.

Be more, a whisper said.

The line of light slipped back from May's eyes and shrank to a narrow golden crease in the darkness. She thrust her face toward it, desperate to stay, but her body seemed to float as if she'd been cast into space. Something held her. She glanced down, expecting a rope or fist to clutch her middle.

But she had no middle to clutch. She had no body.

A limb of hairy darkness stretched where she expected to find her chest, middle, legs, feet. Petal-like eyes dotted the coarse hair where the limb forked away from May. The limb's foundation grew from a grander trunk that stretched high and low. There was no sky, no earth, only a great gray bend in this outer world where countless root-like limbs weaved through a foggy miasma.

All the way up the trunk, the hairy limbs reached for a dark world, its surface crackling with slender lines of light through which to peer.

And May was a pair of eyes. Nothing more.

Her limb curled inward toward the vast trunk, sweeping the miasma beneath her until she could look farther down the column of dark hair, into the endless meadows of eyes. They glanced at her, at each other, and into the light where their adjoining limbs pressed them, but the panic in some and the vacant gaze in others said they had no control. They were pieces of the missing, of strangers.

Except where May caught a familiar stare.

She would know those eyes anywhere. She'd seen them peeking around corners, through window glass, and deeper in the past, she'd stared into them with comfort or longing, before things got bad.

Nica gazed out from a neighboring limb. Her eyes glistened white and unblinking. Could she see? Was she here, or in some dream inside her head, maybe replaying whatever night had brought her here over and over? Remembering May.

Nica, May wanted to cry. She'd been so reluctant to say her name, and now it sank inside her. The voices fell away in this place. They weren't of any use, so why keep them? May could want Nica's help, her understanding, maybe her forgiveness all she pleased, but they were both trapped across the great limbs.

There was nothing Nica could do for either of them.

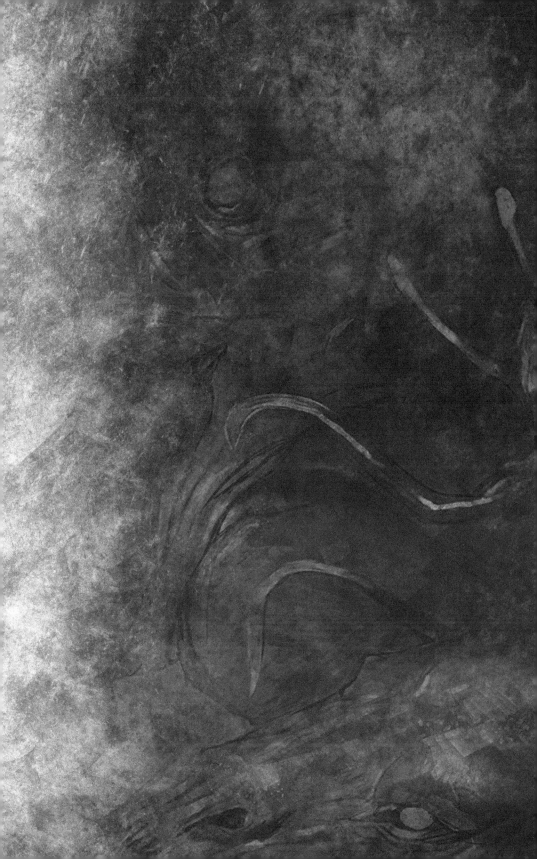

ZONE STAGE

WHAT'S MISSING?

Every morning at 6:13, Martha and Gerald stood at their his-and-her sinks and brushed their teeth. The coffee maker was programmed to start at 6:28. They ate wheat toast at the kitchen table, each engrossed in a book, comfortably unconversational. At 7:20, Monday through Friday, they pulled out of the driveway, Martha behind the wheel. After dropping Gerald at the bank, Martha drove to a building where the window placement guaranteed a view of nothing, the handiwork of a man who regularly designed prisons. There, she processed driver's licenses for the state from 8 a.m. to 4 p.m.

After collecting Gerald from the bank, they headed together to the grocery store, or the dry cleaners, or the dentist, or, if there were no errands to run, home. With a jazz music accompaniment, Gerald prepared supper, working his way sequentially through his newest cookbook, following every recipe's instructions without deviation, while Martha dusted and vacuumed and folded the freshly-washed laundry. Every evening they watched two hours of television, with a strong preference for documentaries or British dramas. At night they lay side-by-side in bed, each engrossed in a book, comfortably unconversational.

The weekends were for doing chores around the house, practicing Tai Chi in the backyard, and playing bridge—every other Saturday night—with Erica and Charles. Once a month they had sex. They went to the library weekly. If asked, they'd both say—with conviction—that they were happy more than they were unhappy. But they spoke frequently, if briefly, about the What Else? Yes, they were happy more than they were unhappy, but both felt a small hole, a concavity like a mini teacup, where something was missing.

Over the years they had discussed making dramatic changes: Having children; moving across the country; finding new jobs. The possible solutions always felt bigger than the empty teacup and once they reached their forties the existential conversations tended to culminate in a trip to a bookstore, or a weekend workshop on meditating or salsa dancing. Until Gerald suggested one Sunday afternoon that they buy a new house.

"A new house?" Martha considered him, and his proposition. "Where?"

Gerald swept crumbs from the counter into his palm, and sprinkled them over the garbage. He rested his hip against the dishwasher, arms crossed, casual not defiant. "Maybe just a little farther out. Have a little more space, but not add too much time to our commute."

Martha mirrored him, hip against a lower cabinet, arms crossed. "With a bigger backyard we could really take a stab at gardening."

"Play badminton. Or bocci ball. Or put up a pair of hammocks. It's something to think about."

"I wouldn't want to have to wake up too much earlier."

"No, our schedule is good. But in a different place...We'll be just a little—"

"Different," Martha said, completing his thought. She smiled. "It's worth investigating what might be out there." He smiled back.

And that's how Gerald and Martha decided to buy a new house.

Over the next several months the careful routine of their lives was disrupted. Intermittently, they both regretted the decision, as the realities of selling a house, buying a house, packing and sorting and moving took over their regular patterns. But even then there lay an undercurrent of excitement, of change afoot. They went to bed each night exhausted, but always shared a few hopeful words about the new things they would do.

The new house was bigger. Martha said it was like looking at a digital photo of their old house, and spreading their fingers to increase its magnification. The ceilings were higher, the rooms broader. They still stood each morning at his-and-her sinks, but there was three feet of space between them. When they made eye contact in the mirror they laughed.

It took longer than anticipated to figure out how to arrange their furniture and things. At first they tried placing everything as it had corresponded in their old house. But that felt wrong, and lazy. They spent weeks experimenting, shifting their old furnishings around in different rooms. At night, instead of reading, they nestled in bed shoulder-to-shoulder and bought new chairs and rugs and lamps online. Martha and Gerald were certain they were transforming not only their home, but their lives.

Their old habits returned as soon as they were settled. Needing twelve additional minutes to accommodate their location, they now brushed their teeth at 6:01, programmed the coffee maker for 6:16, and left the house at 7:08. They still did errands after work, and played bridge every other Saturday with Erica and Charles. Gerald got a small raise at work, and, unrelated, Martha bought them both tap shoes so they could do something purposeful with their one small, extra room. Together, twice a week, they watched a tutorial online and made the walls ring with the brush-heel-shuffles of their Shirley Temples and Buffaloes. But beyond that, nothing in their lives had *really* changed.

They had no regrets, and if asked both would say they were happy more than they were unhappy. But there was no denying that the void hadn't been filled.

One evening Martha said, "Sometimes I feel like I'm seeing the world through clouded water."

"Maybe you should clean your glasses," Gerald joked. He held her hand through the entire last hour of their TV show.

One Sunday morning Martha stepped out onto their back deck to enjoy a moment of fresh air. The yard, as Gerald had envisioned, had a large grassy area for playing games, bordered by perennials and small shrubs. They hadn't quite gotten around to planting tomatoes or beans, or a pollinator garden to attract butterflies and bees, but it was on their to-do list. Martha had intended to sit on one of their two lounge chairs and meditate, but an unexpected object drew her attention.

By its prominent place in the center of the deck, Martha immediately assumed it was a gift—a surprise—from Gerald. She approached it with cautious delight, uncertain of its purpose. It appeared to be a round globe, a fish bowl perhaps, set upon a sturdy monolithic pedestal. As she got closer to it, the mysteriousness excited her even more. There was a small opening at the top of the orb, and she was certain now, by its murky contents, that it was from Gerald: a quixotic response to the comment she'd made the week before, about seeing through clouded water.

When she first pressed her nose to the bowl she saw only unfathomable darkness. Then, as if her vision were acclimating to the gloom, shapes started to emerge. She saw dainty leaves billowing against the curved glass. Something within the water sent out a ripple. And a bubble. It startled Martha at first, but she was more intrigued than ever.

"Hello? I can't see you."

She tried to imagine what her husband might have gotten—a small turtle, koi, a pair of frogs? Her smile started to waver as the something swam toward her face. She caught a glimpse of...fins? a spiny tail? claws?

"Oh." She took a step back as the thing in the globe stretched toward the opening.

"Oh!" Worse than the fact that it was escaping came the impossible reality that it was growing.

Martha turned and ran for the house. She slammed the screen door and looked outside, still curious to see what had emerged from the tank, but more confident to do so from a safe distance.

Except it wasn't a safe distance.

The thing was growing, and advancing. She shouldn't have stood there gaping, but the shock of it mesmerized her. Its shape remained fluid even as it continued to grow, as if its lifeforce was the essence of a beating heart. It was a mammal one moment, an amphibian the next. Now with lengthening talons, now with dripping stilettos of teeth. It had two eyes on the sides of its face; it had many eyes on uneven stalks, clustered near its gaping mouth.

It headed for the house, for the door. For Martha.

The enchantment she'd first felt was now a solid block of terror, heavy in her gut. So heavy it was slowing her down, but she sprang back to life and threw herself against the unwieldy door, slightly misaligned and a challenge to close on the best of days. She turned the deadbolt and affixed the chain...But she knew none of it was enough—the doors, the locks. The thing was growing, and it would follow her inside no matter what she did to block its way.

She raced for the stairs and charged up to the second floor, screaming her husband's name.

Martha and Gerald huddled on the far side of their bed. Their bedroom had only a flimsy door with an even flimsier mechanism in the knob meant as a "privacy lock."

"What is it?" Gerald whispered, terrified by his wife's fear—and the ascension of a monstrosity slithering and squeezing its way up the stairs. The wooden steps groaned under its weight and shivered with quick snapping sounds that reminded Martha of the tap lessons they practiced in their hollow room.

"I don't know!"

They knelt there—riveted, imagining the thing that was making their house creak. It reached the top of the steps and started toward them. Sometimes it had nails that clicked against the hallway floor like an overgrown dog. Sometimes it labored to force its slippery mass over the angled surfaces of their new house. It carried the primordial perfume of rot and bloom.

"It's coming." Gerald gripped his wife's arm.

In perfect synchronicity, as if this dance was a product of the monster's singular music, they ran for the adjoining bathroom.

This door was older—thicker—with hardware like a miniature anchor, set sideways, that turned a small steel shaft into a groove. It was better than the bedroom, but Gerald giggled as he locked them in. Martha clutched his elbow, also laughing.

"This isn't funny," he said.

"No." They laughed anyway.

They sat like spoons, leaning against the door, fascinated by the sounds. Somehow, a wall was making a stretching noise, tight and rising in pitch. Next came a loud *pop* and Martha and Gerald understood the thing had gotten the bedroom door open and was squishing itself through. Again came the clicking and slithering as it moved around their bed, growing momentarily quiet as it crossed over the throw rug.

Martha and Gerald pushed off with their feet, sliding on their bottoms across the cold bathroom tile. They were stopped by a wall. The thing reached the door; they heard it breathing. A snuffling, gasping sound with the low vibrato of a growl. It was five feet away now. Only an old slab of painted wood stood between them.

Gerald darted around the room, looking for something they could MacGyver into a weapon. Martha jumped up and hurried to the pane of frosted glass. It was a small window and they'd yet to open it more than four inches. In theory, shouldering it together, they could force it all the way. In theory, if Gerald shoved her when she got stuck—as she surely would—she could worm her way out. But then what? Fall two stories to the ground? With Gerald left behind? No, she wouldn't leave him.

The thing crushed its mass against the door. The symphony of resistance—the groaning, squawking, howling—wouldn't last long. It would soon fill their gaping doorway, and keep advancing. Was it still growing?

Without speaking, they reached the same conclusion and abandoned their search for a figurative, or literal, way out—though Gerald grabbed a can of hairspray. With their fingers interlocked, a death grip, they backed away from the wheezing door. A tentacle wriggled under it, but quickly withdrew as the thing exerted pressure and once-flat planes became convex, ready to burst.

Martha and Gerald looked at each other, and the laughter erupted again.

"What are we going to do?" Gerald asked.

His unremarkable question gave Martha an idea. Nothing had been visible in the dark water before she greeted it. In a similar way that she'd enticed it out, could she suggest it retreat?

She remembered how intently she'd peered into the bowl, eager to see it. It seemed right to repeat her actions. Gerald tried to pull her back as she tiptoed forward.

"It's okay," she said.

While he didn't let go, he loosened their finger-lock enough to let her get within a foot of the door.

She hunched down, trying to get a glimpse of it through the stretching, pulsating cracks. She saw mangy fur and scaly skin. "Goodbye. I can see you."

They were the opposite words she'd spoken upon glimpsing its bubbles in the orb.

With a quick leap backward she and Gerald huddled together again, giddy with excitement and anticipation.

The thing stopped pushing against the door. It slunk backward, and Martha was sure she could hear it shrinking. It *flub-flubbed* and *click-clicked* out of the room and down the stairs.

"Come on!" Martha threw open the door and chased after it.

Gerald, barefoot, had to be careful as they scampered down the steps, which were littered with splinters of wood.

As gleefully as children spying on Santa in his workshop, they watched from the back door as the monster returned to its home, growing smaller and smaller. It leapt onto the globe and looked back at them.

Martha held her breath, afraid to speak to it and cause another reaction. It was so diminutive, a feral wolf pup. Tentacles as slender as needles. A newborn creature.

"I love you," Gerald whispered; Martha was almost sure the words were meant for her.

The thing dove into the murky water and disappeared.

Grinning, husband and wife turned to each other, their skin aglow, their thoughts racing, their hearts pounding.

"Thank you," Martha said, just in case it really had been a gift from Gerald.

Life returned to its familiar routine—coffee, wheat toast, work, the library on Thursdays—but they didn't talk anymore about what was missing.

They were comforted to know that if any sort of malaise returned, all they needed to do was gaze into the globe's dark waters and whisper hello. Though they did add one element to their schedule: at 5:58 each evening they stepped onto their deck hand-in-hand and stood in silent wonder near the mysterious object, a short vigil that preceded their supper.

Occasionally, as the sun began to rise or set, Martha or Gerald would visit the orb alone. With shallow breaths they'd watch for a ripple, a bubble, some sign of the creature's life, as their lips made the shape of an unvoiced greeting.

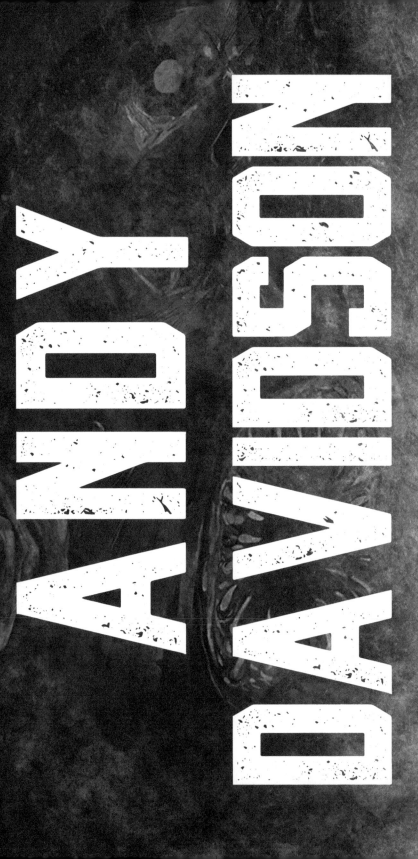

STILL LIFE
WITH BONES

Hobe and me, we hang around the valedictorian's childhood home until we've had our fill of horseshoes and cornholing. We say we're skipping the barbecue supper, and the valedictorian—two stair-stepped kids and a nit husband with a swank job, Facebook photos of the whole clan in white, a backdrop of sea oats—tells us, "Now, remember, we all sit together at the game. Kickoff's in two hours!" We'll be there, Hobe tells her, and winks at me, and then we take our class reunion on the road. First stop's Airport Liquor: a bottle of Old Grand-Dad and two fistfuls of Slim Jims. Next, it's the old spillway out by the dam and a spot deep in the bottoms where Hobe lost his virginity to a girl whose name he misremembers, insisting it was Carly when it was Charlie. Hobe says they got arrested on one of these roads, a few weeks after graduation. Driving drunk and naked in her daddy's pickup. The judge was lenient. He never saw that girl again. "You was off in basic by then," he says.

The sun's gone by mid-second quarter. We cruise past the stadium in Hobe's momma's shitbox Tercel and the windows are down because they won't roll up, and off across the stark-lit field you can hear the steady primal pound of snares and toms and suddenly we're called back to seventeen, Friday nights full of promise, and Hobe says, "You remember them bones?"

Autumn leaves scatter over asphalt, whirl behind us.

"I remember," I say, and take a slug of whiskey.

I switch off the radio, where a preacher calls the game out of the press box on a local station. Soon, we're passing out of town onto the bypass, then a turn or two and it's the long straight blacktop of a county road, the old munitions plant, Quonset barracks where the National Guard used to train, now abandoned. Highlines amid the onrushing dark of dense pine thickets and railroad tracks. Train cars still and silent along the roadside, like beasts that slumber upright. At last: the little church in the piney woods, empty shell of a building. Graffiti scrawled on the inside walls and the pews carved up with names and vows and curses. Cigarette butts and broken needles, blood and spit, sweat and spunk, the smashed bowls of crack pipes.

In back, the cemetery, ringed in crooked iron.

This haunted dirt.

The bones are still there, right where we found them nine years back. Amid the sunken, unreadable tombstones, a broken slab of granite all but swallowed by bahiagrass. The bottom of the slab a gaping hole. I remember how Hobe sat there, put his feet over the edge, into the grave, like it was a swimming pool. How we both hung down in there to have a look. Smell of moldering leaves and cool root-cellar dark. We shined a flashlight and saw what was left of a human being, laid out. Tonight, we go right to it. Hobe with his Maglite from the job he works, night watchman at the paper mill. "Ain't been touched," he says.

I can hear it in his voice, the urge to do it. Like he wanted to all those years back, when we were kids and it seemed like the stupidest thing: steal a corpse and ride it around in the trunk of your momma's car. No more consequence to Hobe than watching his old man's porn on a weekday afternoon. I was always the cautious one. Always the voice of reason. My mother's child, for the most part. Tender-hearted and thoughtful. But there was always the itch of transformation, out with Hobe. That thing beneath your skin that rakes its claws through fat and tissue, wants to rip its way out. Trash some shit. Hurt someone. Steal some bones.

In the Army, they search out that beast, tame it with pain.

I buried mine so deep, they never got it.

Thank you for your service, the valedictorian's husband said, shaking my hand.

I almost broke his nose.

We sit with our feet in the grave, trading hits on the bottle.

"You remember that guy," I say, "Rex Swanson?"

Hobe holds his hands out on either side of his head, like he's measuring a span. "Head out to here?"

"That's the one. He spit in my face once, when I was thirteen."

"I don't remember that."

"You were out sick. Chickenpox. He walked right up to me in the lunchroom and, for no reason I ever understood, just hocked one right in my eye."

"He's in prison now, I think," Hobe says, drinking. "Or maybe he runs a lawn service."

We laugh. He tells me about his brother, Jason, how he's got a job with the county sheriff, how Hobe's thinking he might apply, come spring. I tell him about a girl I've met through an online dating site. She has a black belt and breaks boards. I take out my phone, show him the video. A dojo, the girl in a white gi, three pine boards sandwiched in a stand. Whip-crack and the boards split and she dances away on the balls of her feet. She and I fling messages back and forth in chat boxes. It's all just pixels on a screen. She's into bondage, domination. I've tried to picture it: getting tied up, blindfolded. I imagine it like one of her dojo videos. My heart is a board. It will never work.

We don't talk for a while, just sit and drink. The night out here is as black as any at Fort Hood, but the stars seem dimmer, distant. It's October cool and

I wish we had a fire. I think about the planned, post-game bonfire, back at the valedictorian's house. Ten years out of high school, a class of fifty, and only a dozen showed. One or two smart kids, come back to lord it over the rest. Dentists and lawyers. Some nurses. One guy we all laughed at for getting his dick hard in class and standing up in his desk when our civics teacher's back was turned. A smile and a handshake from him, wrist tattoos from a stint in jail after a knife fight in a motel parking lot. One of the girls I never really knew, Janelle, she's a science teacher now, at our old school. Freshman year of college, she had a baby. Rumor was it belonged to her stepfather. Everyone passed the story around by email in the months after it happened, how they found the baby one Saturday morning in a Dumpster in back of the Baptist Student Union. She'd hidden the pregnancy, wrapped her belly all through it in tape and Ace bandages. Monday after she delivered, campus police arrested her in freshman English. At horseshoes, Janelle and I got paired up. "I really like teaching," she told me. "What are you up to these days, Wes?"

"Back home with my parents," I said. "Helping Dad, around his shop."

"That's nice," Janelle said.

"We don't talk," I said.

We finished the game in silence. She won.

There's no headstone to say whose bones they are. Hobe wonders how it is, they've been here all this time, within easy reach and not got stolen. "Lord knows," he says, "it's been plenty of traffic out here. All the used rubbers in there." He nods at the church. His words are slurring. I look at him in the Maglite's glow, shadows beneath his nose and chin. "Clearly," he says, "no one gives a shit about this place."

"Let's take 'em," I say.

Hobe says, "Fuckin-A," and trudges back through the long grass to the

Tercel. From the trunk, he fetches a duffel full of underwear and T-shirts he's been meaning to wash at the Wondermat.

I go in on my belly, like I'm back in the desert, all arms and elbows in the craggy dark. Sound of my own heart huge.

Hobe shines his flashlight.

I toss back a femur, a scrap of pelvis. An arm.

At last, the skull. We stare at each other. No jaw, just a handful of teeth scattered like acorns among the leaves. In the chiaroscuro of the Maglite, a still life with bones.

Hobe wants to wire it all together, drive through the post-game traffic and make it wave through the car's open window. But this would be a desecration even greater than the broken headstone, or our theft. The people in letter jackets, walking for their cars, they wouldn't see it for what it was. What it meant. They'd laugh and point with their foam fingers, carrying their cups of Booster Club cocoa. It would mean even less than the lawn jockey Hobe once stole and threw through the window of the principal's car. Or the time we put peanut butter in the bell of our band director's trumpet. Just a stupid prank.

They'd never know who it was, riding in that car, waving at them.

We stuff the bones in the bag and toss the bag on the backseat.

Hobe's too drunk to drive so I do.

The night air whips through the car.

Beyond the headlights, the woods lie dark and fretful.

We're late to the bonfire. I wake Hobe and we pass the last of the Old Grand Dad between us as we wander up to the blazing pit, around it the long shadows of the ones who've returned. Everyone but the one who went to jail, and the dentist. The valedictorian and her husband sit side-by-side in aluminum lawn chairs, a football blanket spread between them. Beers in hand. I slide into a chair by Janelle, who smiles at me, and there are sparks dancing in her eyes. She's as lonely as I am in this place, and I can see how the night might go, if I wanted it to. Hobe sits cross-legged on the cold ground and picks at grass.

The valedictorian smiles and starts sentences with "Remember...."

Out beyond the firelight, ghosts hold sway in the dewy grass. Ghosts of the selves we could have been, if we hadn't stayed. If we hadn't come back.

The fire mesmerizes, pulls me in.

Janelle asks me about the Army, what it was like. I don't answer, thinking of the last cave I ever squeezed into, a dark slash in the desert rock. The skull I found there, perched high on a shelf of stone, no other bones about. How it begged to be picked up. Taken down. How I wanted, so very briefly, to do just that. Remembering a weekend in San Antonio, before I shipped out, when I visited a medium along the River Walk, who turned over card upon card in an alleyway stall, the last one "Death." That ragged collection of bones wielding a scythe, all contradictions inherent within that simple image. We are born, we die. Death makes way for what's to come. The bones are alpha, omega, life itself the ritual of cleansing.

"Hey," I say, suddenly.

All around the fire, pockets of chatter cease, and there is only the sound of the flames licking air, popping wood. "We have to do something," I say.

Hobe's looking up at me, bleary-eyed.

I walk out of the light to the car, grab the duffel bag from the seat.

When I come back, everyone's silent, waiting.

I set the bag on the ground. Unzip it.

Hobe and Janelle stand over me, watching.

I take out a femur. Hold it up where all can see.

The valedictorian's husband says, "Jesus, is that—"

And the valedictorian gasps.

I throw the bone into the fire.

Then a rib. The sternum. Humerus, tibia, ulna. On and on, until they're all burning save the last.

No one says a word as I hold up the skull.

"Reckon it was a he or a she?" Hobe says.

"It's us," I say.

And toss it in.

Janelle stands close. Slips her hand into mine, squeezes, and her grip is startling, terrifying.

In the morning, I will wake up in my childhood bed and be something new.

We all will. Hobe. Me. The valedictorian. Janelle.

We'll reek of smoke and fire. We'll be powder. We'll be ash.

We'll be free.

THE THINGS
WE DID,
WE DID,
WERE ALL
FOR REAL

I remember going to bed as a child. Clad in pajamas, sent to the top bunk in the room I shared with my brother, long gone now.

I remember wrapping in blankets on winter nights, mummifying myself to keep in the warmth.

I remember how cold it was initially, how delightfully warm it became, and that awful/awesome transition between the two.

I remember the yelling.

Disembodied voices screaming at me in the darkness. Shouting at me to pay attention, to do *something*. I never knew exactly what they wanted or why they were shouting.

When I got older and started my practice, I spoke about this to a colleague, and we decided it was probably my parents, young at the time, arguing now that the kids were asleep. Me integrating this into my dreams.

Seemed reasonable. Even now, it seems as if that's what it *should* have been.

But now, in the spinning center of the encompassing desert, surrounded by sand—tans and beiges and deep browns stretching from horizon to horizon—I know what it really was.

I hang up the phone, fall slowly to my knees and weep.

It wasn't a dream.

Those voices *called* to me.

Have been calling to me ever since.

Tonight, I called back.

I'd heard about the phone from a waitress in the little café I visit for breakfast most every day. Right off the main drag in the dusty little southwest town of Modrega. You know the place, very artsy-craftsy. Chunky, eclectic folk art everywhere. Beaming sun faces, glowering moons. Lots of terra cotta and macrame. Lots of shared art from all the other artsy-craftsy places in town.

What is it about the desert that draws creatives together to eke out a living? Especially here in Modrega. There's a little tourist trade, but we're pretty far from Taos or Santa Fe. These artists—middle-aged, retired men or widowed women—they're basically selling to and buying from each other. It's incestuous, but I guess it's a living.

Not me, though. I have a thriving little mental health practice I run out of my house, almost entirely Zoom or Skype sessions. Great for me that most creative types need counseling of some kind at some point.

I live outside the main part of town, down a dusty, rutted road, at the entrance to a small box canyon. I love it, keeps most folks from visiting. I have what could charitably be called a tiny house these days. Just a small trailer for me and Mr. Cat. That's the whole of his name. I couldn't be bothered with more.

Yeah, my little, aching Midwestern heart loves the desert. So searingly bright in the day, so majestically dark at night, with the universe circling above. How many cool nights I've spent in my lawn chair, a cup of Irish coffee in hand, and watched those same stars, glittering like vaguely shielded eyes.

Who was that Greek god who had all the eyes? Ae-something or another. Can't remember back to my school-boy days. But I think about eyes a lot.

I feel them at night, glaring down on all of us, but on me in particular. Wondering what I was doing, what I might do. What I *should* do. The weight of it all, the pressure of all that inspection, that intrusion.

Physicists say the mere act of observation makes things real.

I think observation of my patients makes them real, makes their challenges real. But perhaps it's the other way around.

Perhaps their observations make *me* real.

The stars, though...all that observation from those trillion upon trillion cold eyes...makes me feel uncomfortably real. Forced into being.

Anyway, I'd called it a morning after the last appointment had boggled my mind sufficiently. Instead of proceeding with the day, I put my pen down, closed the journal I'd been writing in, and went into town for a late breakfast.

Today the house special coffee at the Las Placitas Café was "This is the Story, Morning Glory" blend. Despite the name, I ordered it, and two eggs, over easy with corned beef hash and rye toast.

Juana, the old lady who owned the place, came with the coffee pot.

"Warm up, eh, doc?"

"Sure," I said, offering my cup.

"You look..."

"Charming? Handsome? Devil-may-care?"

"Out of sorts," she said, measuring me with more intent than the mindless slosh of coffee into my cup.

"Really? I guess you're the charming one, then."

"Just an observation. What are you sitting here mooning over?"

"My place in the universe. Hell, my place in Modrega. You know, heady stuff like that."

"Hmm, you need to talk with the higher up," she said, raising her eyes toward the ceiling.

"I thought *you* were the higher up," I laugh, taking a searing sip of "This is the Story, Morning Glory." It was delightful, despite the name.

"Oh honey, I mean *the* higher up, the higher powers. Who else can someone like you bring his problems to?" she said. Now she sounded like a true Modregan.

"Oh? Do tell."

"You need that phone out in the desert."

I stopped a forkful of hash on its way to my mouth. "The what?"

"Just a phone out in the desert. You make a call and tell it your thoughts. Problems. Wishes. They call it the God Phone."

"And?"

"Maybe you get answers," her smile intensified. "Or maybe just the satisfaction of having spoken your thoughts out loud."

"To someone?" I said, still a little confused.

"Or *something*," she shrugged, then walked away.

I finished my breakfast, reading the news on my phone. More bad stuff, lying politicians, lying corporations, lying religions. When I'd had enough good breakfast and bad news, I rose, went to pay my bill.

Juana was at the cash register now. The place wasn't busy, and I wondered if she was the only one there. She rang me up, pushed a receipt across the counter at me.

"Nah, don't need that. It all comes in over the phone."

"It sure does," she agreed. "Take it."

I took the receipt, flipped it over. On the back was sketched a rudimentary map, the interstate and some major crossroads noted.

"Thanks," I said. "I'll try to get out there and give whomever a call."

"Whomever is waiting for it, doc, I'm sure."

If you think I drove right from the café out to that phone in the desert, you don't know me very well yet.

Nah, I went back to my house, tossed the keys and some spare change from breakfast into the little ceramic bowl on the table near the front door. I also fished out the crumpled receipt with the map on it.

Smiling at Juana's crude drawing, I thought about throwing the paper out. Instead, I let it slip from my fingers into the bowl. I went inside, fired up my laptop and went to work for the day.

I forgot about the entire encounter for more than a week.

I went into town about ten days later. I needed more Moleskin notebooks for my job. I keep copious notes on each of my clients. I box these up when they're filled and take them to my unit in that storage facility off I-25.

I go through a lot of them, taking notes, jotting reminders, doodling during my virtual consultations, my preferred type here in these pre-post-Covid days.

There was a little stationery store a few buildings down from Las Placitas, called Memories and More. Ridiculous, Hallmark-style stuff—figurines, plates, holiday cards. You know the kind. I had a standing order for twenty-five of the big classic softcover notebooks each month, and though I was a few days early, I knew Rena would have them in stock, ready to go.

The plan was to swing by, pick up my stuff, maybe a smelly candle or two (hey, laugh if you want), then go grab a late breakfast.

The shop bell tinkled as I pushed the door open onto air already twenty degrees cooler than outside. After living in the desert for almost two decades, AC always hits me as instantly appreciated but gradually annoying.

Rena was on her hands and knees trying to put together a complicated cardboard display unit for some kind of glass garden doodads.

"Need some help there?" I said.

"You caught me," she said, turning to see who it was. "Took me ten minutes to get down here, probably take me just as long to get up."

I offered her my hand.

"Oh, you," she said, rising to her feet. I heard her knees crack, and she grunted as her hips bore her weight. "You're early."

"Yeah, lot of notes this month," I said.

"Let me go get 'em," she breathed, waddling away. I could smell her perfume, some soft, old lady floral stuff, and her acrid coffee breath.

"You need some help with this?" I said, nudging the slump of cardboard she'd been working on.

"If you want," her voice came from the back room. "I can't make heads or tails of it."

I knelt, took stock of the instruction page, written in that charming, exuberant pidgin English Chinese companies are masters of. *Place Tab A into Slot B with delicate. Then fold Tab A down strict crease.*

Okay, I think I got you. I inserted and folded and went from there.

After a minute or so, Rena returned. I heard her stertorous breathing before she stopped near me. "Huh. Well, you got further than I did."

I inserted and folded a few more tabs, until I got a structure I figured she could make the most of. Standing, I followed her to the counter.

"Put this on the card on file?" she asked.

I nodded, and she rang it all up, slid the notebooks into a reusable tote bag with her store's logo on it.

"You really fill all these notebooks you buy?" she asked.

"Sure do."

"Hmpph. I'd have to see that to believe it."

"Patient-doctor privilege," I tsked.

"So, she told you about it," Rena said, out of the blue.

"Who told me about what?" I genuinely had no idea what she was talking about.

"Juana. The God Phone."

"Oh, that," I laughed. "She sure did."

"You been out there yet?

I pictured Juana's scribbled map, balled up where I'd left it in the little bowl inside my front door.

"Nah. Why would I?"

She handed my receipt across the counter.

"A lot of people here in town get great comfort from it," she said. "You might, too. I mean where does the man who offers comfort turn for it himself?"

She waggled her eyebrows at me, pleased at the perceived depth of her comment. I stuffed the receipt into the bag with the notebooks.

"A phone in the middle of nowhere that rings who knows who? Maybe nothing. And talking into it offers comfort? Maybe I should tell my patients, save them some money."

"Shhh, you don't want to tell everyone your secret," she said, smiling.

"Mum's the word," I said, turning toward the door. "See you in a month."

As the bell jingled, she called after me, "You'd be surprised what power simply being heard has."

The cold air ended at the doorway, and I was out in the dusty heat.

Where does the man who offers comfort turn for it himself?

I thought of what Rena had said. It might have been an offhand comment, but where *do* those who offer comfort turn to for comfort? Not just doctors or first responders, but all of us, all of humanity?

I think back to those voices I heard tucked into my childhood bed. Mom, Dad. Fighting. Seems to me they should have turned to each other for comfort, but I rarely saw that.

When I really looked at it much later, I realized that my parents were crying out for help. Floored to realize they were as helpless as I was. As helpless as we all are. Their cries fell on my ears, but I could offer them nothing.

I wasn't cold or indifferent, just powerless. And they were as powerless as me.

There we were, all three of us, orphans crying out for help to a universe of ears unable to hear, unable to provide succor.

Or unwilling.

My entire career was devoted to building a place where need meets comfort.

But I realized while I could offer my patients help, it was temporary, illusory.

There's nowhere for any of us to turn to in need.

At least that's what I thought.

I awoke around one a.m., the fire still sputtering in the pit outside the trailer. I was slumped in the Adirondack chair, feet pointed toward the heat of the fire. The small table near me held three things: a plate with the remains of my dinner, a small crystal glass, empty, and a bottle of whisky, also empty.

My head, though, felt remarkably steady and clear, weird because I knew that bottle had been at least half full when I carried my dinner here. Maybe I spilled some? But when you spill whisky, in my experience, you generally remember.

I let my head loll back against the solid wood of the chair. The night was clear and cool, as nights mostly are in the desert. The crooked arm of the Milky Way flexed across the sky, its trillion pinpricks of light glowering down on me.

For a reason I cannot, even now, pinpoint with any degree of accuracy, I thought of the crumpled receipt in my key bowl, the phone out there in the desert. I grasped the arms of the chair. It was as if the light of all those stars wrung me like a dishtowel, distilling something in the well of my brain.

I stood, upsetting the table, spilling the remains of my food, the fork and knife. The paper napkin fluttered into the fire, vanished in a curl of heat.

Somewhere, a coyote howled.

I went inside, dug for the flashlight, then hopped into my car, the receipt held tight in my hand, wrinkles smoothed, showing Juana's map.

I drove west for about twenty minutes, a few car beams coming down the two-lane from the opposite direction. The windows were open. The cool desert air, minus the warm smell of colitas, pushing into the car. Tom Waits' rough, mournful voice carried me into the night, following the sketchy map.

Twice, I stopped to consult the drawing in the washed-out dome light of the car, backed up and turned onto a road I overshot. I saw no signs, though I was sure I must be on tribal lands. I slowed down even more, paid attention to where I was.

The last turn I made was one I missed, drove back, missed again, then returned. Barely a road, more like a trail, just two rutted slots in the desert, scruff growing in the hump between them. The car shrugged and jounced, but I was too far gone to go back.

I went on for nearly two miles. I'd turned off the stereo in order to think more clearly, and my eyes scanned the black desert to see something... anything.

Just as I was about to turn back, angry at Rena and Juana for sending me on a fool's errand, there it was.

It jutted from the flat, arid plain, lit by a fixture hanging on a gooseneck above it. A plain, old-style phone booth enclosed on three sides, attached to a grey, metal pole. The phone was on a steel plate mounted to the pole, glass panels on either side went from just above the phone down to about three feet from the ground.

It looked like a typical phone booth you'd see on a typical street corner in a typical urban setting. Except this wasn't a street corner, typical or otherwise, and it certainly wasn't urban.

Plus, there was no logo, no AT&T icon or anything noting what company had put the phone out here.

Incongruous against the desert night. Starkly lighting the nearby bushes and cacti all blue-white, as if frozen in a lightning strike.

I stopped the car, considered my next move.

What was there to do when encountering something as unusual as this?

You either nod, put the car into gear and leave, telling yourself it was all nothing, it meant nothing.

Or press on and see where it leads.

I left my car door open, the engine running, easier for me to hightail it out of there if things got too weird. A few steps brought me to the phone booth, but again being cautious, I didn't get between its unmarked glass panels. I felt moving into it was akin to kneeling at an altar or saying the final word in an incantation.

Being inside gave it power.

I circled it instead.

Nothing at all set it apart from any other phone booth I'd seen, save it was *here*, all lit up in the middle of the desert.

And it was as clean as a whistle. Usually, these things were covered in graffiti, scratched into the metal, etched into the glass or tagged with spray paint. Not this one.

More, it was pristine, as if it had never once been used. No scratches on the clear glass, no scrapes or dings in the metal. The silver buttons were clean and free of smudges, the handset smooth and unblemished by the grip of hundreds of greasy, desperate hands.

Nothing, not any piece of the entire thing, was covered in dust or sand.

I went cautiously into the enclosure, feeling the alcohol I'd consumed leech into every brain cell. It momentarily staggered me, made me wonder how I'd driven out here without feeling any of its effects.

Losing my balance, I reached to steady myself, found my hand clenching on the cold, plastic handset, much colder than the surrounding night would suggest. Instead of resting there until my head cleared, though, I lifted the receiver, brought it to my ear.

The light above the booth buzzed and flickered.

There was no sound from the earpiece, and I reached for the little flipper to hang up, maybe dial a number.

Before I could, though, a high-pitched wail screeched from the phone, echoing into the desert. Instead of holding the receiver away or dropping it to hang from its spiral metal cord, I pushed it to my ear.

The sound augured into my brain, filled it with a burst of green-violet light like a scatter of Mardi Gras glitter. Then, as if on a bungee cord, it paused, came back, imploded in a silent concatenation of light.

In that light, an eye opened, regarded me with insectile interest.

Then another. And another.

Dozens. Hundreds.

Unbelievably, I recognized them.

Under the weight of their combined gaze, I passed out.

The sun coming through the slats of my bedroom blinds woke me. I lie there staring at the flocked ceiling of my room, sparkling like stars where the light hit it.

Shooting up, I remembered the night before.

I launched from the bed, tore out of the trailer. The car was parked askew near the firepit. The fire was out, the remains of my dinner scattered on the ground. The empty whisky bottle and glass sat undisturbed.

Fumbling in my pockets, I found the receipt with the map drawn onto it.
Had to be a dream.

Didn't it?

Only one way I know to acknowledge a dream and that's to deal with it in the light of day. So, I grabbed my car keys, followed the map again.

There were the same number of suspicious turns and back tracking. But I found my way, this time under the blaring sun. It was around 104 degrees outside, and the AC in the car barely made a dent.

There it was, like something from a Dali painting, so deeply incongruous it made me blink trying to focus.

A phone booth on a metal pole in the middle of the desert.

I considered it from the cool safety of the car before finally getting out, going towards it.

I'd left my sunglasses, and the pounding daylight was blinding. Shielding my eyes, I made my way to the phone.

It was just as I remembered—*dreamed?* Unusual only in its absolute banality here in the desert. Pristine, as if just installed.

Just a gleaming pay phone here in the middle of nowhere New Mexico.

The sun shimmering from the steel and glass reflected straight into my eyes, but I grasped the handset and put it to my ear.

No signal of a working line, no static or tones of any kind. Frowning, I pushed a button. It bleeped, satisfyingly recognizable, but after that... nothing.

I hung up, then immediately retrieved the receiver and, on a whim, dialed my own number. Each button made its familiar tone as I pressed it, and when I entered the last number, there was silence.

As I prepared to hang up, go back into town, there was a click, barely audible, then the thin hiss of static. It sounded distant in the way some phone connections can be. Like they're coming in from Mayberry RFD in 1958.

Through that static, a sound came, riding over it like a surfer skimming a tremendous ocean wave.

It was unintelligible as a word, glottal and full of consonants. It rose above the static until it dominated it, then faded away, repeating.

Whatever it was, it punched through my skull, reverberated there like a rung bell.

I dropped the receiver—*again?*—staggered backward out of the booth.

Not bothering to shield my eyes from the sun or the glare from the phone booth, I stumbled to the car. What I did next was surreal even after hearing a nonsense word from a payphone in the desert.

I fished in the backseat until my hand encountered the hemp tote Rena had dumped my monthly shipment of notebooks into. I grabbed one of them, pulled a pen from the center console of the car, and started scribbling onto the first clean page of the notebook.

When I looked down again, I was on the last page. I lifted the pen, flipped through the pages.

They were filled with writing in a language I didn't know, had never seen. There were drawings, too, much better done than I could ever do. They weren't just doodles or scribbles, either, but detailed sketches somehow tied into whatever the writing discussed.

I closed the notebook, lifted my head, and let out a loud sigh. The engine wasn't on anymore, and the air inside the car was oven-hot. The door was still open, and the desert was now fully inside. Dust covered my clothes, the dashboard, the steering wheel.

A stack of books slumped across the passenger seat. All the rest of the notebooks from the bag.

I reached over, opened one at random.

More weird writing, more drawings.

I opened another.

You get the picture.

Every page, every book, all twenty-five of them.

I closed the car door, started the engine, left.

A quick shower, then a Google search and a few phone calls to local service providers. No one had a pay phone out there...or anywhere near there. There was also no cell tower providing service in that area.

City Hall said the property where the phone was lay in unincorporated land, not owned by any person, corporation, or government—state, federal, or tribal. It was just a small slice of land belonging to no one.

When I finally put the phone down, closed my laptop, I knew one thing.

The air was cool inside Las Placitas, smelled of all the usual wonderful things. I waved toward Juana, then took my usual seat, pretended to look at the scuffed, laminated menu tucked between the napkin dispenser and the off-brand ketchup bottle.

"Hey, you," she said, pouring coffee into my cup. "Been a few days."

"Iced tea, please," I croaked, putting my hand on hers and eliciting a soft gasp, a tensing of her hand holding the coffee pot.

"Sure thing," she said, withdrawing. She came back with a tall plastic tumbler of iced tea, sweating already, and removed the coffee cup.

"Are you ready—"

"I went there, you know."

"You went where?" She seemed genuinely puzzled.

"The phone in the desert."

"Oh?" Now she was bemused. "And? Did it clear things up for you?"

I shook my head. "Clear things up? Why did you send me there? What were you hoping for?"

My tone of voice, low and guttural, took her aback.

"Oh, honey, you were out of sorts, that's all. It's a joke, really. Just a disconnected phone some hippie put up in the desert. Said it was an art installation or some such nonsense. Evidently, they have one at Burning Man. People just go there and tell it their troubles. Helps some. That's all I know."

I nodded, a little too enthusiastically I guess, because she turned and left without taking a lunch order from me.

It was late in the afternoon, so I just drained the tea, put a five down on the receipt, went to leave.

Rena was not around for me to apologize to. One lone customer sat with his back to me at the counter. I looked in the window to the kitchen, through which the orders came.

I saw the cook, who I think was one of Rena's sons, scowling back at me, steel spatula in hand.

I went outside in the glare and heat of the sun.

Once home, I collapsed on my couch, threw my arm over my head. It was cool in the dark of my house, not as frigid as Las Placitas, but more welcome. There was too much to process, too much that defied easy explanation.

I fell asleep, overwhelmed by it all. I had dreams of floating in space, infinite, depthless black in all directions.

Something was there with me, unseen, a presence so huge it filled space itself. It dwarfed me, made me feel even smaller than had I been alone.

Then, it noticed me.

I felt the enormous *thump!* of its regard strike me, hold me in place, a wriggling butterfly impaled on a lepidopterist's needle. I struggled to evade it, to twist away, to somehow pull myself into something smaller, less likely to be discerned.

But it wasn't to be.

Blaring like a foghorn erupted in my head, a note so low it wasn't heard at all, but felt within my bones, from the stapes of my inner ear to my pelvis.

As soon as the final syllable sounded, it began again, insistent, so deep it made my dream-head throb, my bones disassociate.

A single eye opened in the dark, as big as a moon, a planet, and I instantly snapped awake.

I flailed, my limbs no longer weightless. I fell to the floor, and that landing momentarily cleared my head.

Scrabbling up, I went to my small desk in the front room. Atop it, held by two bookends in the shape of Rodin's Thinker, were the current notebooks I'd been transcribing thoughts about my clients' problems. I grabbed one at random, pulled it out.

Its pages are blank, as white as the light pouring through me at my last encounter with the phone.

I fumbled another loose. This, too, was blank.

That one tossed aside, and another, and another, and another.

All blank, even though I was positive most of these had at least some notes in them, marginalia, scribbles. Insights into my patients' innermost secrets.

The remaining notebooks slumped between thinkers. Soon, I'd gone through all, found them blank.

I'd spoken to these people, listened to their problems, offered suggestions, made notes. None of that was reflected in these blank journals.

That wasn't possible. Flatly not possible.

Was I having some sort of breakdown? Was I experiencing a fugue state?

Hell, maybe a stroke, some sort of transient event messing with my memory?

I thought of all the boxes and boxes of notebooks I had in the storage facility, all neatly packed, neatly labelled, neatly stored.

I grabbed my car keys.

Hours later...how many?

It's oppressively hot here in the storage facility. I'm sitting in a sea of empty, battered storage boxes that have disgorged their contents onto the concrete floor. Hundreds of black-covered Moleskin journals, mountains of them, spilling out of the garage door of the unit I rent and onto the road.

I'm soaked with sweat, my hair plastered to my head, every inch of my skin slicked with it.

None of the hundreds of journals here contain one jot of writing. No notes, no witty commentary on the state of my patients' psyches, no scribbles, drawings, ink stains.

Every page, every motherfucking page is white, lined, empty.

I feel like laughing.

I feel like crying.

What have I been doing all these years? According to these journals, nothing at all.

Have I actually helped anybody?

Myself?

Crawling back to the car, leaving the spill of journals and cardboard boxes, I examined myself in the rearview mirror. Disheveled, haggard, looked like I hadn't slept in days, even though I had...at least I think I had.

I closed the door and let the air conditioner dry me. As I reclined, my right hand fell back over the console and into the backseat. My fingers tickled the carpet, encountered something solid, closed on it.

A journal, the one I'd thrown there after the second encounter with the phone. I grabbed it, brought it forward.

It was still filled with writing, drawings, from front to back.

Only this time, I could *read* them.

They organized themselves into sentences. The drawings became immediate and instructive. The words of some ancient god-thing, older than Christianity or Islam or Judaism, older still than cave paintings in France or stone tools in Africa.

Older than the earth, than the sun, maybe even our galaxy.

It was the story of what I felt floating free in the vast blackness, an indescribable bulk of presence dwarfing me, dwarfing even the space that contained it.

But I wasn't transcribing *its* words, *its* history.

They were *my* words, I knew. I recognized the voice, the cadence of the speech even in the strange language.

They were my words, for I realized it had been on Earth before and I had been there with it. How it came, how it left, I didn't immediately know. How I could even be around that long ago, I didn't understand. I just knew I was involved. Intimately involved and an unutterably long time ago.

Now, it wanted to return.

Wanted a *way* to return.

I felt the skin of my neck turn to crepe.

All that I'd done—this rewriting of its vast history, this *remembrance*—was the key to that lock, the way back.

I had *noticed* it.

And it, very definitely, noticed me.

I felt the tumblers inside slide into place.

Much later, night again, I return to the payphone.

That one thing I knew?

It was my patients' need for me, my awareness bringing them into reality, that saved them. Now, that cosmic thing needed something similar from me.

But more so, I needed it, and this presence offered its observation to me. Under its gaze, I felt more alive than ever.

I would bring it back, happily, *joyously* just to have its regard pull me more fully into realness. What it meant for others, good or bad, I didn't care. I wanted to be as real as I could. More real than anyone or anything else.

Where does the man who offers comfort turn for it himself?

I made the final phone call.

There in the spinning center of the encompassing desert, surrounded by sand—tans and beiges and deep browns stretching from horizon to horizon—I hang up the phone, fall slowly to my knees and weep.

Those voices weren't a dream.

They were never a dream.

Those voices *called* to me.

My head bowed, I think of nothing but the vast, black space behind my eyeballs, between the firepop of distant stars. The space between minds, between creation and destruction, between Eden and Apocalypse.

The circular space between *having done* and *will do*.

I wait for those eyes to open and see me again, make me real.

When the familiar touch of that caller falls on my shoulder, like the hand it isn't, I don't flinch.

I don't flinch.

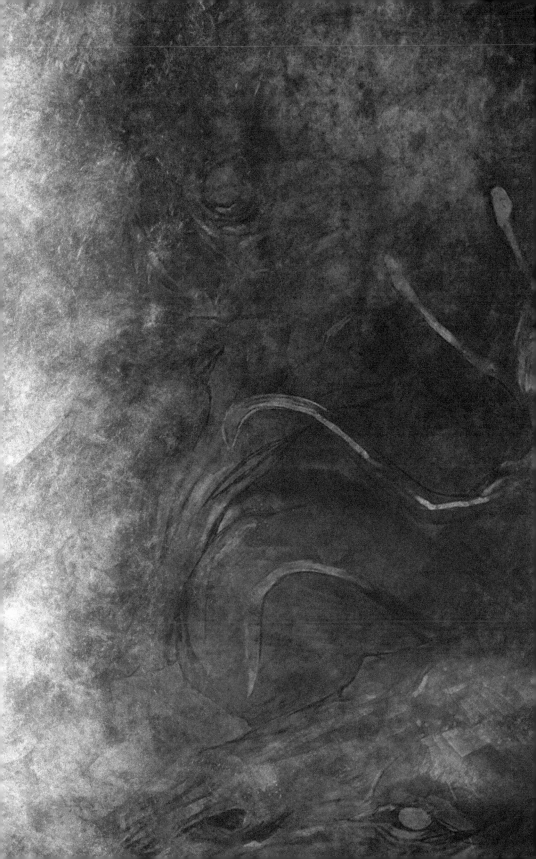

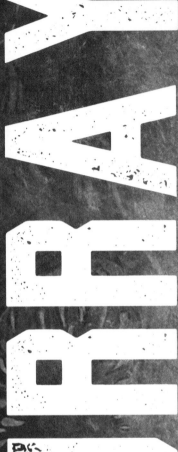

LEE MURRAY

MOONCAKE

The stairwell stank—a mixture of cigarette smoke, take-out grease, and mediocrity. Only the handrail was shiny, polished slick through a half century of comings and goings by the flats' occupants. Stacey stuffed her hands in her pockets as she climbed the gum-pocked stairs to the second floor. On the landing, the balustrade's chicken-wire barrier had been replaced with metal struts, clumps of grey lint lace clinging to the uprights. Otherwise, nothing had changed in the two years since Stacey had last visited, that time she'd argued with her grandmother and stormed out. What else could she do? The toxicity, the wheedling, *the expectation* had been too much. At eighty-seven, it was as if Por Por were plucked straight from some ancient dynasty.

"You'll understand when you have some babies," she'd said.

For her own sanity, Stacey had had no choice but to bail. She'd spent the past two years trying to put all that behind her by travelling, studying, *experiencing* all the things that were not about having babies—including the things you didn't tell your grandmother about. But tradition was a fucking overstretched rubber band, wasn't it? You could pull and pull, but resistance only got you so far. Sooner or later that band was going to snap you back. Her grandmother needed help, so here she was.

Stooping at the door to the flat, Stacey drew back in disgust. The fibres of the mat were so caked in crud that it had become a flattened brick of grime. No way she was going to touch that. Instead, she nudged the blackened slab aside with her shoe, exposing the key, which was still there, same as ever. She picked it up and unlocked the door. It opened, but only partially. Something was blocking it.

Stacey peered through the gap into the hall. She couldn't see a thing inside; it was so dark. A thick stench rolled towards her, and her eyes watered. Just ten days since Por Por had been admitted to the mental health unit, and already it reeked like an abattoir. Stepping back onto the landing, Stacey took a gasp of fresh air. Then she turned and shoved at the door with her shoulder. Something inside gave way, and the door opened.

Stacey waited a second for her eyes to adjust, taking care to breathe through her mouth—not that it helped with the smell. She didn't go inside. There was nowhere to go, just a tiny tunnel, barely wide enough for a child to pass, snaking into the heart of her grandmother's precious hoard. Stacey hadn't left the sill and already she could see a pile of used takeaway containers, half a dozen black bin bags, a broken standard lamp, a rusting toasted sandwich-maker streaked with brown, and four stacks of yellowing newspaper. On either side of the hall more plastic boxes than there were shipping containers on the Auckland waterfront were stacked in towers, each pillar leaning perilously inward. The flat had two bedrooms, but Stacey couldn't see their doors for the trash. In fact, only the cinderblocks near the ceiling were clear of clutter, and those were festooned with greying spider webs and desiccating fly carcasses. Fly shit and god-knows-what-else smeared paintwork that had once been white. Scuttling sounds carried from somewhere deep under the hoard. Stacey shuddered. What monstrosities were breeding in the detritus?

By some chain reaction, a greasy cardboard box near the ceiling detached itself from the pile and hurtled towards her. In an instant, Stacey twisted to one side. An overzealous guard dog, the box thundered by, grazing Stacey's shoulder and making her grunt as it rolled onto the landing. It hit the balustrade and broke open, spilling its viscera of clothes, bags, and books. A score of black roaches scuttled across the concrete.

Stacey stood back and exhaled hard. She'd been wrong. Things *had* changed; they were much, much worse. Por Por had hoarded herself out of the flat and into care, paramedics taking the fire escape and lifting her through the living room window when the stretcher wouldn't pass through the front door. No wonder the council wanted nothing to do with clearing the place—fifty years of rent be damned.

"Please ensure all Mrs. Ching's personal belongings are removed and the apartment left in a clean and tidy state by Tuesday 12 October, or incur a fine," the email had said. The number they'd cited had made Stacey's skin itch. She would've been happy enough to get the contractors in and have the whole lot hauled away, but what about the family documents? Birth certificates and photos, and so on. *Por Por had to have saved something of Mum's somewhere in this hellhole. She'd fucking saved everything else.* Stacey would wade through a sea of dead insects and more for something to remember her mother by.

Her phone buzzed in her handbag. Leaving the door open, Stacey moved towards the stairwell, the stench fading further from the door. She rummaged for a wet wipe, scrubbed her hands, then opened her phone.

It was Louise, a quasi-friend from way back. The only one who'd been in touch since Stacey had got back into town. "So how is it?" Louise asked, sans preamble.

Stacey sighed. "Know anyone who owns a bulldozer?"

"That bad?"

"I can barely see past the front door; the trash is piled so high. I'm going to be up to my neck in it. *Literally.* I can't believe she lived like this, Lou. The place is a death trap."

Guilt festered beneath her ribs. Stacey pushed it down. It wasn't as if she hadn't tried to get her grandmother to change her ways. She'd called in specialists, tried intervention. None of it had helped. Her grandmother didn't trust Western doctors, who knew nothing about balancing humours, about yin and yang, about Qi.

"I could come down," Louise said. "You shouldn't have to do this on your own."

Except she did. Louise wasn't Chinese so, of course, she didn't understand. Being Chinese came with a double helping of filial guilt. Like a tumour, you either learned to live with it, or you got it cut out. Stacey had run, left it to fester, and now her guilt had metastasised. "Better that you don't," she told Louise. "The piles could fall any moment, and the place is a massive fire risk…" A roach wriggled out of the toasted sandwich maker. Stacey grimaced. "Plus, who knows what diseases you might catch in here? You have to think of the baby."

"Well…that's true. You're sure you'll be okay on your own?"

"I've got more PPE in the car than all of Middlemore Hospital put together. Not to mention enough disinfectant to fill a swimming pool."

"There you go. Think of it like a grand treasure hunt. I remember your grandmother had some interesting collectibles back when we were kids. Carved jade and ivory. That sort of thing. You'll want to find those. Pity you only have a few days."

"I've ordered a dumpster for later this morning. I'll have them set up a construction chute on the landing, so I can toss the trash directly into it. I tell you, Lou; I'm going to Marie Kondo this flat in no time."

"Make sure you don't Marie Kondo anything valuable. I'll be calling you for updates. If you don't pick up, I'll assume you're buried under an avalanche, so expect the cavalry."

Stacey grinned. "Thanks."

"And Stace?"

"Yeah?"

"I hope you find something that sparks joy."

Like autumn's golden mooncakes, you came dusted with double happiness. I loved you so much. I only wanted to keep you safe. But I was smothering you, and so we argued. You called me old-fashioned and set in my ways. You had your own dreams, your desires. That's how it is these days, isn't it? You young ones are never satisfied. Always hungry for more. Wanting more.

Around lunchtime, when Stacey had barely finished clearing the hall, someone knocked on the door frame.

"Hello?" a woman's voice called from the landing.

Getting to her feet, Stacey lifted the goggles, pulled down her mask, and turned to face her. "Yes?" Arching her back, Stacey massaged the base of her spine with her fingertips.

It was a Marge Simpson sort, only without the bouffant hair. "Chrissy Sutton," she said. "I live next door." She tilted her head, indicating a grubby door. "You must be the granddaughter?"

Stacey joined the woman on the landing. She snapped off her gloves and tossed them into the dumpster. "Yes. I'm Stacey."

"You're the pharmacist."

The ball of pressure grew under Stacey's ribs. "You know about me?"

"Just that you and your grandmother had a falling out."

What the hell? Stacey was about to snap her goggles back into place when the neighbour held up her hand. "Sorry, that was rude of me." She handed Stacey an insulated cup, steam spooling from the edge. "Look, I made you some chai tea." She gave Stacey her best puppy dog eyes. "Peace offering."

Warm cinnamon clouds carried over the cloying stench of the hoard. It smelled so good, and Stacey was thirsty, so she smiled and took the cup. "Thanks."

She stood beside Chrissy, both of them contemplating the dumpster, and took a sip.

"It looks like you're making progress," Chrissy said eventually.

"It's slow going."

"I wouldn't say that. You've already half-filled the dumpster."

"Except I haven't even begun to clear the rooms yet, let alone made a start on the cleaning." All she'd done was scratch the surface, removing things collected over the past few years. The real treasures, mementos of her dead mother, would be buried deep.

"You know you could sell some of this stuff?" Chrissy said. It was true. People listed all kinds of junk on Trade Me. Louise had said as much. Said there could be good money in it if Stacey wanted to sort through it. She didn't. She waved her hand at the dumpster. "Take anything you want. I'd give it a good wash first, though."

Chrissy nodded. "Thanks." A pause. "No chance of your grandmother coming back, then?"

Stacey shook her head. "The doctors say her dementia is advanced. She can't look after herself anymore." Stacey tried to suck back the guilt that flooded her veins. No chance. You could rule the world with the power of women's guilt. It'd worked for centuries.

"I hadn't realised things had gotten so bad," Chrissy said. "If I'd known, I would have called the authorities sooner."

Stacey looked up. So *this* was the neighbour who'd responded to Por Por's cries.

"I could have checked in on her more," Chrissy went on, "although I'm not sure it would've done any good. Your grandmother was a very private person. Probably ashamed of the hoarding. They say it's the result of past trauma, don't they? That'll be your mother dying in that car accident, I imagine."

"Hmm," Stacey said, hiding her face in the mug. After a morning hauling trash, the hot tea was welcome—the side of psychobabble not so much.

Chrissy was still chattering. "The thing is, when I heard your grandmother's shouting that night, I almost didn't call the police. I figured if she'd had a fall, her boarder would help her."

"Her boarder?"

"The young woman who lives with her. She wasn't here in the daytime, not that I'd noticed—probably worked in town somewhere—but at night I'd hear the two of them arguing: shouting and carrying on."

Stacey frowned. There was no space for a guinea pig, let alone a boarder. "You're sure it wasn't the TV?"

Chrissy shrugged. "Sounded like a woman. A girl. Always shouting at your grandmother, she was. The neighbours talked about reporting her, but no one wanted to upset your gran."

"Her hearing isn't that great," Stacey said. "I'll bet it was a soap opera, the volume turned up. She always loved those."

Chrissy sniffed. "Maybe."

A man from the downstairs flat hurled something into the dumpster, the clang of metal on metal. Cheeky so-and-so. Stacey prickled with annoyance. Still, she couldn't be worried about a few bits and pieces, just as she couldn't be standing around here gossiping all day.

"I should probably get back to it," she said. "Nice to meet you, Chrissy, and thank you for the tea." She handed back the cup. "Tell the neighbours they're welcome to anything from the dumpster."

Your father was weak. After your mother died, he couldn't bear to see you. To be fair, his second wife might have had something to do with it. I did what I could, but you needed more than just me to sustain you. You needed a family. Was it really so bad to want that for you? You didn't say it, but deep down, I know you wanted it, too. You used to want babies so much... Seems I made a mistake, silly old woman that I am.

After emptying the box of magazines—faded *Little Treasures* issues from the 90s—into the dumpster, Stacey checked her watch, before attacking the pile again. Close to four o'clock. She'd been up to her elbows in trash for eight hours straight. She hadn't eaten since breakfast—she'd lost her appetite. It was probably a good time to attack the bathroom, but the fairy ring of mushrooms sprouting around the toilet put her off. What were those mushrooms even growing on? Besides, nobody in their right mind stored heirlooms in the bathroom.

Stacey shook open another trash bag and shuffled through the piles of filth, picking up what might once have been a roll of paper towels. Saturated in dark liquid that had long-since dried out, it was crawling with ants. She biffed it in a trash bag, then shook off a shower of insects. How could her grandmother have lived like this?

The next layer of debris included a rotting sack of rice, a curled-up scratch-and-win ticket, and a plastic bread bag stuffed with…human hair. Its greasy musk made her stomach roil.

A cardboard box. Taped shut. Like the kind you might store photos in. Stacey cast around for something sharp, and, finding a pencil, used it to break the tape.

Over the rustle of mice and insects, a baby's cry emerged from the piles of garbage. Stacey straightened. There it was again. Not a baby, obviously, but an animal. A cat or a possum or maybe a rat. Mewling. Did rats mewl? Well, whatever it was, if it had managed to get in, then unless it had gotten itself stuck somehow, it probably knew how to get itself out.

Crouching again, Stacey lifted the lid of the box and checked inside. Nothing of interest: some old handbags, a scarf, and a bag of buttons. She shoved it out of the way.

Shit.

A dead cat lay underneath. Not the source of the noise. It had been a long time since this animal had made any kind of sound. Its mummified corpse was crushed, the tortoiseshell pelt still intact, and its bloodied face, fixed in a silent howl, flattened like a macabre flower pressed between the pages of a book.

She stood up.

A dead animal. For fuck's sake. There's a dead animal in Por Por's flat.

Her phone rang. Stacey kicked through the junk and took it on the landing. "Yeah."

"You sound rattled."

"I found a dead cat, Lou. God knows how long it's been here. The bloody thing is mummified. And there's another one in there somewhere. I can hear it mewling."

"Euuw."

"You're telling me. I feel like Alice chasing a White Rabbit. There are toadstools growing knee-high in the bathroom."

"Stace, call it a day for today. Go home, have a shower, and get some sleep. You can make a fresh start tomorrow."

"I can't. There's too much to do."

"You don't have to do it all yourself. Just look for the valuables and leave the trash. Commercial cleaners can do that."

Stacey gripped the handrail. "No."

Not yet. If she gave up now, she gave up on her mother.

On the other end of the phone, Lou said. "Well, if you won't leave, I'm Ubering you some pizza. When it comes, you take a break, okay?"

"I'm too filthy to eat."

"Why do you have to be so stubborn? You need to eat."

Stacey grinned. She hadn't remembered Louise being such a good friend. "Okay, okay. I'll eat."

When you were small, it was easy enough to protect you from the world, but when your mother died it changed everything. I did my best to nurture you, to give you everything you wanted, but girls these days are demanding. To think that once you'd only wanted babies. Now you want choice, freedom. If everyone does that, who's going to look after the old ones?

On the landing, Stacey flung the pizza box over the rail into the dumpster. The skip was already full. Beneath it, wedged down the side of the container and out of sight, was the cat's corpse. Good thing she'd ordered a replacement dumpster for tomorrow morning, or some poor soul might uncover their long-lost pet.

Breathing deeply, Stacey raised her arms above her head, then twisted left and right, stretching out the kinks in her back. Lou had been right; the meal break had done her good.

Time to get back to it.

Stepping into her overalls, she zipped them up, then fired off a text to Louise, thanking her, and telling her she'd work another hour and then head home. She didn't mention her plan to push on through the night. They weren't that close that she had to share everything. Anyway, worry wasn't good for babies. She pressed [send] then slipped the phone into her pocket, pulled on a fresh pair of gloves, and flexed her fingers inside the rubber.

Once more into the breach...

This time, she closed the front door behind her. No need to disturb the neighbours at this hour. She trudged through the rooms, weaving through the trash, and clicking on the lights. Now that night had fallen, the flat had taken on an eerie aspect, the teetering piles casting deep shadows in the electric yellow glow. The rustling of the mice—*she hoped to god they were mice*—and the scuttling waves of black cockroaches didn't help, either. The place was straight out of serial killer heaven. But at least that incessant mewling had ceased. Stacey had left the place open when she went across the road to the park to eat, so the cat must've found its way outside. Thank goodness. One dead cat was enough.

Where to start? So far, she'd cleared the hall, created a deep track into the heart of the living room, and cleaned a section of the kitchen bench, so she could boil the kettle and make herself a cup of tea in a mug she'd scrubbed and disinfected. She'd shifted a mountain of stuff out of Por Por's bedroom, too. Still nothing of Mum's, though.

Chrissy Sutton's comment about the boarder came back to her. Why would she think Por Por had someone living with her? Stacey peered through the door into the spare room, which shared a wall with the flat next door. Not that she could see it, given it was barricaded behind a mountain of boxes and trash bags. She couldn't see a TV anywhere either. A radio? They were smaller. A portable radio could be tucked in a cranny somewhere. Stacey sighed. She may as well make a start in here. Grabbing the closest box, she rummaged in her pocket for the pencil.

When I fell, and the men carried me through the crack in the wall, I tried to explain. I tried not to let them take me. I kicked and thrashed and cried for you.

"Please stay calm, Mrs Ching. We're here to help you," they said. Their voices were kind, but you think I couldn't see their disgust? I'd built a temple to my daughter, for you my mooncake, and all they could see was the crazy old woman wallowing in her own waste.

Maybe they were right, and that's all I am. Still, I tried to hold on—for your sake.

An hour later, the mewling started up again. Stacey stopped her fossicking and strained to hear. Whatever it was, it was somewhere in this room. Near the back wall from the sounds of it. Stacey lifted a couple of plastic containers out of the way, clearing a path deeper into the hoard. More scuttling. Strange. The floor here was relatively clear. As if the boxes had been moved recently. Stacey gazed up at the trash tower and caught a dark reflection on the ceiling. Something large moving on the other side of these boxes?

She sucked in a breath. "Hello? Anyone there?"

There was a low wail. The hair lifted on the back of her neck. That wasn't a cat. Someone was in there. The boarder? *Ohmigod. It's been days.* They'd be starving. Dehydrated. Close to death.

"Hang on. I'm coming," Stacey tore at the pile, scrambling to push through. A lowboy dresser blocked the way. She climbed over it. Still a wall of trash confronted her. But, from between the stacks, came a crack of light. Flickering. Stacey felt a pang of relief. Whoever was in there was still moving.

Stacey turned back to the jungle of junk. There. An old broom. She dragged the lowboy aside to retrieve it, then thrust it into the gap. Using the handle for leverage, she prised the boxes apart, shifting them, little by little. A waft of stale air escaped through the crack. Stacey didn't let that stop her. She heaved, and heaved again, breathing deep, ignoring the stench. "Hold on." She grunted. "I'm going to get you out."

The gap was so narrow it took her a while to wriggle through. But, at last, she popped out the other side, her eyes blurring at the reek. They cleared and she gasped. *What the hell?* She was up to her knees in bones. Hundreds of them. Thin and delicate. Thousands of tiny skulls. All of them picked clean.

A shadow passed over the ceiling light. Stacey almost sagged in relief. An owl then. But that wasn't right because surely there would be feathers.

Slowly, Stacey raised her eyes.

It was a ghost-woman. Or part of one. Just her torso hovered above Stacey, trails of viscera glistening in the dim light. She had sallow skin. Tapered talons. Greasy tresses concealed her face.

Stacey shook her head to clear the illusion. No. This wasn't happening. She'd inhaled too much noxious shit. Mould spores and fumes and the like. They were fucking with her brain. But the creature screeched and flew at her, its yellow teeth bared.

She was fucking real enough.

Stacey scrambled backwards through the boneyard. There was nowhere to go. She pressed her back against the tower of boxes, against the too-tight hole she'd entered, while the monster slammed its talons into the cardboard boxes on either side of her head. Stacey could smell the rot on her, feel her cold breath as the she-monster hammered at the cardboard in short sharp stabs, its head only inches from her own.

"Sssttacey."

Stacey trembled. The undead half-woman knew her name.

"Hungry," it said. "Hungry." It stabbed some more at the cardboard, its tresses parting, revealing her face. Stacey almost choked in recognition.

The fuck? She ducked away, retreating to the other side of the boneyard, ripping her gloves, scraping her knees. Blood bloomed on her overalls.

What the hell was this? A sister? Her head raced to find the reason. Something rational. But already she knew. Chinese women and their guilt: you either embraced it, or you ran. Double happiness meant double the pain, didn't it? Here was her mother's legacy. Her grandmother's, too. A monster of lost dreams, of lost hope. The price you paid, so a daughter might have freedom.

The ghost-girl crawled towards her, lowered her face to suck on Stacey's knee, like a child sucking at the breast. Stacey screamed and kicked her away, unearthing a nest of mice. Her sister pounced on the escapees, skewering one with a talon. She raised it to her mouth and crunched down, shattering its bones.

Stacey watched her starving sister and her heart filled with pity. She'd come back searching for a hidden legacy, and she'd found it. She couldn't just turn around and abandon her. Now it was Stacey's turn to nurture her grandmother's hopes.

"Por Por's gone. Hungry," the ghost-girl wailed. Blood oozed between her yellow teeth.

Don't blame your mother. She only ever wanted your happiness.

Stacey stalked up and down the hall, her ghost-sister hovering at her shoulder as they waited for the dawn. At six o'clock, she called Louise.

"Stace, what the hell?"

"I'm at the flat."

Stacey caught the rustle of sheets as Lou shifted her bump up the bed. "Did you find something valuable?"

"Depends on how you look at it. Seems I had a sister."

"Oh." There was a pause. "That's interesting. I thought maybe... A sister. Wow. Any clue to what happened to her?"

"I think she died when she was young."

"That's such a shame."

Beside Stacey, a cockroach skittered up the wall. She breathed deeply. "Yeah, so look Lou, I was wondering if you could come down, after all. There's something valuable here that I need your help with."

Louise sucked in a breath. "A collectible?"

"Um. Yeah."

"I'll have breakfast and be right down." Louise rang off, and Stacey popped her own phone in her pocket.

Trails of viscera grazed her shoulder as the ghost-girl slithered closer to the door. Well, what else could Stacey do? The monster would need feeding—a few mice wouldn't sustain it—and she had no daughter to give.

See? I told you, all would be well, my darling mooncake.

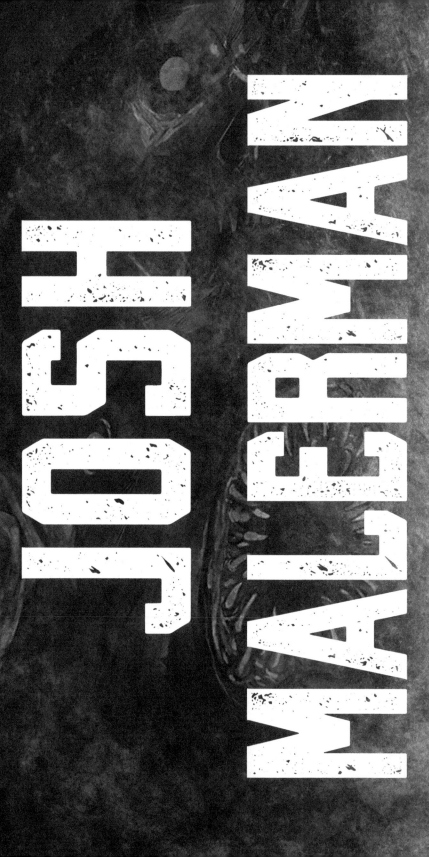

DUNGEON PUNCHINELLO

We were all supposed to die down there.

Anything that's happened since then doesn't matter. Certainly not the decade I endured, the endless grind of Time upon me, as I felt myself growing thinner, smaller, lesser. Not just my body, but my *person*, you see, as I spoke less through the years, took no walks, saw no old friends and made no new ones, cut myself off from my family and former place of employment, isolated myself in a city I never had any interest in calling home. What was an apartment, what was money for that matter, after having escaped? When the breaths you take are no longer recorded in the ledger of Time, when you exist beyond when you were supposed to... what does location matter?

And what of morality, too?

Ah, *ten years*, yes, and what a dance I've done. Quiet and alone, with these visions of that madman. Memories of an experience so singular, it's as if we visited an island, not a mountain range, the four of us kept prisoner in a place nobody else could reach.

Myself, Terrence, Billy, and...

Shawn.

Shawn, yes, whose behavior in that prison has come to confound me, to irk me, to occupy my thoughts even more than that of the madman who kept us in darkness, who starved us, who...

Oh, never mind that. Never mind what was *done* but rather how we reacted, not each of us in turn, but rather Shawn himself, he who faced absolute darkness with a levity that can only mean one thing to me now, as I've had ample time to consider that horrible stay.

Shawn was hiding something.

And you cannot convince me otherwise.

Just look here, *here!* An invitation mailed by the very Pollyanna, this peppy handwritten letter declaring what an honor my *presence* would be, as if being present, being *alive*, bore significance any longer. And the nerve, the absolute gall, to include exclamation points and a small drawing of a small smiling face, there at the bottom of the page, to mock me, no doubt, just as his literal words were intended to do:

I told you, John!

Yes, yes, Shawn told me. He told me one hundred thousand times if he told me once, but there was no *place* for that down there, no *room* for optimism in that hole, nor any room in any of us unfortunates, no space for the things Shawn said, for how he purported himself, even as his arms and legs were chained to the same stone walls as our own.

Does he flaunt exclamation points at Death as well? Does he say: *Come take me!*

Oh, the smug little quake, the ignorant little *man* who holds over me to this day *his* reaction, *his* behavior, *his* insufferable optimism as the rest of us sank into despair.

For those few days, there was no place else to sink.

He hides! Yes. He hides something. Hides it from me and from the others, eternally, Shawn *hides*. What did he know? And how did he know it? And how could one remain stout in the face of that madman in that hole in that ground by those mountains?

A foreign country, a concrete room buried, a psychopath.

And the four of us: taken prisoner.

Myself, Terrence, Billy, and...

Shawn.

I feel sick with the memories of my friends, their arms above their heads, chained to the stone. And for what crime? And to what end? The whim of a lunatic we knew nothing about... the four of us on a vacation of spontaneous friends... landing instead in the fantasy of a stranger.

Well, Shawn has proven he still has no reason if he thinks this invitation is anything I want to receive. An anniversary get-together. Do you see? The nerve. To mark the occasion: the ten-year commemoration of the darkest moment of our lives.

Damn you, Shawn. And Damn your offensive cheer.

Here, tell me what *you* think.

Here:

We'd met at college, two sets of close friends, each duo with a bunkbed and a room, between us a shared sitting space, all this in the dormitories of Middle Michigan University. Terrence and I had grown up together about halfway up the mitten, a smaller city called Chaps, in which we'd attended elementary through high. Terrence was always willing to perform for the sake of the moment, always *on*, as is true of most bright ones, present above all else. Yet, no puffed optimist was he. Terrence's cynicism could cut most collegiate philosophy in two, and I loved to watch as he diced. He was a big thinker, but also: the ideal college roommate, as, just about the time we were through with Chaps, both of us were ready to embark upon an adventurous life.

I've often tried to recall: what were my first thoughts of Shawn? The very day we met at MMU, who did I think he was?

Well, not much, to be honest, as the pair had come north from near the border of Michigan and Indiana, the two with some country bumpkin in them, despite the high marks they both received in school. They were a book-smart duo, and certainly respected when it was time to study. I'll give them that. And I'll give them a little more: Billy, though quiet, was interesting when he wanted to be, and often Terrence and he stayed up late in the living room, watching films, a shared taste for the absurd films of Norm DePlume. And Shawn... well, I mistook his naïveté as humor, something close to southern comfort, his country-side glaring at times when I suspected he was unaware. In those days I found him quaint. Terrence felt the same, once referring to him as a "biscuit" as we lay in our bunks in the dark, our smirks unseen, our laughter unheard.

Yet, note: there was no *animosity* then. Terrence and I would never have begun talks in earnest of traveling to Europe with the two of them if there was.

Despite our differences, the four us became friends.

It's something I struggle to understand now, even as I hold the tone-deaf invitation from Shawn to return to Michigan, this ten years after our...

Vacation.

I won't call it anything else.

Yes, we were friends. Our different upbringings didn't feel quite as different a year into attending University together, and we decided to live together once more, for our sophomore campaign, off-campus, in a small shitty home on Academic Place. And it was in said sty that Terrence and I became Shawn, Bill, Terrence, and I, as the lines between us all were blurred and we felt more like a quartet than two duos sharing the same living space. Friends! Yes! Who else would you cross the Atlantic with but friends? And who else but *college* friends to attack the future?

I see now my naïveté, these ten years to *think*, how stupid to find anything in common with Shawn.

I told you, John!

Oh, the fucking *gall*. I daresay I took pleasure in playing the pessimist to his rose-colored takes on all things worldly, as the four of us drank wine about that misshapen plank we called a table in that wretched kitchen he professed to like. Understand, however, that his worldview never quite reached insufferable, not then. It wasn't until we found ourselves actually suffering that his optimism I could take no more.

Rather, I recall that soft look in Shawn's eyes. The way he laughed off all concerns. The go-to phrases he employed: *One day this will all be our story and we'll enjoy even the hardships.*

I remember Shawn's father passed in our sophomore year and it felt as if he was consoling *me* when I expressed my sympathy. I remember, too, that Billy had to return home for a serious matter and Shawn accompanied him. In their absence, Terrence said, *It won't be so bad as he's got Shawn to pick him up.*

This sounds like the makings of a good man. But do you believe in such things? For, today's judgments are tomorrow's reconsiderations.

Here:

We saved enough money for the flights; I recall them exceeding one thousand dollars each. How we agreed upon the Alps was actually quite simple: Shawn had always wanted to go. His enthusiasm was infectious as we spun the globe in the MMU library. We debated all its destinations, from its tropical pockets to its Nordic drapes framing the window of the Baltic Sea. Shawn was interested in the rail that traveled that legendary mountain range and he painted a picture at once fascinating and educational. We were all just spontaneous enough then to award victory to the most passionate opinion.

Had I to do again, I would have reduced enthusiasm to blinders, and chosen on logic alone.

But off we went.

And it was with these energies flowing between us, our quartet a young conductive square, that we did indeed fly and did indeed travel by train across the Austrian Alps, spending the evenings in the cities along the way.

I barely remember the sights. Nor do I recall the range itself.

It's the city name St. Johann that sticks. For this was where we found a cheap inn. This was where we drank in a dim tavern. This was where we relaxed, the four of us piqued, from the pressures and excitements of travel.

This was also where the madman must have spotted us.

Perhaps it was from under a dark awning bordering the cobblestone streets. I try to recall silhouettes in the windows. Cigarette smoke from an alley. Footsteps that might give me a clue as to exactly where it began.

But, truth is, I can't remember the details. I hardly remember the room in which we slept. I see the shadowed corners of a high ceiling. I see a bookshelf on the wall with no books upon it.

I feel the sink into sleep.

And then I open my eyes in a room of stone.

My companions' arms are above their heads.

Billy is not yet awake. His head hangs at a bad angle.

Terrence has horror in his eyes.

And Shawn...

Shawn looked determined, like he'd been awake some time, an expression that suggested, even then, *even then*, that we'd get out of that place alive.

I'm on a plane now. Haven't taken one in close to five years. That was to visit my own father up in Michigan as he got ill. I haven't been to MMU since we left it for our trip. I don't know if I've missed the cities, the dunes, the farmland, the long and gorgeous drive from the south to the north. Yet, the state has wormed its way into my dreams, respites, I suppose, from the nightmares of St. Johann.

Now, on my way to Michigan, I'm responding to Shawn's invitation after all.

And why shouldn't I? Why not face the man I've thought of for ten years, *ask* him how he knew, *what* he knew, how he kept his spirits high in a place so low?

The first question I will ask:

What are you hiding?

Because I can still smell Billy's dead body, as it began to decay, lifeless against the stone, the three of us without food or water for what must have been three days in full. Yes, we eventually determined Billy was already dead by the time we first woke. He must've experienced a brutality I've intentionally tried *not* to guess at. And was it for our benefit that one of us must die from the get, so that the others understood the severity of our lot?

I think it's that. I think Billy was killed for the same reason people hang drapes in their homes, place throw pillows on a couch:

Mood. Ambience. Setting the table and setting the stage.

I say it was three days that we hung there, our arms growing numb for the lack of flowing blood. It could've been longer, but I've studied the effects starvation (and no water) have upon the body and while I've factored in the fear, I still believe it was about seventy-two hours. Terrence became my mirror, him being chained directly across the space from me, Shawn some distance to his right. And to my left? Billy. The smell of him filling the subterranean space that had no windows, lit only by a single dirty bulb high above.

"No door," Terrence said. It's the first thing I can remember any of us saying. "There's no door in here."

"There is," Shawn said.

I knew he had to be right, of course, as we were placed down there *somehow*. But more importantly, the slimmest shred of optimism was both desperately needed and wholly, frighteningly, out of place.

"My head," I said.

We'd been drugged. That much we knew.

But these revelations, these piecemeal observations, came in brief bursts. I remember Terrence saying Billy looked dead. Yes, he was the first to say it. And Shawn? Shawn studied the walls, it seemed, intent on proving the existence of that door.

I think it was me who pointed out the fact it might be better if there weren't one. For, a door would suggest the possible appearance of whoever put us there.

And those initial hours went in this manner; the three of us trying not to look at Billy, sometimes calling out for help, even calling out for food. And to make it all worse, as if to mock us, the only other object in the prison beside ourselves and our chains was a green rubber hose. Coiled upon itself not five feet from the tips of Shawn's shoes. Water, it seemed, *life*, not only just out of reach, but impossible to turn on, even if Shawn were somehow able to make contact.

Yes, we called for help. Terrence and I did so with increasing desperation. But Shawn...

I don't think I saw him sleep in those first few days, as I nodded in and out of exhaustion, my nose and throat dry, as if the stone that held us also filled the air with grit. I would close my eyes and open them and who knew how much time had passed and who knew which of us was yelling for help, but at each interval, there was Shawn, eyeing the walls, the hose, nodding to the beat of some hidden drummer, something that, at the time I mistook for optimism, but have come to believe was *knowledge*.

For how else could he have maintained his wits, his worldview, in a place like that, if not for the certainty he'd survive?

"I'm gonna tell his mother," he said, at some point in the crush of those first few days. "As his friend growing up, that's on me."

It was the first time we'd argue about our chances.

"I don't think you'll be seeing his mother again," I told him.

I expected silence, the way a period expects the sentence to end.

But Shawn responded. Of course.

"I will, John. And so will you."

"Billy's dead," Terrence said. "We're next."

I agreed. But still, Shawn...

"We're going to get out of this," he said. "We may not know what that looks like yet, but we will when the moment comes."

Shawn's comments got the silence I believed my own deserved. Here was our Michigan bumpkin, commenting on the state of a stone prison in Austria.

We posited theories, our voices like weak fog cast from our delusions. Terrence looked for a camera. He suggested someone had to be watching us die. I hypothesized we were being starved for something worse to come.

I don't remember Shawn having any theories of his own.

We resolved into inevitable silences. And it was during once such hush, in the near-death haze of starvation, that I saw a rectangle of stone tremble, before the sound of grating slate indicated there was a door indeed.

"Good," Shawn said.

An unfathomable choice of words. As, with the sound came the inward swing of stone, and space enough for our madman to show himself.

We didn't speak. Not even Shawn would've been dumb enough to say anything before hearing what this man had to say. But while his presence was enough to ice me, it was the fact that he wore no mask, no hood, that stole what remaining hope I had.

This man wasn't afraid to let us know what he looked like.

I'll do my best to put down what I remember.

Here:

He was of average height. That surprised me, as I was expecting intimidation in every trait. Short dark hair, mussed up. I remember some of him both ways: eyes too close together, one eye on each side of his head. Shirtless that first time. And how many times did I see him? How often did he enter and exit that stone cell with a pan of gruel in one hand, a ladle in the other? Three times? Three thousand? He never spoke.

But the most striking element for me, the piece that's lodged in my memory, along with my growing disdain for Shawn, and perhaps *responsible* for that disdain, is that the madman looked...

American.

I'd seen men like him all over Michigan. That strange blend of deep-woods libertarian with an oddly sympathetic visage. I knew that, if he *were* to speak, I'd recognize it as a midwestern accent.

These days I wonder if it wouldn't have sounded just like Billy and Shawn.

But, again... he didn't speak, not even when he stepped to Terrence, scooped some gruel, and lifted it to Terrence's lips. I recall the rattling of my friend's chains as he tried to free his legs for a kick, his arms for a grip of that pan, to use against the quiet madman's skull.

Shawn said,

"Eat, Terrence."

Was bumpkin Shawn suddenly so adaptable that his first thoughts were of what we might need, even if delivered by the man who had already begun killing us?

"Don't do it," I said.

Because who knew. Because Billy was already dead and maybe he'd eaten from the same pan, the same stuff cooked on the same stove.

The man held the ladle to Terrence's lips.

"Eat," Shawn said again.

"Get away from me," Terrence said.

And he thrashed.

The madman stepped from him and held the same slop to Shawn who gulped it down.

"I could use some water," Shawn said. "We all could."

I eyed that rubber hose in the corner.

The madman carried the pan to me. Over his shoulder, Terrence looked to me, wide eyed, as if saying, *John, do something!*

"You gotta talk to us," I said. "We're all wealthy students from America. We have money. We have connections that will be angry if anything happens to us."

The madman touched my lips, my teeth, with the ladle.

His face was so close to mine:

I recall a partial mustache and beard. Patches of hair upon an otherwise youthful complexion.

"Eat," Shawn said.

And I ate. Despite telling Terrence not to. I ate.

Shawn nodded encouragement (in that place!) and the madman set the pan down near my feet.

He stepped to the hose.

"You have to let us go," I said.

I didn't like the way he uncoiled it. Like he'd been in this prison many times.

Beneath the coil was the handle, a gold nugget amongst dark slate.

The madman turned it on. And water, sweet water, poured forth.

He dragged the hose across the stone space and lifted it to Shawn's lips.

Shawn drank. His gulping still echoes in my mind.

Finished, he said, "Thank you."

I'll never forget that.

Thank you.

The madman brought the hose to me, and I opened my mouth for it, and while it tasted of rust, it tasted of life, too.

He rolled the hose up again, turned the handle, and replaced the rubber.

"Hey," Terrence said.

The madman took the pan and made for the rectangle in the wall.

"*Hey!*" Terrence shouted. "I need water, too!"

As the stone closed behind him, with no sign of a door, I remember thinking, even then, that Shawn was right.

Terrence should've eaten.

"We're going to figure this out," Shawn said. His voice was a little stronger for the food and water.

"We need to get Terrence something," I said.

"It'll probably be tomorrow," Shawn said.

"How would you know that?" I asked. "It had to have been days before we saw him this first time."

"*Fuck*," Terrence said. He didn't need to say anymore. His voice was hoarse in comparison to ours.

And whether or not we'd got our fill of food, we had eaten.

We all looked to Billy then. Even Shawn. As if we'd all drawn a line from Terrence to Billy.

I started shouting for the madman again. I cried out with my newfound strength, even as my arms grew number, the blood traveling through my body in ways it was not designed to do.

Terrence looked more afraid than I felt myself, which, in turn, scared me to near paralysis. At the time I believed it was because he faced the same unknown. But I now wonder if he'd come to a conclusion quicker than I:

Terrence had been punished for refusing the food.

And so, with that, I suppose we, or at least Terrence, knew something about our captor we did not know in the hours before his arrival.

Whatever he looked like didn't change our circumstances.

The fact that he *punished* most certainly did.

"He put a tool within our reach," Shawn said. It was dark, the bulb out. We had no idea if this meant it was night.

"Our hands are useless," I said.

"But you still could've got it with your mouth," Shawn said.

"And then what?"

"That's not the point."

We were mostly whispering but the echo made it all too loud.

"I'd say that's definitely the point," I said.

"It's the fact that he's sloppy," Shawn said.

"Billy's dead," Terrence said. His voice splintered wood in the dark.

"That's okay," Shawn said.

"What do you mean, *okay?*" I asked.

"That's happened," Shawn said. "And so now we're past it."

"We're not past anything."

"It's all about recalibrating," he said. And I sensed some feeling in my fingers yet, as I wanted to reach across the space and slap him. "Whatever's happened has happened and so we start over, start everything over, at that point. It's the only way to move forward."

I laughed. My chains rattled.

"No time to mourn?" I asked.

A few nights ago, we'd been laughing at a tavern. Lying down to sleep at an inn in Austria.

Now?

"You can move forward *as* you mourn," Shawn said. "Listen, I mean it: he's careless. We're going to pull this off."

"This isn't a football game, Shawn."

Then the grating stone again.

We went quiet as the door opened and the madman's shoes scuffed against the floor.

"What's going on?" Terrence said. "What are you doing?"

What was he doing?

"Terrence!" I cried. "What's happening?"

"I don't know! He's breathing by my face!"

I heard a quick slashing. Terrence cried out. The shoes scuffed to where Shawn hung.

A second swipe. Shawn grunted.

Had he slit their throats? Had he gutted my friends in the dark?

He came toward me.

"*No no no!*" I shouted. "*Please don't!*"

But he did. I felt the blade across my chest.

And the sound of the madman exiting was eclipsed by the rattling of our chains.

Off the plane now. In line to rent a car. There is no airport near Sleeping Bear Dunes and so I need to make my own way there. I imagine Shawn in khaki pants, a blue shirt, feigning the part of beach lover, acting the part of *survivor*, at peace with the house money, the extra time he'd found on this planet, in this life.

But we both know he didn't survive any more than Billy did.

Shawn was in on it.

Had to be.

Shawn *knew*.

I opened my eyes to see the bulb was on again. My chest hurt. And… yes… I remember seeing Terrence's bloody shirt, a long line of red.

"Are you okay?" I asked. My voice was hoarse now, too. How long had it been since we were offered food and water?

Terrence didn't respond. One eye half open, one closed. He only seemed to stare back across at me. I think it was in that moment that I, too, went mad.

I understood, with absolute certainty:

We would not get out of there alive.

I looked to Shawn, and saw no mark, no blood on his shirt.

He was looking to the hose, to where the door was that no longer looked like a door.

"Didn't he cut you?" I asked.

He looked surprised.

"Yes."

"Where?"

"Across my chest."

But... no mark.

"When he comes back to feed us," he began, but I cut him off.

"Why weren't you cut?"

"John. I *was*. Now, listen to me. When he comes back–"

Terrence coughed and spat blood to the floor.

"We need to put ourselves in the position of power," Shawn said. His bumpkin eyes as bright as ever. As if we were lab partners, working to solve an equation.

"We can't use our arms or legs," I said.

"That's okay."

"*Nothing* is okay right now!"

"That's okay," he said, as if now adding my pessimism to the score he was counting.

The stone door opened.

I rattled my chains, intent on grabbing the madman by the neck.

I saw my hands had begun to go purple.

There was a brief pause before the madman entered. Shawn squinted into that darkness, and I knew he was searching for a meaningless edge. I could almost hear him telling me there was a chair beyond the door, as if therein might lie our salvation, in an object we had no way of reaching.

But the madman entered at a quick pace and I cried out, believing this was it: he'd kill me with that blade.

He went for the hose instead. He knelt a few feet from Shawn's shoes, turned the gold handle, and dragged the rubber toward Terrence. My boyhood friend groaned and opened his mouth, asking for water.

And the madman gave it to him.

With one hand he pulled down Terrence's chin and inserted the hose with the other.

He fed it deeper.

Deeper.

I pleaded for him to stop. Terrence thrashed. But the madman had done this before.

He trotted back to the handle and turned it all the way on, so that the rubber became a bloated line.

I couldn't turn away.

Even as Terrence thrashed. Even as the water began to pour out the sides of his mouth.

I remember two things clearly, and I think of them now as I drive northwest to Sleeping Bear Dunes:

The red wound on Terrence's chest becoming a frown as his abdomen swelled.

The sound of him choking, trying to speak.

I closed my eyes. I pulled my purple hands against my cuffs. I heard an unnatural pop.

I do not remember Shawn speaking. Not even as the madman turned off the hose. Not even as the stone door closed behind him.

Terrence was dead.

I won't describe his expression. I won't do that to him.

But Shawn's...

Bright, focused. Engaged.

"Okay," he said at length. "Okay."

He eyed the bulb above.

Was this part of the show? Was this *the* show?

Shawn feigning the piecing together of an escape...

I recalled our late-night debates in the house on Academic Place. Me, the proud cynic, he, the eternal, blind optimist.

I recalled, too, all my canny laughter as I mocked him for his country bumpkin ways.

"I'm telling you, John. We're going to get out of here," he said. His voice echoed off the stone. Four dead ears did not hear him. "It's going to be okay."

I look to the invitation he sent. It's alone on the otherwise pristine passenger seat of the rental car.

I see the words, the punctuation most of all:

I told you, John!

Yes.

You did.

Only I didn't realize how much you told me at the time.

I have asked myself,

Was Billy even dead?

How long I stood awake in the dark, my arms above me, my feet barely touching the stone, I do not know. How long I heard the quiet scuffing of Shawn's shoes against that same stone, I do not know. I wonder what he did in the dark, as he pretended to struggle with his chains. He grunted, quietly, over and over, whispering to himself. Then he would pause, breathe slowly for many minutes, before struggling all over again.

I mistake the echoes of his chains rattling for a belt beneath the hood of this rental car. I worry I've rented a lemon.

I worry I won't make it to Sleeping Bear Dunes.

You're gonna make it, Shawn would undoubtedly say, if he were seated beside me.

And that's exactly what he told himself down in that prison, whispering as he worked. Yes, in the darkness, over and over, his voice, pleading with himself to stay strong, so that Billy and Terrence wouldn't have "died in vain." I recall him saying we would escape together.

And I... I didn't weigh in. I didn't agree we would any more than I said we wouldn't. I only listened, dumbstruck. Terrence's belly. The madman's sure manner, as though he worked at the slaughterhouse, and us... livestock.

Billy was really rotting by then. His smell grew stronger, in concert with my fear. I couldn't cover my nose and mouth and so I blew out, blew the smell away, the sound of which Shawn must've heard, for, across the stone space he said,

"John? Are you awake? Listen. My cuffs are rusted. I think I can break free."

I did not respond. I'd heard his brand of idealism so many times it had become a children's show to me, full of all the phony lessons and songs of my childhood.

"You must be asleep," Shawn said. "You must be having a bad dream. But don't worry, John. We're going to get out of here. We're going to get back home."

I imagined myself entering this place through the stone door, doing what I wished with the optimist chained to the wall.

He worked at his cuffs. Or feigned the act. I remember the sound and I remember picturing a large rat, the googly eyed idiotic Malcolm from the puppet show on television from our youth, the Rat in the Cap, all smiles across the way in the dark, rubbing a nail file against the cuffs that kept his rat arms above his head.

I refused to believe Shawn, of all people, could possibly have discovered a way out.

What are the odds the optimist is proven right? Are they higher or lower than the probability the optimist knew the outcome beforehand?

"He's going to hear you," I said. Because suddenly I was drawn with a fear of Shawn making this worse for me. Yes, I believed, then, that he could only make it worse.

"John!" he said. Was he smiling? Was he... *smiling?* "You're awake!"

"He's going to hear you."

"That's fine."

Fine?

"I don't want him coming back. Do you understand that?"

"I'm close."

Close to what?

"You're not close to anything."

"We're going to get out of here."

"No, we're not. And the sooner–"

"Yes, John." He continued working. Continued grunting in the dark. "We're going to free ourselves and we're going to hang out in the sand at Sleeping Bear Dunes."

"You have lost your mind."

"Would that be so abnormal? Down here? But I have not. Keep positive, John."

Positive?

"You make me sick."

"That's okay. So long as I get us out of here."

"You make me *sick.*"

"That's okay."

Then... from Shawn, a small, quiet: "Oh!"

He went quiet and I listened for the stone rectangle to begin its inward swing. Was the madman standing outside that door?

I felt cold. Exposed. The slash across my chest burned as it healed.

Without warning, without deciding to do it, I pissed myself. My urine flowed down my my legs, to the stone below.

"Hey," Shawn said. "Hey, John."

I didn't respond. The pep in his voice; I could see him smiling, sitting in the torn chair in our living room on Academic Place, facing me on the couch.

"Hey, John, what do you say to someone who has to pee while their hands and legs are chained?"

The words, so unfathomably out of place, and I felt I might throw up. The smell of Billy's rot. The memory of the bloody frown forming on Terrence's chest.

"*Urine trouble*," Shawn said. "*You're in trouble.*"

Did he expect me to laugh? I believe he did.

It was at this moment I began suspecting Shawn was involved.

A joke...

Down there...

A *joke.*

And a sound, too, the stone sliding.

I braced myself, believing, surely, one of us would die.

"It's okay," Shawn said. "It's okay."

The madman entered, the sound of his shoes unmistakable now.

He stepped deeper into the space and we were flooded with sudden light.

I squinted at Terrence but had to look away.

I remember looking to the ground. To the puddle of my piss gathered at my shoes.

But the ladle at my lips brought me to lift my head, and with it, my gaze.

Behind the madman, Shawn lowered his arms.

I looked to the madman. To the ladle. I opened my mouth.

Shawn moved slow, silent, his wide eyes fixed to the madman's back.

I ate slow.

Shawn crouched behind the man's shoulder.

I ate slow, slurping the one scoop.

The madman shoved the ladle forward, cracking it against my front teeth.

Shawn rose behind him, the hose in both hands.

How could he use his hands?

"More," I said, not wanting the man to turn around.

But it was one scoop and one scoop only down there.

He turned, yes, lowering the ladle back into the pan, as Shawn…

"Shawn wrapped the hose around his neck," I say, pulling off the highway. "He looked insane as he strangled the madman, tying the hose tight until the man fell to his knees. I can still hear the clatter of the pan falling to the floor. I can still hear Shawn grunting, see survival in his eyes."

I turn right at a sign pointing the way to Sleeping Bear Dunes.

"And I watched. Chained to the wall. I watched Shawn snuff the life out of the madman. Watched as the man fell to his side. His head cracked against the stone."

I turn left at another sign.

"Then… Shawn smiled at me. His face, lit from within. And he turned to the light bulb above and closed his eyes and howled with freedom. 'I'll get you out,' he said. And he crouched beside the madman and reached into the man's pants pocket and pulled out the keys. First try. Like he knew where they'd be. And he unlocked my chains and I fell into his arms, me, ten times weaker than he. 'We gotta get out of here,' he said. 'We gotta leave Billy and Terrence.'"

I turn right at another sign. These small Michigan towns are quaint in the same way I once believed Shawn was quaint.

"He draped one of my arms over his shoulder and helped me out through the open rectangle. He talked, constantly, reiterating that we'd made it out, that the man was dead, that we only had to get back to the world, the real world, and we'd be done with this, away from this forever. He helped me until I could do it on my own and the two of us hurried through a long, stone corridor that ended at a flight of wooden steps, illuminated by light coming through slats above. A door."

I turn right again. A dirt road. Some sand at its edges.

"Halfway up the steps, Shawn said, 'We don't know what we're going to see when we walk through that door. So be ready. Okay? It could be anything. But we're going to make it. Okay?' I recall nodding. I recall thinking it was impossible. Not what had happened to us, but that Shawn, of all people, had figured out a way. That Shawn, of all people, was proven right."

I turn left and I can see the beginning of the dunes now. Possibly Lake Michigan beyond.

"We climbed the rest of the way. Shawn opened the door and entered a room and I followed. The door closed behind us. We stood in a kitchen. The door we'd just come through nothing more than a pantry door. No different than the kind your grandmother had in her home as you were growing up."

I drive. I drive. I drive.

"We were silent as we moved through the house. As we exited through the front door. As we stepped out of the madman's house and into the semi-darkness of early evening in St. Johann. And once we were there, outside, without speaking... we ran."

A sign tells me I am mere feet from my destination.

I pull the car to the side of the road.

"We ran far that night, up and down streets, searching for the police, searching for help, needing to tell them what happened, needing the authorities to know that two Americans were killed in the faux-pantry cellar prison of a madman. But..."

I eye a seagull. I think, *Michigan.*

"But neither of us thought to remember the address. Neither of us thought to look for it. At the time, and as we answered the questions posed to us by the St. Johann police, I believed we were justified in not knowing. Who would think of such a thing as they fled for their life? But... Shawn. I can still see him responding to the police. Lit from within, yes. But for having found a way out? Or for some other reason?"

I rev the engine. Two seagulls now. Free in the sky.

"In the end, we weren't able to show them where the house was. And in the end we flew back home regardless."

I pull back onto the road.

I pass a sign:

WELCOME TO SLEEPING BEAR DUNES

I have arrived.

We're going to free ourselves and we're going to hang out in the sand at Sleeping Bear Dunes.

I eye the invitation in the passenger seat.

I look ahead.

No, we never found that house. It was never found.

And so somewhere in St. Johann, Austria, our friends turn to bone.

Where we should've died.

"But I'm here," I say. "And Shawn is here, too."

I told you, John!

The address is on the invitation. It's a small cottage on the grassy edge of the dunes. Maybe he lives here. Maybe he rented it for the occasion. I do not care.

I sit in the car, the engine off, watching him move through the cottage, passing the windows, as if preparing.

Did he believe I'd come?

How far does his optimism go?

I imagine his mind in there, a phony place, where the impossible is believed, where will is more powerful than odds.

The car window is down and I catch a rancid whiff from the dirt road. Out the window, a dead seagull. I think of Billy's head at that angle to his shoulder.

I exit the car.

I eye the dead bird. I eye the cottage windows.

Through the glass, Shawn sees me. His face a rendering of surprise and gladness.

I walk the short walk to the cottage door.

He opens before I do.

He says,

"John! My God! I'm so glad you came."

I say,

"What are you hiding?"

His smile doesn't falter. If he were innocent, I would think he was shocked by the question.

"Come in," he says. As though I didn't ask what he was hiding.

"What are you hiding?" I ask.

Now, a change in his face. The sun upon it.

"John? What do you mean? Are you okay?"

Okay? I can barely resist reaching for him, taking him by the neck.

"What did you know, Shawn? What are you hiding?"

"Know? John... listen. It was the scariest thing imaginable. I think it's okay if–"

"*Shawn.* You're not answering me."

"John..."

"It's not possible. What you were down there. It's not *possible.*"

"What was I?"

"You knew we'd get out. Even as our friends were rotting."

He tilts his head the way people do when they realize there's more to the situation than they thought there was.

Yes, Shawn. I've been thinking about this for a long time.

"Maybe you should come inside. We should eat. Drink. Are you sure you want to talk about this... right away?"

I do not respond. I wait for the answer.

"Listen," he says, again. "I just wanted us to get out. That's all. I had to get us out."

"What did you know? What are you hiding?"

"Nothing! I don't even know what I could be hiding!"

"It's impossible."

Something clicks in his eyes. He gets it now.

He steps out of the house, joins me on the grass. I see behind him, along the side of the cottage, a green rubber hose, coiled upon itself.

"Hey," he says. "I don't really remember a lot of it myself. But if there's one thing I knew, it's that we weren't going to get out of there by letting things go the way they were."

"How did you get out of your chains?"

He swallows. A bad memory? Or time to lie...

"They were rusted. I remember *that* clear as day. I dream of rusted metal a lot."

I step toward the cottage. Get closer to the hose.

It strikes me: I didn't come here to ask Shawn these questions.

"I don't know what you think happened," he says, sincerity in his voice. Warmth, too. Is it real? "But I guess I... I understood, right away, that we were in the worst place in the world. And that we didn't have time to be shocked by that. Does that make sense?"

"No. No sense at all."

"Come on. Let's drink. Or maybe not. Maybe we should talk first."

I'm upon him before he finishes this last word. I don't think of witnesses. I don't think of anything except snuffing out this lie.

"John!"

But I've got him on the grass now. My knee in his chest.

The hose in my hands.

"You *joked* down there, Shawn. You made a *joke!* It was hell down there! Worse! And you... you..."

I bring the hose to his neck.

"John, please... stop!"

"You were a clown down there! And *there is no such thing*. There is no *dungeon Punchinello*."

I wrap the hose around his neck and he thrashes like Terrence once thrashed against his chains. I recall that red line growing, turning down at its ends, as Terrence's belly bloated with water from the dungeon hose.

I hear the pop from within him again.

"John!"

I have the hose around his neck.

Tight.

I bring my face close to his. When I speak, spit falls to his lips like gruel in a prison ladle.

"It's impossible! The way you behaved. The way you carried on. *What are you hiding?*"

I squeeze.

As Shawn turns his head slowly.

No, he says without being able to speak. I was hiding nothing.

And I...

See...

In his eyes... in him...

That he means it.

I let go of the hose.

I stand up.

Shawn coughs on the grass behind me as I walk to the car.

"John," he says. His voice hoarse. "Please. Come on. You don't have to deal with this alone."

But I got my answer.

And I can't stay here any longer.

At the car, I don't look back to him. I don't respond.

His voice is a little stronger when he says:

"John. We went through something. Something bad. It's okay to feel this way."

But I'm already in the car.

And the car is started.

And I'm pulling away.

"I'm so scared," I say, feeling it. Crying now, too. The dunes and the Great Lake receding, behind me.

And my tears are rust flavored water that only tastes good because there is no other.

I cry.

And the only thing more frightening than learning a madman exists, is discovering you believed a man like Shawn could not.

BELOW THE WILDFLOWER HILL

Silence fell after the April rain, quiet as an empty attic
and the luscious soil begged our bodies to strip naked
of skin and lie with our sinews touching wet dewdrops

Sunshine emerged between gray clouds, uninterrupted
daylight promised for a time, beckoning lilacs to streak
false cosmic rainbows of blue, white, and purple across
the rotten bodies we imagine are not holding our weight up

Take comfort in the soft aftermath of war, imagine we sew
togetherness the way spring stitches wildness into hearts
too young to understand how death will follow here

Below the wildflower hill grows a cellar in the dirt,
the housecat escapes a broken door and stands guard,
a deity watching over the underworld, yet you remain
apple-bright as I drag your corpse across soaked fields

All this splendor nature conceals, as if mint grass and spring
onions sprouting from meadows could only harvest beauty,
but invisible evil blows just as sweetly across raw lips

Countryside fauna paints idyllic promises, but the tomb
I kept secret for so long, decorated in powdered butterfly
wings, awaits the last seasonal sacrifice, and you never
did pay enough attention to the way my irises turned black

The bleeding blush of your body is divine, and my deity
licks her fangs as she crawls out from beneath soil,
shaking off the dirt where ancient sleep and hunger linger

Beneath her teeth, your bones crunch like dried twigs
echoing throughout the catacomb as the ground thunders,
summoning more like her, splitting through clay to emerge
anew, to take back a world once belonging to their darkness

No more will they slumber unseen and unheard, no more
will seasons change silently as their descendant daughters
pluck wildflowers, wondering where earth's magic hides

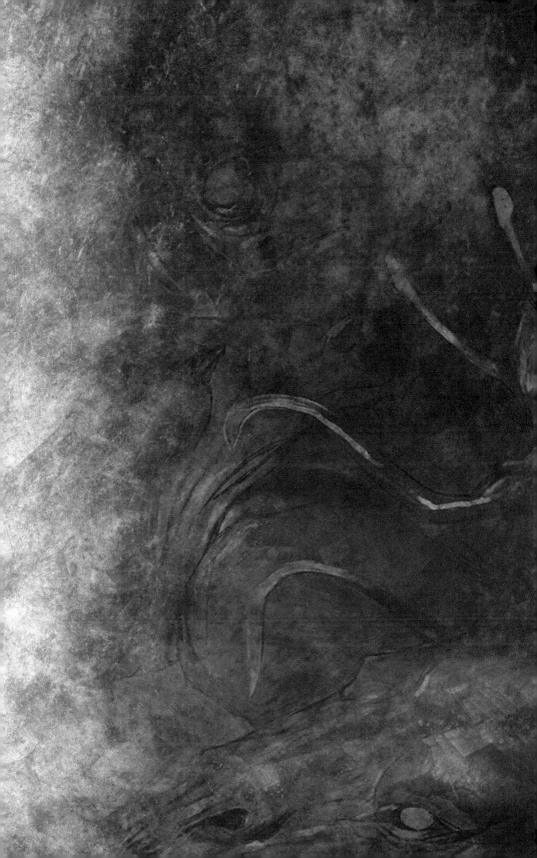

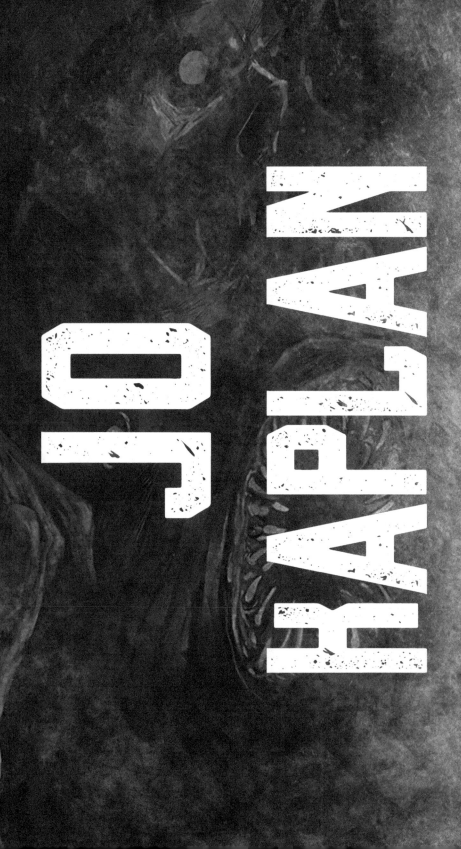

DON'T OPEN THE CELLAR DOOR

When the scratching started, she tried to pretend it wasn't there. She sat on her bed doing homework and imagined the scratching was her pencil on paper, until she pressed so hard on a math equation the graphite tip snapped off—but the scratching continued. She blasted a headbanger metal playlist through her earbuds, letting the riotous anger numb her into a callous, but when she turned off the music she heard it scraping against the silence of her eardrums: broken fingernails on the underside of old floorboards that groaned where she stepped. It reminded her of Mr. Crowley, her childhood cat, who had scrabbled at the bathroom door whenever it was closed, wanting to be let in. Only this scratching was begging to be let out.

And it was nothing so innocent as a cat.

"*Come down here, Hailey,*" his voice uttered from underneath the floor.

In this old house, nothing much made sense, least of all Hailey's bedroom. It might have been converted from an oversized pantry decades ago. The entrance to the cellar, a hinged door that opened from the floor, sat in the middle of her room. Its only use, now, was to hold the booze she stole from her mother.

She longed to creep down those rotten stairs into the cobwebbed dark and drink from her stash. But she couldn't—not with *him* down there.

Her skin itched. Pulling up one sleeve, she picked at the scabs that lined her arms.

Miles Miller had been under her bedroom floor for weeks, and he still wasn't dead.

Of course she'd noticed the way his gaze lingered on her when she bent over. She liked having someone look at her with appreciation. The boys at school looked straight through her, and so did her mother: a woman prone to falling hard in love and losing sight of all else. Miles, her current beaux, had a smile somehow both too wide and too bright, and when he turned that smile onto Irene Wachowski, she became a creature of servitude. She hadn't even asked her daughter about the long sleeves she'd worn all summer.

Even Miles had mentioned it—on a warm September day when he saw Hailey's baggy sweatshirt. "You're such a pretty girl," he said. "You don't need to hide yourself like this."

The compliment made her glow. She was seventeen, and she'd never had a boyfriend. Her closest relationship was with the little box of razors she kept in her nightstand. The ones she used to carve lines in her arms. Tried to carve that hollow loneliness from herself, as if she could bleed it out.

When Miles had started scratching at the underside of her floor, Hailey had automatically pulled a razor from its cardboard housing, thinking only the bite of the blade could smother the sickness in her heart.

"*Just open the door, Hailey*," his muffled voice slithered up from below.

She leaned down, pressed her ear against the floor, tried to hear his breath between the cracks, if he were still breathing. She thought maybe he wasn't. She thought he had to be dead by now. A rancid musk of spoiled meat permeated the warped wood. "What happens if I do?" she whispered.

His voice sounded strange, sibilant. "*We can be together*."

A bubble of hysterical laughter threatened her throat. What would she do if she opened that door—call an ambulance? Tell them she'd locked her mother's boyfriend in the cellar for weeks without telling anyone? What would happen to her then?

If she opened the door and looked down there, and saw what remained of him after all this time—how could she ever look her mother in the eye?

She hugged her knees to her chest. She hadn't meant for any of this to happen.

Pulling out her phone, Hailey burrowed down a rabbit hole of true crime blogs, trying to convince herself she wasn't looking for ideas. But she couldn't help the thoughts that slipped past: the fact that Miles didn't have a car (the bus stop was just around the corner) so there was no way to tell whether he'd skipped town. The fact that her mother never entered her room anymore, had probably forgotten all about the unused cellar.

If she could wait him out—wait until he was really good and dead—then she could simply dispose of the body. No one would know.

But each time the scratching receded, and she dared to wonder if that was it, his last bit of life spent, she couldn't help but think he was only playing possum. Waiting for her to open the door and let him out.

Irene's job as a strip club waitress kept her out late most nights. When Miles returned from what could only be another dull day as a bank teller around six o'clock, he and Irene absconded to the bedroom for an hour until she had to go to work—which left Hailey alone with him.

Typically Hailey spent the evenings studying in her room, sipping vodka, and that's what she was doing when she looked up to find Miles leaning on the doorframe, watching her mark up her history textbook.

He flashed his signature too-white smile. "Still at it?"

She shrugged. "The world has a shitload of history."

Laughing, he took a few loping strides into the room and leaned over her. He smelled of spicy cologne, a hint of sweat. "How do you lug that thing around? What is it, six hundred pages?" Put a hand on her shoulder. "That *is* a lot of history. And there's more of it every year."

Heat flushed from his palm on her bare shoulder to her face. She realized she was wearing only a thin, loose tank top and a pair of shorts. Feeling embarrassingly unclothed, scars on full display, she balanced the book in her lap and folded her arms over her chest. "Seems kind of unfair, when you think about it," she said. "People a few hundred years ago had a lot less history to learn."

"Maybe I can help." She felt his breath brush her ear.

The way he said it gave her spine a little shiver.

When his hand migrated from her shoulder down her back, she tried to pretend this was a normal gesture. Then it crept around to the edge of her breast. With a shock, Hailey flinched away, willing to pretend it had been an accident. Until his hand found her bare thigh, planted itself there.

"What are you doing?"

"Oh, come on, Hailey," he said, his voice playful.

She laughed awkwardly, tried to wriggle to the other side of the bed. Miles grabbed her ankle and yanked her towards him, her shirt riding up as she slid across the rumpled comforter on her stomach.

"Don't be such a *tease*," Miles hissed through his white teeth, and in that moment the thrill disappeared.

"Let me go," she said, reaching for the nightstand to pull herself to the other side of the bed, away from him—and then he was there, on top of her, his breath on her face, something hard pressing into her thigh.

"Don't pretend you haven't been flirting with me for *weeks* now. I bet you have all kinds of fantasies about screwing mommy's boyfriend, huh?"

"Get *off* me!" she shouted. She reached out to pull herself free but succeeded only in yanking the drawer out of the nightstand, rattling its contents. Nothing inside she could use to fight him off. Just some old makeup, an ancient iPod, a scattered handful of spare coins, a half-empty bottle of vodka she'd brought up from the cellar for her study session, and—her hand lit on it—the box of razor blades.

When he tried to plant his spongy pinkish lips on her mouth, she slashed at him.

Miles reeled back. "Son of a *bitch*." One hand covered his eye while the other found Hailey, wide with fury. "What the fuck is *wrong* with you?"

Hailey rolled off the bed, pulse beating in her ears. She dropped the razor.

The rest happened so fast. Miles came at her again, leaving naked the dripping gash that slanted from his eyebrow down through his lips; his eye welled red, wept blood; his hands were around her neck. She slipped away gasping and grabbed, swung the hefty textbook, which connected with his head like a brick. There was a sharp crack she hadn't expected, his neck snapped back, and Miles landed on the floor.

For a terrible moment, Hailey thought he was dead. She knelt on the bed and peered down at him, trembling. Then he groaned. Reached up.

Piloted by instinct, Hailey pulled open the cellar door, and even as he groaned and reached for her, she pushed him to the hole in the floor. He tumbled down the stairs and landed on the concrete with a wet smack.

Hailey slammed the trapdoor shut and dragged her bed frame over it. He wouldn't be getting out on his own.

Maybe she should have called the cops. Maybe she should have called her mother. She wasn't thinking clearly, and she didn't *want* to be thinking clearly, so instead she curled up on the bed and drank the rest of the vodka from her nightstand, washing it all away, until she passed out.

Hailey woke with the kind of headsplitting hangover that coated the world with a surreal glaze. She wandered through the motions of getting ready for school, saw her mother's door closed and assumed she was sleeping, walked to the bus stop. It wasn't until the effects of the alcohol had completely worn off that afternoon, during seventh period, when a hollow sort of clarity came over her: what had happened last night wasn't a dream.

When she got home, she went to her bedroom and pressed her ear against the trapdoor. Heard nothing.

A footstep made Hailey spin around so fast she thought she might vomit. Her mother stood in the doorway wearing a silk robe, hair mussed into tangles. "Hi, hun," she said. Her eyes were lined with dark bags. "Have you seen Miles?"

Hailey's heart gave a sick thump. "Isn't he at work?"

Irene shrugged. "He wasn't here last night when I got home."

"Maybe he went out."

Her mother nodded absently. "Yeah, you're probably right."

But when six o'clock rolled around and there was no Miles, Hailey found her mother sitting in the kitchen as twilight fell. Hailey played with the fraying ends of her sleeves and poured herself a bowl of cereal.

"Where could he be?" Irene murmured, more to herself than to her daughter. Rarely did her mother talk to her directly. Sometimes Hailey felt like an incidental presence, someone who was only half-there. "I tried calling him, but it went straight to voicemail."

Hailey's stomach lurched. Where was his phone? In his pocket, probably. What if her mother tried him again? What if she heard the ringing coming up from under the floor? What if Miles woke up and answered, told her what Hailey had done?

Gripped with terror, she forced herself to finish her cereal, mechanically chewing what tasted like wet cardboard. "Probably just busy."

The hour dragged on. By the end of it, the kitchen had fallen into darkness and Hailey was gripped with a feeling of staticky dread that she thought could only be mitigated with booze. Except Irene hadn't replenished her liquor cabinet, and Hailey's stash was all down in the cellar. With him.

The smell came: old meat, a whiff of rotten vegetables as when her mother left potatoes in the crisper for months on end. Gagging, Hailey lit half a dozen scented candles ranged around her room.

Even with the smell of something dead rising from beneath the floor, the scratching continued, like nails on a coffin lid. When she went to sleep at night, she could think only of him somewhere underneath her, both dead and not-dead, like Schrodinger's cat. Flies took up residence in her room, slipping between the cracks around the trapdoor. And that was how she came to think of him: he was simultaneously dead and alive, fractured into two possibilities that coexisted unobserved. Reality wouldn't collapse into one or the other until she opened the door and looked inside.

Cognitive decoherence. Was that what it was called? No, cognitive dissonance. She could go on with her life and pretend what had happened hadn't really happened, because it still existed in that possibility space of the cellar, not in the realm of the real. There was still a chance she might open the trapdoor and find... *nothing*. Discover it had all been a dream. That Miles really *had* skipped town.

"You're not real," she said quietly.

For a moment, there was no response. A profound calm wove its way through Hailey.

Then a scraping sound—but a different sort than the scratching. Something low, guttural. It took her a moment to place it.

He was laughing.

"*Oh, Hailey,*" said the voice from under the floor, "*Everything is real. Even things you can't see. Especially things you can't see. I'm more real than you are.*"

She started picking at her scabs to distract from the churning in her gut. There was something dark and rotten inside of her, stuck to her insides like glue.

She squeezed her eyes shut and forced herself to stop picking. "Do you even care about my mom at all?"

"*Do you?*" That chuckling again, like broken glass. "*You killed her boyfriend.*"

"You—" She swallowed. "You tried to..."

But she couldn't drag the words out of her throat. Couldn't make it real.

"I'll tell her," she tried again. "I'll tell her everything."

The silence below was enough to know what he thought of the lie.

"I called his work. They said he hasn't been in." Irene rubbed her face. "Maybe I should call the police. Report him missing."

The hour which had been Irene and Miles's was now the hour when mother and daughter sat in the kitchen as it fell into darkness.

Hailey bit down on her tongue until she tasted blood. She had to tell her. She *had* to. Sucking at the metallic taste, she said carefully, "What would you do if something bad happened to him? If he didn't just up and leave?"

"I don't know." Irene sighed. "I'm so worried about him."

"Mom." Hailey swallowed, nerves fluttering. "I need to tell you something."

But Irene was still shaking her head, staring into the distance. "I just can't imagine he would leave like that. It's not like him."

A nasty little worm wriggled in Hailey's gut. "Really?"

That drew her mother's sharp gaze. "Really what?"

Poking at the rubbery microwaved meal with her fork, Hailey muttered, "It's just... it wouldn't be the first time."

"The first time *what?*" When Hailey didn't respond, Irene slapped the table. "Spit it out. What are you trying to say?"

Hailey pushed the plastic tray from her but could not finish her accusation—unable to vocalize the simple fact that Irene's boyfriends had a habit of taking from her, taking and taking, and then leaving when they'd drained her dry. Like vampires.

"Miles wouldn't do that," Irene said, her voice low, inferring her daughter's unspoken words. "He's different."

Hit with the memory of his hand on her shoulder, his dry lips on her neck, his breath in her ear, how *different* he really was, Hailey felt sick. She dumped the rest of her meal in the trash and bolted to the bathroom, threw up what little she'd managed to get down. By the time she came out, her mother had left for work.

When she returned to her room, Hailey could hear Miles laughing as if he already knew she had failed to come clean.

"*Come down here with me,*" he said, "*and you can be alive and not-alive too. Isn't that what you want?*"

"I want you to leave me alone," she said.

"*But you're so lonely.*"

Hailey opened her textbook and stared at the page but took in nothing of its contents. Were those her only choices? To be lonely, or to be haunted by Miles?

"*Come down here,*" he said. "*You're such a pretty girl. You won't be this pretty forever.*"

From the corner of her eye, she noticed something on the floor.

No. Something coming *out* of the floor.

Like a worm, like half a dozen worms poking their blind heads up from the cracks around the cellar door: searching tendrils rising, black and wet. Hailey dropped her book and scrambled back on the bed.

"The worms crawl in, the worms crawl out," Miles said in a singsong. *"They invite their friends, and their friends too. They all come in to chew on you."*

The long black things rose and rose, sinuous as slender snakes.

With a shout, Hailey jumped down from the bed and tried to stomp on them, but they wriggled out of the way. Then they probed towards her—she felt one wrap around her ankle, slither and caress its way up her leg.

Miles was laughing.

"Let me go!" she shouted, tearing herself free. She pulled open the nightstand drawer and fumbled for a razorblade, then lunged across the floor to stab at the rising tendrils, slicing them off at the root. They fell, squirming, and wriggled back through the cracks in the wood, vanished underneath.

Hailey stood, panting.

Below, Miles was chuckling again.

When no more black worms emerged, Hailey crawled onto her bed, wrapped her arms around her knees. She pinched the comforter with her toes.

The darkness, when she finally turned off her light, seemed to amplify the scratching under the floor and the voice that whispered her name through the cracks.

On Irene's night off, Hailey found her in the living room lit only by the television, which turned tears to rivers of light on her cheeks. A bottle of vodka sat on the table beside a glass with melting ice.

Hailey hadn't drank in weeks. She hovered awkwardly between the tiny living room and kitchen, where she had been heading when she'd found her mother crying in the dark.

Instead she sat beside her mother on the couch. Irene did not look at her. When she finally spoke, her voice was thick. "They always leave me."

The rotten thing inside of Hailey reached its tendrils into her heart. "Maybe he wasn't right for you," she said. "He wasn't good for you."

Irene shook her head and poured another drink with unsteady hands. "No," she said before knocking back the vodka. "*I'm* not good enough. Not a good wife. Not a good mother."

Though Hailey's instinct was to tell her she was wrong, the words lodged in her throat. Why did it fall to her to comfort her mother? Was she supposed to lie, to make her feel better? The truth—had she the courage to say it—was that Irene was right. She *wasn't* a good mother. She never had been. And something about that made Hailey want to curl up with the squirming darkness inside of her and never come out of herself again. Always she had to comfort her mother when her latest boyfriend cheated or took off, and never did she receive comfort in return.

"Mom, I need to tell you something," she tried.

Her mother didn't seem to hear her. "There's something wrong with me," she said.

Hailey forgot what she was going to say. She suddenly felt she understood something about her mother. It was like Irene had pulled the words right out of Hailey's own mouth.

Irene looked at her, directly at her, with a gaze of terrible intensity—and maybe that was why she didn't often turn it on her daughter, because she knew what could be found within that gaze. Then she asked in a small, plaintive voice, "Why can't they ever love me like I love them?"

The sickness in Hailey's gut turned to an ache—a sore, unhealed wound. She said, "*I* love you, Mom."

The intensity of Irene's gaze diminished. She gave her daughter a thin parody of a smile. Her voice turned bland. "I love you too, sweetie."

It was the way she said it, like it was only something she was *supposed* to say, that sent Hailey to her room fighting back tears. She closed the door as she heard her mother unscrew the cap of the bottle and slosh more liquid into her glass. Barely thinking, Hailey pulled open her nightstand drawer and fished out the little box of razor blades, pulled out a fresh one, pushed up her sleeves.

Then she stopped. She knew it wouldn't help. But she didn't know what *would* help. What would make the demon twisting tesseracts in her gut relinquish its hold. She dropped the razor, filled with self-disgust.

Sitting on the floor, she looked at the scars that crisscrossed her forearms and thought about what it would be like to be both alive and not-alive. Wondered if she was actually both and just didn't know it. What was the difference between not-alive and dead? Between not-dead and alive?

Then she felt a tingling in her arms.

A dozen sharp pains.

Her scars reopened.

Something thin and black poked out of the freshly bleeding wounds—searching tendrils weaving into the air, birthing from her flesh like they had from the floor. They curled and coiled as their sticky length unspooled from the aching mouths of her split skin.

A moment of helpless terror consumed her as she saw her own rot burst free.

Mute with horror, Hailey grabbed one and pulled—and pulled—grabbed a few more from that arm and pulled them too—a foot, two feet, a yard emerged. Their length seemed impossible, interminable. She wondered if they had an end, or if she would keep pulling until she had disgorged all of her insides, had unraveled herself like a pulled thread on a poorly-sewn sweater.

She remembered what Miles had said—*I'm more real than you are.* And she felt sure she would collapse into a pile of worms at any moment.

Then, with a final tug, they came free.

Her left arm was empty, reopened cuts throbbing like the hollow of a missing tooth. Dropping the tendrils, she grabbed the ones still probing the air from her right arm and pulled them out, too, with excruciating desperation.

Long black worms fell to the floor, found the cracks around the trapdoor, and wriggled through.

For a moment she sat against her bed, panting, blood dripping down her arms. She felt empty. Purged. As if she had thrown up the final effects of food poisoning.

But she was still here. She hadn't unraveled. She wasn't a mess of worms masquerading as a human. She was *real*.

"You can't hurt me," she said to the floor.

She thought of him down there. The terrible thing she had bred in the cellar, made both dead and alive in its Schrodinger's tomb. She had to look at it, like she had looked into her mother's eyes, to see the truth.

She pushed the bed aside, its feet scraping against the floor, and opened the trapdoor with a creak.

A rank, fetid darkness rose to greet her.

The pungent smell hit her with obscene physicality. Shirt over her nose, she crept down onto the groaning stairs. Turned to the trapdoor standing open. Saw the long gouges in the underside of the wood.

Light from the room above spilled down, diffuse, so that as her eyes adjusted she could see the grayish forms of the shelves below, bottles enrobed in spiderwebs—and the body which lay in a pool of rot. A gelatinous face. Skeleton showing through meat which had mostly liquified. One bony hand raised, as if trying to scratch that faraway door, even from all the way down here. Long nails split, embedded with splinters.

She could not tell if the worm-like tendrils were emerging from the black, tarry rot of him or if they were the ones she had pulled from herself now seeking a new parasitic host in what remained of his gooey organs. Only that they wriggled into and around the corpse, made it sit up, made it stand, upheld by dozens of thin black strands like puppet strings.

It looked at her, jaw hanging open to reveal bright white teeth.

The tendrils moved the jaw up and down, plucked what remained of the rotten vocal cords to make the corpse say, "*Hailey.*"

"You're dead," she told him. Maybe he only needed to be reminded. She was observing him, wasn't she? Wasn't reality supposed to collapse, to pick either dead or alive? Why hadn't it picked? Why was the corpse lumbering towards her, that bony hand reaching, reaching—the head lolling on its neck, propped up by tendrils of rot—?

Hailey backed into the steps and started crawling up them without turning away from Miles's corpse as it came for her. Black worms poked out of empty eye sockets and puppeted arms up and forward, grasping.

But it stopped at the bottom of the steps, hesitating at the edge of darkness. "*Don't be such a tease,*" it said. "*Come down here with me.*"

She froze as she realized it would not come up. "You're afraid," she said. That was why it hid in the dark. Why it thrived in the secrets of her soul, like mold. Why it preferred to be covered up, under sleeves, under the safety of the cellar door. "You're afraid to come out."

Grinning with savage glee, Hailey reached for it, grabbed the corpse by its hand, and yanked it up into the light.

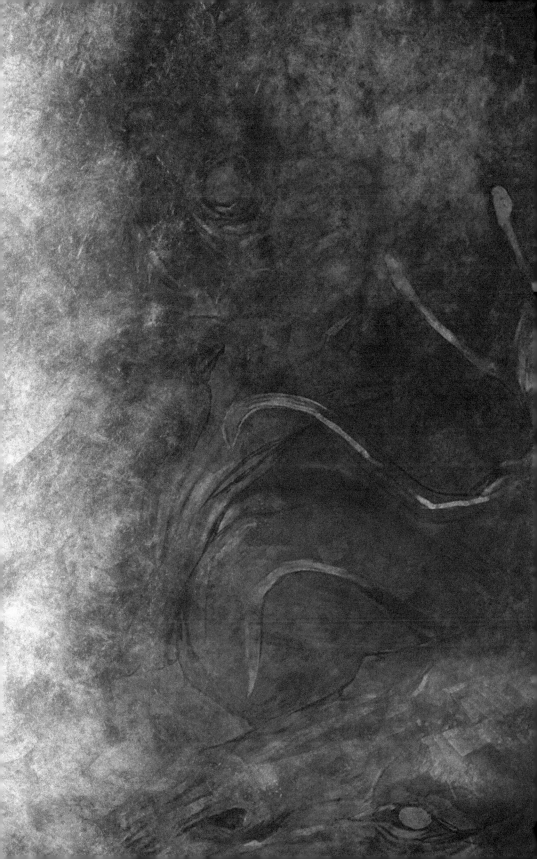

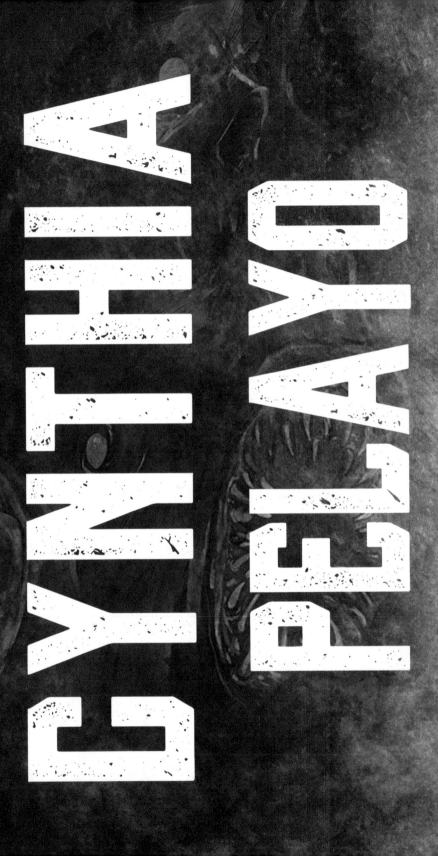

ROSES
IN THE
ATTIC

$\mathfrak{C}$an I have a mirror?" I ask Mother whose mouth quivers a bit when I say this. Her hands are folded delicately on her lap.

We are seated on the wooden floor with a wool blanket laid out beneath us because it is lunch time. Around us is an audience of the forgotten; mismatched chairs, old sofas covered with white sheets, light fixtures missing their bulbs, sagging cardboard boxes, plastic bins, and wooden crates stuffed and spilling over with a lifetime of forgotten things.

It's been ages since Mother has sat with me during a meal, and I am very pleased to have her here with me. I want to ask her all of the questions about the outside world. I wish I could reach out and touch her smooth hand, or embrace her, but Mother says I must never touch her.

I eat my sandwich, first giving thanks to Mother for making it for me. Lunch is typically a peanut butter and jelly sandwich with a glass of milk. Breakfast is often warm milk and crackers. Dinner, well, dinners used to be steamed vegetables or white rice, but these days dinner comes less and less. This morning Mother had forgotten breakfast. She said she was busy. She's become busier as time moves on.

"I'm sorry, Rose. I don't know where I can locate a mirror. They've all disappeared, like I told you, as if by magic."

Mother brushes a lock of smooth, straight hair away from her face. Mother's hair is a brilliant gold, a sparkling piece of sunshine in this dank, dark room. I reach for my hair, wishing instead I could touch Mother's. My hair swoops in great waves this and that, and is like the color of the scratched and dented floorboards beneath us.

"Right," I bite my lip and look down at the book resting beside me that I was reading before Mother arrived. She has brought me more books today, but nothing will ever compare to my favorite book. A book of fairy tales I found hidden deep in one of the trunks tucked in the far back of the room. The book's cover is yellow and worn, and the pages are tattered from all of the times I have read it. I don't know why I read it over and over really, with its wicked characters and cruel endings. Perhaps because within those lines there's always a glimmer of hope of a happily ever after.

"Because the Evil Queen hid away all of the mirrors," I add.

"That's right," Mother says. "Remember, the Evil Queen declared that all children of your kind should remain locked away and hidden until...it is safe." Mother stands up and smooths out her skirt. She looks about the room and then pinches her nose. "It smells in here," Mother says and then stares down at me.

"You really should read something else..." She points to my book. "I've brought you these...perhaps this is enough for you to fill the time."

I feel my eyes begin to sting, and my thoughts drift away, thinking of the adventures I have read about in all of my books, of green pastures and great oceans, snow-covered mountains, cities beaming with light and laughter, and of a family seated around a great table covered in delicious food, roasted meat and fruit-covered tarts.

"Will it be safe for me to leave this room soon?" I ask.

"You are different." Mother is already at the door, her hand on the doorknob. She sighs heavily and without turning around says: "You are in this room because you are *different*. You will never leave this house, Rose."

I open my mouth to plead with her to tell me more, about the outside world and the dangers she speaks of. I will beg her to let me out. I will promise to be good and kind. I will be the most perfect and brilliant child that I can possibly be, but Mother is already gone.

The door is shut, and I hear the lock click.

I am once again alone in this large, cluttered room full of moldy boxes and crates stuffed with objects that are like me, ignored and forgotten, gawked upon only when remembered by chance. I turn to the single bulb that hangs from the rafters, my only source of light besides a small window whose view is obstructed by gnarled and twisting branches.

I look at the crate beside me. It has been months since Mother has brought me new books and I know I should be thankful for the small things she gifts me, but still, my chest aches and tears stream down my face. I would rather be out there with her and with a family, than in here with only an ancient tree looking over me from the outside and inside all of this clutter, of things people packed away long ago, hoping to need but never will.

She has visited me less and less since I asked her: "Who is my father?"

Her eyes flashed with a rage I have never witnessed before and she spat: "A man I thought I loved once, but soon realized was undesirable and unsuitable for this world or any."

I dig through the box, but these books all seem to be written for children younger than myself, board books of lullabies, lessons on colors and learning to count. All of these things I know already. I kick at the crate.

I'm frustrated with all of the discarded and overlooked things in this messy attic. I hate this room. I hate the dust that floats around me, and through me, filling my lungs, and covering the boxes and crates and creaky old furniture in layers. I hate the cobwebs that catch on my hair and brush against my cheek as I navigate this space. I hate the spiders that crawl across my arms and legs at night, and I hate the stillness and silence of it all, and of feeling as if my only purpose is to fold in with the objects around me that are no longer needed, as if I have become one of them.

I look in the crate Mother left behind once again, and notice two books at the bottom I had not seen moments before. The first is smaller than the second, *Flowers in the Attic* by an author named V.C. Andrews. The cover shows a wide-eyed girl looking out of a window, and I feel like she is looking directly at me, waiting to tell me all of the secrets that lay within her attic. The other book is thick and heavy. A picture of a sea creature stares back at me from the cover, *The Complete Tales of H.P. Lovecraft*. I set them both aside knowing that all I have is time and that I will read both soon.

The next day Mother does not come to my room, or the next. When I raise my hand to knock on the door, I am frozen by one of her earlier warnings:

If you make a noise they will hear you, and if they hear you great and terrible things will happen.

Mother never explained to me who *they* were.

I read. I sleep. I wake. An endless cycle of misery in this room. I do not know how long I have been here. All I know is what my books have taught me, including the two newest books Mother left for me. One tells me about a little girl in an attic in a faraway home full of dreadful secrets and gruesome possibilities. In my other new book, I learn of monsters from galaxies far away, and that lurk in this reality as well. In one of those stories, I read about a horrid being that was locked away for years in endless twilight, in an old and infinite castle full of accursed rats and disappointment. One night, this desperate creature escapes its tower, and happens upon people who are aghast at its presence. When the creature looks into a mirror, it sees its own nightmarish reflection for the first time.

When moments of boredom come and when I have completed reading about those horrifying things in my new books I search the attic, picking through bins. I thumb through photo albums, looking at pictures of smiling adults and children who look a little bit like Mother, with her shinning hair and fair brilliant eyes. I open large wooden chests and am attacked by the fluttering of moths who have made their homes tucked within silk gowns with sparkling beads and cotton dresses with pretty silver buttons. I wrap myself in these great clothes, and while they swallow me up as they are too large for my form, I still dance and play in them pretending I am a princess living in a beautiful kingdom.

When I tire, I sit on the squeaky red sofa with broken wooden legs, and read through newspapers, old diaries and journals. They speak of internal conflicts and wars, of bullet-hole- ridden bodies that fill the streets, cities on fire, and of people that aren't really people, but that are different.

I carefully turn the pages of the yellowed newspapers crumbling under the weight of time with bold headlines that speak of man as monster who has no place in civil society.

With each turn of the page, I can feel my eyes wandering off to the door wondering if and when Mother will return with my meal.

The days fold in and out.

My stomach groans with pain until all pain ceases. My lips become dried and cracked, unsure that they would ever feel moisture again, and just as I am sure I will never see Mother again there is a soft knock at the door.

"Mother?" I had not spoken in such a long time my own voice sounded foreign to myself.

I scramble to my feet, but she does not answer.

The door opens a few inches, and a porcelain plate is pushed inside and once again the door is shut and locked. On top of the plate sits two small, powdered donuts and a glass of milk, which I devour.

Another day rises and another night falls.

Again, another and another.

I begin to sleep beneath the window, for while it is a drafty place to rest, the tapping of the branches against the glass feels comforting, as if the tree is speaking to me — my only companion in this darkness.

During the days, with whatever little light I have, I reread the same books over and over, my fairy tales and stories about children secreted away and a monster alone in his castle. At night I don dresses and dance and twirl, silently, carefully so as not to make noise. I imagine I am a princess locked in a tower, who reads enchanted books whose words flutter off the page and whisk me away to a far away place with green grass, blue skies, and a golden sun.

After some days there is once again a light knock. The door opens, a porcelain plate is shoved inside with powdered donuts and cold milk. The door shuts, but this time I do not hear the lock click.

I wait for a few moments, for the sound of retreating footsteps. I consume the food quickly. I turn back to the great darkened room of shadows and cobwebs, old letters and forgotten books. I look at the gnarled branches outside my window and ask my ancient tree friend to give me strength for what I am about to attempt.

I place my hand on the cold doorknob, close my eyes, turn, and the door opens.

I open my eyes and begin walking down a short hallway that leads to some stairs. I place my hand on the railing and descend all the way down until I arrive at another floor. Here the walls are white and the hardwood floor before me is without a spot or a scratch, shining and pristine and free of all dust. I find another stairway and from the top I hear...voices and laughter. I remember what my Mother has told me across all of that time I have lived in the attic, that people should not see me, that no one should gaze upon me because I am different.

I move down carefully until I find myself in a large, open room with plush seating and large windows that look out into a sea of green grass and full trees and flowers bursting in bloom. Radiant sunlight streams in through the great room. I stand in front of those large windows and close my eyes, taking great pleasure in the warmth of the sun on my skin. I breathe in deeply. The room smells so sweet and so fragrant, so far away from the foul odors I have known my entire life.

And then, I hear a plate crash to the floor.

"Mommy..." a small voice says. "What is that?"

There are screams. The sounds of chairs tumbling and glass shattering.

I turn around and see my Mother standing at a table. Two small children are seated beside her. A man stands at her side. The smallest child runs around to Mother, cowering behind her skirt, screaming and crying pointing at me with a look of immense terror.

"Get rid of it, Mommy!" The smallest one stomps her feet and then shoves her face into my Mother's skirt. "Make it go away!"

The little boy stands up, opens his mouth to scream but instead vomits all over the table. He then collapses at Mother's feet in tears. "Get it out," he gasps and gags through tears.

"Why is this ghastly thing in my house?" The man shouts at Mother. "You said you had gotten rid of that...defect."

Mother's voice shakes. "It's been in the attic..."

"In our house?" The father throws down a napkin on the table. "I'm going to have to fumigate everything. Paint the walls. Hell, it probably touched the walls on its way down from upstairs. We'll have to rip out the drywall. Gut the entire house."

The young boy sobs, covering his eyes. "Get rid of it, Mommy."

"Mother..." I say, but my words are swallowed up by cries and screams.

She does not look at me, but instead walks away to another room.

"I can't sit in this house for another minute with that diseased thing. We're going to have to move knowing that rot was living in this house," the father shouts, following after Mother.

The little girl's cries rise above the clattering that was going on from another room.

I take a step forward and Mother appears. "Not another foot!"

I do not know what to do, where to move, what to say. All I have ever known are the ways of discarded objects and abandoned things. The only smell I have ever really known is that of mold. The only touch I have ever truly felt is the delicate caress of a spider's web.

There's all this screaming.

All of this anger, and I just want to hide inside one of my books.

I turn around and then I see...her. She is wearing a moth-eaten cotton dress with gold buttons. The dress is too large for her, but she is a princess no less. She is a girl who looks older than the littlest child hiding behind Mother. A girl with dark hair that falls past her shoulders in sweeping dark brown curls.

Above all of the screaming and all of the crying and clattering of plates that engulf me I smile because I finally have a mirror to look into, and I am pretty.

"Get rid of it!" the man shoves a metal object into Mother's hand.

Mother approaches me. No words, just quiet, and as she raises the flat part of the sharp metal object above my head I turn back to the mirror and see our reflection side by side. I can now see that we really don't look that different from one another after all.

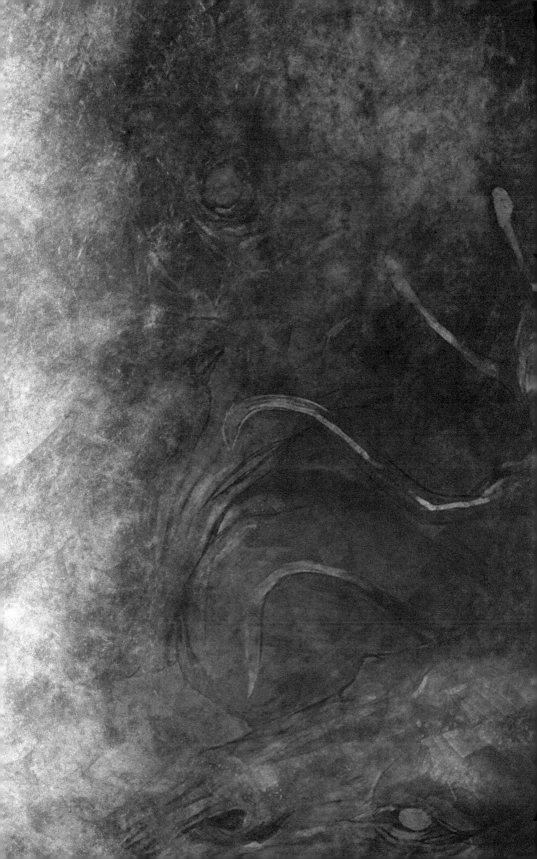

PERIPHERAL
VISION

On the afternoon that the creatures revealed themselves to me, the sun hung high in the cloudless sky, birds chirping, spring flowers in bloom, the mile loop a hiking circuit that I frequented to get some fresh air, a bit of exercise, trying to get away from the pressure of school and my parents. Eighteen at the time, finishing up high school, I was still trying to figure out the future, and these walks helped to clear my head. As a young boy, I loved to hike, spending as much of my time outdoors as I could, joining the Boy Scouts so I could camp, and cook, and fend for myself. Years later, as I grew older, those skills, that awareness, would come in handy. I was impressionable then, going through the unpredictable changes of that age, seeking answers to the weighty questions of life. I was an open book waiting to be written. In nature, I saw beauty, an order to things, and a chance to interact with something greater than myself. Usually, I'd take the family vehicle, an old minivan we called Bessie, a sturdy companion, a tank with a heart of gold. I drove with the windows down, the smell of pine and cut grass rushing in. In no time at all I had parked, and locked up, taking a water bottle and backpack out into the woods to see what it might offer up to me—a rare rock, or possibly a deer, an arrowhead, or unique flowering bud.

I had barely crested the headland at the halfway point of the trail when the stench of decomposition washed over me. My body physically recoiled from the odor and I spat repeatedly to rid my mouth of the awful taste. Something was dead. Something close. I paused at the wooden footbridge over the pond, trying to find the source of the stink, scouring the scummy surface of the water for dead fish, searching the trail for scat, or something worse. I'd heard of suicides in these woods, but thought they were urban legends—hooks for hands and curses come home to roost. But I didn't believe them. Until now.

Off to one side, there was a familiar path that I knew would lead back to the car, through the high grasses where the deer would rest and hide from the prying eyes of predators, past a massive stand of dead snags, before winding along a trickling creek to the parking lot. Instead, I kept going, and the deeper I got into the forest, the more it consumed me, surrounding me with lush foliage, swarming insects, and the claustrophobia of nature responding to my presence. In the past, she'd been a friend, Mother Nature, but today, she felt like a foe. I walked on through the woods, pushing aside dense vegetation and thorny bushes, before catching a glimpse of a dark cloud of gnats hovering over a small clearing beyond the lush pine trees.

I had to see what was up ahead, curious about what had transpired.

There, in a patch of flattened grass, in the centre of a circle of white pine, scotch, and spruce lay a cornucopia of death and dismemberment. I stood transfixed for several minutes, as the noises of the forest disappeared one by one, a quiet descending over me, wrapping me in a cold sweat of uncertainty. I wasn't sure what I was seeing, but against all instincts, I moved closer, until the atrocity came into focus, the sour smell of decay making my stomach churn, bile rising in my throat.

At first glance the dead animal appeared to be a wolf, lying disemboweled on one side, its thick grey fur matted with clotted blood, a swollen tongue protruding from its gaping mouth, eyes like glass marbles, its dilated pupils fixed on oblivion. It had been a magnificent, dignified animal at one point in time, but now, its corpse was emaciated, a skeleton with a pelt glued to its bones, as a horde of buzzing insects swarmed around me.

The rest of the tableau only confused the situation.

The creature's stomach had been ruptured, the half-digested contents spilling out onto the trampled grass. It was most certainly the ingredients of its last meal—the long ears and hind legs revealing it to be a brown rabbit, partially putrefied but somehow still whole, my head swimming as I tried to figure out how the wolf had managed to swallow the creature in one piece.

The tiny rabbit was also gutted, the series of corpses opening up like Russian dolls, nesting one inside the other, sinking this horror down another level. Its pink eyes had frozen wide in shock, as if the hare had been birthed from within the dead lupine. Inside this eviscerated rabbit lay a dead grey mouse, its tiny head poking out of the deflated stomach of the once fluffy animal, its little teeth jutting out, its limbs stiff and twisted. While I puzzled over the oddity of a herbivore devouring a mouse whole like a snake, an echo of sounds drifted to me from beyond their collective grave here—a bark and a howl, a whine, a chitter, and chirp.

The rabbit started to move, and I stepped back, as its guts bulged and strained, finally bursting open as something fought to get out. Crawling out of the torn stomach of the field mouse was a large, black beetle that was moving slowly away from this shrine, its pincers clicking together, as it lifted first one leg, and then another, at a glacial pace, holding my gaze, as if trying to communicate some cryptic message.

I straightened up, suddenly feeling much less alone, and scanned the surrounding trees for some sign of life. Nearby treetops shook and the undergrowth rustled with the rising wind, and then at eye level, I noticed for the first time, a set of claw marks raked across the trunk of a stout evergreen, slicing through the thick bark, a deep wound that still leaked sap.

There were no bears in this part of Illinois, and yet, these claw marks told a different story. Glancing back at the creatures lying in the grass, viscera strewn around them, dirt dug up from under the weeds and pine needles, my gut clenched in protest.

In that moment I was just one link in an evolutionary chain, very aware of those smaller animals at my feet, and the threat of something larger moving about in the woods.

Eat or be eaten.

Survival of the fittest.

Darwin, at play.

A fluttering of wrens launched into the sky as a lone cloud drifted across the sun, throwing its shadow over the woods, my skin chilling under the expanding umbrella of something massive hovering overhead, descending closer, breathing in and out. Bushes shifted, the ground trembled, a weight looming over it all.

Whatever this was, it was much bigger than any bear I'd ever seen. I wasn't going to wait for it to reveal itself to me. By then, it might be too late.

So I ran.

Careening down the path, tripping over roots, panic rising as I did calculations in my head about various routes, faster and slower, hills and dips, I glanced back over my shoulder, and lost my balance. I sprawled in the dirt—hands and forearms scraping on rocks—the world around me shifting and rotating, blurring, tears filling my eyes. At the top of the treeline something came into focus.

Deep in the woods, a thin sheen of pink silhouette rose up high, spreading across, and behind, and through the trees. The creature was several stories high, but thin as paper, slender legs raising and lowering, two long antennae extending, stalks with black dots for eyes, a shimmer in a flash of blinding sunlight, and then it was gone. It flickered in the sunlight that broke through the clouds—there one minute, and gone the next. I turned away, scrambling to get up, as the main trail was only a few feet away.

Glancing back one more time, there was nothing to see, the grasses swaying back and forth, the purple flowering chive dotting the greenery, a fish landing in the murky pond with a splash, and then gone.

On the drive home, I would pull over, and vomit onto the side of the road—retching and straining like an animal. I would tell myself for many years that what I'd stumbled across had been merely some bizarre midden of dead animals, nature just being weird and brutal, nothing more. I had obviously been tired, perhaps with a fever, or sickness.

Nothing more.

Nothing less.

Periodical cicadas spend most of their life underground surviving on xylem fluids from the roots of trees. But after seventeen years—using an internal molecular clock that allows them to sense the passage of time through subtle changes in the tree sap—they explode in unison to the surface to quickly breed and die.

Many years later, I am upstairs shaving, dragging the sharp razor over my stubbled face, when my wife unleashes a blood-curdling scream from downstairs. My hand jerks at the sound, slicing the blade across my cheek, droplets of blood spattering on the white porcelain of the bathroom sink.

It is the kind of scream that would suggest that she has fallen and broken something, or possibly tumbled down the wooden stairs to our concrete basement below. Or perhaps her chef's knife has caused an accident, cutting vegetables on the butcher's block, mistaking one of her tanned fingers for a slender carrot.

When Jennifer screams again, one might think she has left the back door open again, and that pack of rabid coyotes that has been prowling the neighborhood, eating cats and small dogs, has come to claim its first human victim.

I grab the machete that lies under our king-sized bed, and rush down the stairs in my boxer shorts, drops of blood coining the steps, paying the price for safety, a prayer working its way over my chapped lips.

When I reach the living room, the back door is open, and she is standing on the faded tan couch, her eyes bulging, filled with fear.

"What is it?" I yell.

"There!" she says, pointing to the table. "Can't you see it?"

I approach slowly, peering around the rectangular ottoman, looking for a long, yellow python, or perhaps a yipping red fox from the woods down the road.

I don't see anything.

"What?"

"The moth, the bug!" she yells.

This has happened before.

I approach the low upholstered seat, as she breathes heavily, her terror palpable, her face flushed.

There on the black leather surface is a giant silk moth, and she is magnificent—a mottled mix of gray and brown, with fake eyes on her wings. Her abdomen and thorax is as big as an acorn, with her wings opening up even larger, to make her larger than my fist. Her little antennae quiver in the air. I put my palm out to her and she climbs up onto it, and I carry her out the back door.

"Kill it!" yells Jennifer. "Squash it!"

"Let me get it away from the house. She might be carrying babies, and we don't want the eggs scattered all over the living room."

Her eyes widen and she retches, covering her mouth.

I know that she is scared, but I also know that this moth isn't going to hurt anyone. When I'm in the middle of the yard, far enough away, I open my fist and let it go.

A common housefly I would also catch, and release into the back yard, instead of smashing it with a flyswatter. They lift off from surfaces like helicopters, and if you swipe your open hand over them, closing your fingers as you approach them, they will soar right into your grip. I feel like Mr. Miyagi when I do this. Horseflies I don't like, they are bigger, and angrier, full of hate, but if I'm quick, they don't bite me.

I'm not always very quick.

I have caught many a field mouse in our basement, until Jennifer spent thousands of dollars to seal it shut—white foam sprayed into holes, blocks of wood nailed in tight, new insulation running around the top of the unfinished basement. They're the ones I like best, just little, fuzzy guys who lived here long before we moved in. I started by capturing them alive and just letting them out the back door, but they came back. Then I took them to the wooden fence that runs along the back of our property, and opened the long, green, plastic trap to set them free. They found their way back inside. Eventually I had to take three mice in a car ride a mile west, setting them free, hoping they were a family, able to look out for each other on the edge of the forest reserve. No hawks in the air, they were let loose. But I didn't tell my wife.

When I come back inside from releasing the moth, she is still visibly shaken.

"Why can't you just kill it? What kind of man are you?" she asks. "What if some intruder came into the house and tried to rape me?"

"I'd chop him to pieces with my machete," I say, waving it in the air for effect. "A moth isn't a rapist, Jennifer. And neither is a fly, or a mouse. That's the deal—you scream, I come running, but the critters go free. You knew that when you married me—who I was, who I still am now."

"Next time I'm going to kill it myself," she says unconvincingly, finally sitting down, glaring at me. "You're useless."

The last word cuts deep into my ego, my heart, as I shuffle crestfallen toward the back door and close it.

"What happened to your face?" she asks.

"You did, my dear. You did."

She squints at me, trying to figure out what I mean.

It is a major disconnect we have—me not truly understanding her fear, and her feeling I don't act fast enough, that I won't kill them for her, destroy them, because I don't love her enough. We both have work to do, it seems.

I finish a load of laundry, the dishwasher already unloaded, the grass cut, garbage taken out, bills paid. For a moment, I think of the garden we're building along the back fence—lavender, petunias, mint, and chrysanthemums—all known to keep insects away.

Later, she will come to me, and apologize, and I will forgive her for lashing out when she was upset. Just like I forgave her for the tennis shoes in the garage that held tiny appendages of the insects she's crushed when I wasn't home, or when I didn't come running fast enough. Just like I forgave her for the wooden traps in the trash can, the pitiful, bent frames of mice she killed pushing a wave of sadness over me when I found them. Ant traps under the sink, bug spray in her purse, the bag of lye tucked in the corner, all manner of poison and death. Their little ghosts linger in the walls of our house, whispering her sins to me in the middle of the night.

With every moon—harvest, blood, super, and blue—I've retired to the back yard after she's gone to sleep, a bonfire built out of hickory and cedar, pine and birch, dried thyme and sage, filling the air with layers of woodsmoke, spices, and hope. I squat in the shimmering moonlight, under the protective blanket of darkness, and apologize to the mice living out amongst the trees, try to explain her violence to the insects that lurk in the grasses beneath my feet, the tens of thousands of them, asking for their forgiveness. I don't know if any of it works, or helps, but I offer it up anyway.

They were here first.

With a hibernation period of up to 100 million years, bacteria discovered on the Arctic sea floor may have the longest life cycle of any known organism.

Our trip across the Painted Desert was a nightmare from the start, the beauty and color of the rolling hills and expanding desert providing a brief respite from a series of fights and undoings.

It was this very vacation where I started to understand why my wife hated bugs so much, why she had such an innate fear of such small, harmless things.

We were driving cross country from Chicago to Los Angeles to see friends, stopping at some of the state parks and iconic landmarks we'd never seen, bonding over the great outdoors.

At a rest stop in Oklahoma, as we worked our way west on Route 66, I went into the hot, concrete bathroom marked for men and she went into the women's. These places always smell, either of urine and vomit, or harsh fake orange disinfectant layered over the stench of it all. In and out, do your business, keep going.

For Jennifer it turned into something else.

I heard her scream, a sheen of sweat glossing over my forehead as I pushed hard to empty my full bladder.

When I shoved open the door to the women's bathroom, she was running in a circle, batting at her head, which was covered in cobwebs. Both stalls were open—one filled with an unholy crap that circled the basin, bathing in a sour, yellow bowl of fermenting piss. There were rat droppings in the filthy corners of the bathroom, balled-up paper towels dotted with blood, as well as leaves that had blown in from the outside, muddy boot prints caked onto the concrete floor.

It was like this place hadn't been cleaned in weeks. Maybe longer.

I rushed to her, her pants unbuttoned, her shirt untucked, and helped her to get the webs off of her head and face. Trying to comfort her, I pulled the sticky, glossy gossamer off her anguished face, as she slowly started to calm down. I held her as she sobbed, a woman walking in, flannel shirt and blue jeans, taking one look at us, and then turning around.

She didn't need this trouble.

It would be six miles down the road when the spider entered her ear. Her hands flying about, body seizing up in the passenger seat, clawing at her head again, lashing out, swatting the rearview mirror askew, nearly breaking the passenger window. I swerved onto the shoulder of the road and before I even had the car in park, she launched out of the vehicle, scrambling over the trash littered shoulder into dead grass, before falling down into a drainage ditch, and getting soaked with stagnant rain water and run-off.

Later, we'd drive for miles into the fading sun, her crying silently in exhaustion and shame, before she'd talk about a friend of hers that had fallen asleep and woken up to a tickling in his ear, shoving his finger in to scratch that itch, only to crush a spider and send it farther back into his ear canal. The rupture had forced an early birth of tiny, black babies that scuttled and dispersed deeper into his head, down his neck, and over his body into his bed. Jennifer would shudder as she told this all to me. I pictured online videos of doctors dragging crickets out of ears with tweezers, pulling tapeworms out of nostrils, scabies burrowing the scalp, or blood flukes swimming in swollen veins.

Over a spurt of sanitizer, we shared a feeble smile, both of us putting down our guard for a moment, seeing each other, appreciating how in this moment we had relied on each other and survived. I had acted fast enough, a true reaction, nothing manufactured or reluctant, and she saw that, was grateful. Maybe it was progress.

We drove in silence, trying to ignore the incident at the bathroom, to forget each other and appreciate the beauty of it all. But the roadkill that lined the highway along the route soured the beautiful landscape, mangled carcass after carcass being devoured by vultures and crows, culminating in a young deer cut in half by a semi, smearing blood and fur across the road, and down into the low grass off the pavement. Everywhere around us was death and decay.

When we arrived at the Painted Desert, we walked down into the valley from the parking lot, as the layers of purple and yellow and orange and red surrounded us. It was unlike anything I'd ever seen. Scattered here and there were petrified pieces of wood—some small, some entire logs, massive and heavy. The further we wandered down into the desert, away from other tourists, the quieter it got, until we stood alone in the middle of a path, the world around us disappearing.

I stood there grinning, her head cocked to one side watching me. I was overwhelmed by what was happening.

Several thoughts washed over me as the world went mute—not a car door, or engine, or plane overhead, not an air conditioner running, or a radio, or distant conversation. There was absolutely no sound. In that moment, my heart pounding, eyes watering, I had three revelations come to me: I was dead, and this was either heaven or some kind of purgatory; the matrix had broken, and I had been shown that this was all an illusion; I was in the presence of something holy, wrapped in the presence of God, and the great beyond. Somewhere in this moment I felt both the vastness of this expanse and a crushing claustrophobia, the desert breathing in and out, deeply, as I did, making everything I thought I knew a giant question mark. I was both contained and fractured, at an atomic level, uncertain of how reality truly worked.

And then the wind picked up, and an engine revved in the distance, a crow cawing as it took off in flight from a weathered guard rail in the parking lot. The illusion had been shattered, allowing the harsh reality of our world to seep back in.

I would share my thoughts with Jennifer as we continued on toward Winslow and further west to Flagstaff, and she would nod her head at my every confession, but I could tell she hadn't felt the same way. And that's why

I didn't tell her about the flickering, pink silhouettes that loomed on the horizon. Or how that translucent grouping of monstrosities lumbered slowly forward over hills, and plateaus, and mesas. Or about the buzzing of their wings. Or how the smallest one turned towards me, the black orbs on the end of two very long antennae, taking in my gaze, its thin, bent legs picking up one at a time, then placed down slowly, this herd of ancient creatures shimmering in the desert sun, barely visible, in and out of focus, and then suddenly gone in a rush of wind.

No. I didn't mention them.

Because I thought I might be going insane.

Some snails that live in the desert can sleep for up to three years. They bury themselves in the ground when it gets too dry, seal their shell to retain moisture, and hibernate until it gets wetter again.

We were getting old, no children for us, the alien invasion of her body something that held no appeal for her. We'd fight about it, and in the end we acquired a series of black Labs, but never our own brood. I wanted to care for something beyond me, to create life out of our love for each other, and she wanted one less mess to clean up, one less responsibility, one less worry. I understood, but didn't agree.

I remember sitting with Jennifer around the fire pit in our back yard, trying to talk to her about the things I'd seen over the years. I told her about my friend Martin communicating to me from the other side after his passing in high school—heavy knocks in the walls that spoke in Morse code, drawers opening on their own, knives arranged in strange patterns. I told her about how I'd rewound time while taking acid in college, left my body, and spoken to God. I told her about the photography project a roommate had undertaken, pictures of candles and pentagrams filling the digital screen—yelling at him for playing with the dark arts—him mocking me as I cut the picture into four sections, and then further into smaller squares—one burned, one buried, one flushed, one tossed. When I woke up screaming and swinging my fists at the menacing silhouettes standing over my bed, he stopped laughing, his face turning pale. So many things I didn't want to acknowledge, even as evidence presented itself to me.

I tried to tell her there were things humanity didn't understand, layers of life and reality, the universe a vast and wondrous place.

I don't think she truly comprehended what I was saying, until the creatures appeared, sending our world into utter chaos.

The day started as an ordinary one, the wife and I in the backyard working on the garden, both of us older now, covering our gray hair and wrinkled skin with hats and long sleeves to protect it from the sun. We'd gotten up early before it got too hot, pruning and weeding, watering the flowers as they swayed in the summer breeze, each one adding welcome splashes of purple, and red, and vibrant yellow to the ubiquitous green grasses and carefully placed dull gray stones.

It began with the fighter jets overhead, the airbase not that far away, just a bit north of us, followed by the police sirens, the ambulances, the fire trucks. We stood up, looking at each other, something not right in the very air around us—some primitive, ancient ability to sense danger that our species lost as we became more civilized, activated in us both. And then they started to appear in the sky, to land, one after the other, across the landscape, these flickering beings, in shades of pink and salmon, almost transparent, wings fluttering and then folded in tight next to their bodies upon impact. One buzzed to a halt next door, filling the entire backyard, its giant exoskeleton dwarfing the neighbor's house. Gunshots rang out in the distance, as scattered explosions and panicked voices became more frequent. Both of us stood there with our mouths open, staring at the monstrosities descending on the landscape, me recognizing them at once.

My wife's familiar scream brought the attention of the creature, its eyestalks bending toward her as she started throwing rocks, tools, anything she could find, picking them up from the ground, from our garden, heaving them up into the sky, tearing through its thin, papery skin, the long skinny legs of it lifting and then coming back down, striding over the fence, to step on my wife, squashing her entire body down into the soil, silencing her for good. None of it was real, and yet, all of it was happening. I was numb, unable to move.

And then it turned to me, hesitating, standing motionless as it scrutinized the insignificant creature below it. It had hardly changed over the years—from the woods, to the desert, to this moment in time. I stared back, craning my neck upward, the sunshine turning pink as it filtered through its translucent body, blinding me for a moment, before everything went dark.

The African lungfish can sleep out of water for three to five years without any sustenance, only to wake up when freshwater surroundings become available.

When I woke up, I found myself deposited on a barren mountaintop, the frigid wind swirling around me, blowing dusty snow over the lumpy, irregular surface of the plateau. Somewhere above me a buzzing faded into the distance, the creature departing in flight. I pushed myself to my feet in the knee-deep snow, shivering uncontrollably in my shorts and t-shirt, overwhelmed by the whiteness of the landscape, my exposed skin burning from the bitter cold. I was surrounded by lumps, an endless sea of frozen bodies. One was in a blue down coat, a knit hat, and blue jeans, black boots laced up tight. It curled in the fetal position, head tucked between its knees. As the wind gusted, it revealed more of them—a woman in a tie-die shirt, and long skirt; a kid in a black leather jacket and white shirt; a peasant in some sort of patchwork frock; a man in flowing purple robes.

As the snow fell heavier, and the storm covered the area, I sat down, holding myself, trying to find any heat, my efforts to take clothes from the others only cutting and tearing my hands, everything frozen and sharp, going numb as I fell over, and started to go under.

The burning sensation on my legs had been replaced by nothingness, the skin having turned bright red and gone completely numb. Desperately, I scanned my surroundings for some refuge from the cold, spotting a bright blue parka on a nearby corpse. I staggered toward it, dropping to my knees and struggled to tear the garment from the young woman's frame. The muscles of my hands failed to respond, my fingers immobilized with the intense cold. It took only moments before I realized that the frozen jacket was too difficult for my aching hands to remove. I pushed myself to my feet and stumbled again toward the nearest fallen body, desperately clawing at the snow to uncover their jacket, my hands twisted from the cold like the talons of a crippled bird, only to find the man's torso covered in what appeared to be a breastplate with a crude rose carved into its mottled surface, its green verdigris creating a stark contrast against the white of the snow, his head half-covered with a bronze helmet. I fell backward, screaming in agony and frustration, and dragged my body away from the bygone man. As I reached yet another cadaver in a deep drift, my breathing growing shallow and weak,

I brushed the snow from its face with my arm, straining to remain conscious, pleading for mercy and forgiveness. In my final moments, lying numb and exhausted in the snow, I accepted my icy fate and marvelled at the face before me—the bulging eyebrows, the retracted chin, the sloping forehead, the impossibly wide nose, and the chapped lips pulled back to reveal its massive teeth—the features of a long-forgotten Neanderthal.

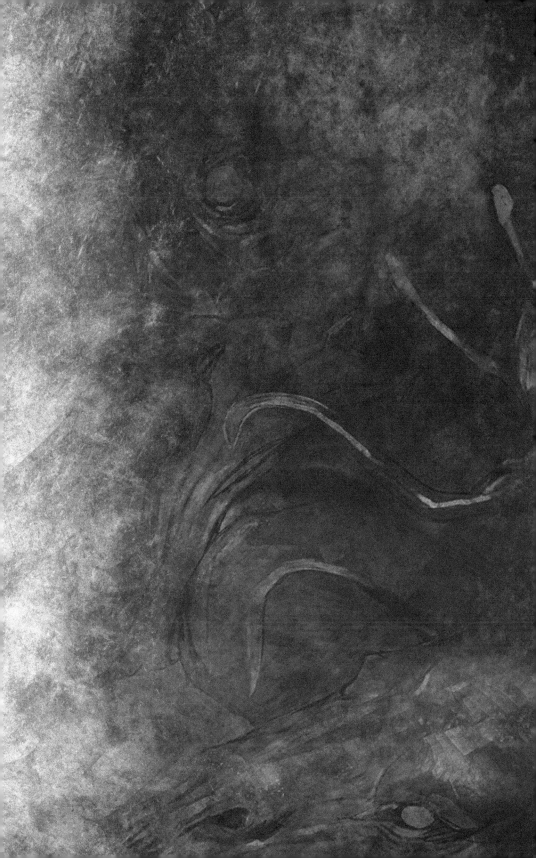

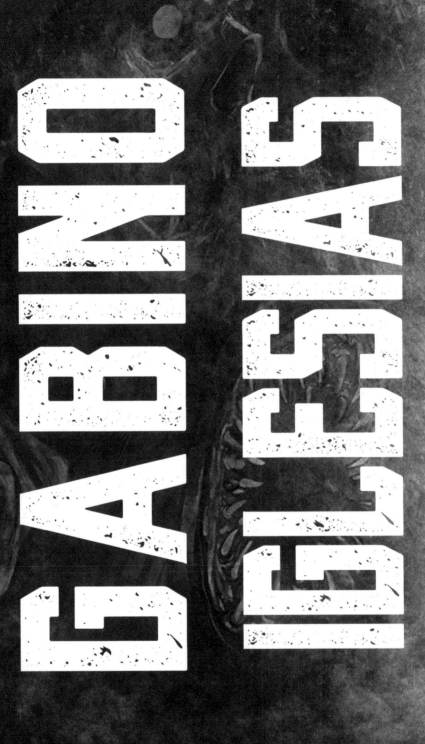

HAUNTED INSIDE

Pablo couldn't pinpoint the moment happiness had become a regular thing he took for granted if he didn't pay attention, but he recognized the feeling that came over him whenever he felt truly happy. That Sunday morning was perfect, for example, and he knew it. Sofia was in the kitchen, her long black hair swaying as she mixed the pancake batter. Mandy was on the floor, her tiny hands banging a giraffe plush toy against the floor. Her movements reminded Pablo of the destructive impulses at the core of every human, but he pushed the thought away. Outside his window, a squirrel ran up a tree that stood like a brown tower in their new front garden. Its canopy was full and round, which made it look like a green cloud against a perfectly blue sky.

The light that came through the window felt like a warm blessing. Pablo looked for particles floating in the light because it felt like the right thing to do, but Mandy's pummeling of the poor giraffe was too cute and he couldn't keep his eyes away from his daughter for long.

Look around.

The voice was calm. It felt like a reminder more than threat, but Pablo understood its true nature. Looking once more around the new house, he wondered how long the happiness would last this time, how long it would take for him to start seeing dark figures out of the corner of his eye and hearing strange things in the middle of the night. He knew this perfect moment was fleeting, transitory, a fragile thing tottering at the edge of a dark, ragged precipice. The darkness would come and the figures would show up. When that happened, he'd have to come up with a new excuse to move. As always, he'd have to apply for a transfer or find a house for sale that he'd convince Sofia they couldn't pass up. He was tired of it, but it was the price he had to pay for all his good fortune. The thing that granted him this perfect moment was also the thing that haunted him, the invisible evil that soiled everything around him.

Pablo looked at Mandy again. She had stopped beating the giraffe and was now sucking on one of its brown ears. For her, he'd move again whenever the darkness found him. For his beautiful baby daughter, he'd move into a cabin at the end of the world and happily live there the rest of his days as long as that meant his family was safe. His old instinct kicked in and he felt like asking God for help, but he knew it'd be useless; you can't undo a deal with a simple prayer.

Two weeks after that wonderful Sunday morning, Pablo was brushing his teeth when he saw a dark figure out of the corner of his eye. The thing slid into the doorframe and blocked the light pouring in from the hallway. Pablo turned, his heart pounding in his throat, but the thing was already gone.

Three weeks. That's how long they'd been in the new house. It was too soon. Pablo sat at the kitchen table. Mandy was asleep and Sofia was in bed with her headphones plugged into her ears and some TV show—surely a series with a historical angle—playing on her iPad. The silence that should've felt like a comfort to Pablo felt more like a warning, a still hammer hanging above the naked fragility of everything he had built. He scanned every corner of the kitchen and living room for the unnatural darkness he feared had already found him again. Its absence should've been something to celebrate, but it felt more like an angry promise of bad things to come.

Three weeks. Pablo had just started at his new position as supervisor of the bilingual department of the insurance company he worked for. They'd approved his move to Dallas because he'd done wonders with the bilingual departments in Austin, Houston, and San Antonio, but he knew they wouldn't allow him to move again. Three weeks wasn't enough time to make any significant change. He could quit and try to find something else, but that would ruin his plans and severely wound his finances. Going back to poverty wasn't an option, and now he had Mandy to worry about, which changed everything.

Pablo closed his eyes, buried his face in his hands, and tried to convince himself he hadn't seen anything in the bathroom. He told himself this was a new house, a clean house. He told himself he was almost 300 miles from his previous home in San Antonio. He told himself the change in light happened because of a car's headlights outside his house. He almost laughed at that one. In the back of his head, the voice that constantly told him to keep his eyes open told him to open them.

Look around.

As Pablo scanned the kitchen and living room again, he thought about how long he'd spent in each place. Austin had been the best. He had gone from losing his previous job and getting an eviction warning letter to landing a great job at the insurance company, Sofia taking him back, and the two of them getting married and buying a house in a new development on the East Side. They'd spent three wonderful years there. In fact, Pablo had started to think luck had truly been on his side and the deal he'd made had nothing to do with the way his life had changed. Then Sofia started complaining about a man peeking into their house at night. A few days later, she became convinced one of them was sleepwalking because she would wake up some mornings to find the fridge open or the leftovers from the previous day scattered on the kitchen floor. Pablo knew better. He stayed awake for three nights and on the third one saw the two shadowy figures come up to his living room window, their faces black holes darker than the night around them that threatened to swallow everything he loved.

Two nights later Sofia woke him with a scream. Pablo sat up and saw her halfway off the end of their bed. She was crying, screaming about how something had pulled at her leg. Pablo held her and soothed her, telling her it'd all been a nightmare. The next morning, four red scratches down Sofia's left leg screamed loudly about how everything Pablo had said in the middle of the night was bullshit.

Sofia went to a motel for almost a week. The company was happy to let Pablo work his magic in Houston, so a few days later they were pushing boxes into their new apartment, the shadowy figures and night attack a thing they both refused to talk about. Despite their silence, the move came with a harsh realization for Pablo: no matter where he went, the thing that was tied to him would follow.

Austin brought them three years of almost constant happiness, but in Houston it only took about two years for the shadow figures to start showing up. This time, Pablo saw them first: strange shadows moving slowly in his peripheral vision, dark bodies with impossibly black holes for faces coming up to his bedroom window at night despite the fact that they lived on the fifth floor. He started planning his next move and looking for a house before Sofia complained, but that wasn't quick enough. He came home on a Thursday afternoon and found her sitting in her car when he pulled into their second parking spot under the building. She'd been turning on the shower after work when a "dark, humanoid thing" had walked into the bathroom and stood in front of the mirror for a few seconds before vanishing into thin air.

This time the move was just as smooth in terms of getting a transfer and finding a new house in San Antonio, but things weren't as easy with Sofia. She started asking questions. She brought a priest to their new house to bless it and made Pablo get up early every Sunday to go to church. She hung a cross in every room of the house and tied a rosary to one of the legs of their bed. Then she spoke to her mom on the phone about the dark figures and asked for help. Her mother back in Puerto Rico found a woman who claimed to be a witch and said she could help them. Sofia sent her mother some money and then got on the phone with the witch. She wrote down a bunch of spells to cleanse the house and bought a dozen huge candles. Pablo let her, but he knew all of it would be useless because the thing that kept making them move was tied to him and would spoil any house they moved to. Houses can be haunted, but in his case, he was haunted inside and carried the haunting wherever he went. Guilt ate at him like a hungry sickness.

The prayers, candles, moon water, incense, incantations, holy water, limpias, and offerings to St. Joseph, the patron saint of homes, did nothing to stop the inevitable. Almost three years after moving into their new home, and just a few months after Mandy's birth, they woke up to the sound of things falling in their living room. Before they could process it, they were both standing in the living room with the lights turned on. Every piece of furniture had been knocked down. Sofia's tears felt like tiny knives puncturing Pablo's heart.

It took them a while to get the transfer this time, so Sofia went home to Puerto Rico for a few weeks. She said it was so her mom and dad could spend time with Mandy, but they both knew she was running away, scared of those dark faces they saw in the windows and the shapes that would show up in the dark corners of the house at night. Pablo sold the house at a loss and spent some time commuting all the way from New Braunfels, where he rented a small apartment that was packed to the ceiling with their life tucked away in boxes. When Sofia said she wanted to come back, Pablo had to convince his bosses this was the last transfer for a while and spent three meetings talking about everything he had accomplished just to get them to agree to one more transfer.

Now it was all happening again, just three weeks after they'd moved.

Pablo sighed and realized he'd been sitting there, staring at the inside of his new home in fear, for a few hours. He left the table, left the lights on, and went to bed, knowing sleep, if it came, would be a fitful, nightmarish mess.

Desperation makes people act strangely, pushing them to do things they normally wouldn't do. Pablo was not much of a drinker, but after being walked out of the building by a security guard—standard procedure, according to the HR woman who'd delivered the news—he drove to a bar instead of his house.

There's no easy way to deliver bad news to the people you love, and calling Sofia to tell her he'd been fired wasn't something Pablo could fathom doing. She was in Florida visiting her sister and they'd had a huge fight about something he couldn't even remember just before she left.

Pablo drank and wondered what to do next. He could work at the gas station by his house, which had a sign that said "HIRING" right outside the door. He could ask one of his friends, an immigration lawyer, to throw some translation work his way. None of that would pay well enough, but it was something he could do while applying to other jobs...

After a few beers, a young man walked up to Pablo and said "I can help." Pablo turned to him.

"How do you know I need help?" Pablo asked.

"Look at you," said the young man, "You look like your dog just died and took your mom with it."

Despite the dark ruins of his inner world, Pablo smiled at the comment. He knew the man was right.

The conversation was quick, but Pablo remembered every word of it.

"Just say what you love most is mine and everything you want can be yours," said the young man.

"That's fun—"

Before Pablo could get the word out, an invisible hand wrapped itself around his throat and two others held his face firmly in place. When he tried to lift his hands to remove the hands he couldn't see, Pablo's hands refused to move, held in place by a pressure that held his entire body hostage. The young man smiled and moved a bit from side to side as if to force Pablo's frantic eyes to stop bouncing wildly from side to side.

"Relax, Pablo," said the man. "It's okay. No one else can see me. If they look at you, they'll just see a weirdo having a drink and apparently watching a tennis match only he can see. Look at me."

Pablo looked at the man. His eyes had gone entirely black.

"You can say no and I'll walk out of your life. You can spend the next few months working the counter at that gas station or sucking dick for money and becoming homeless as Sofia slowly becomes a memory or you can say yes and get a new gig tomorrow. Big money. Think about it. You can return to your shitty life, which I assure you is about to get worse, or you can have everything you ever wanted. The only thing you have to do is tell me the thing you love most is mine."

Pablo had seen movies and read a few stories about people selling their souls and he knew this was it. Somehow, he'd ended up living inside a horror story where a bored demon was offering him a happy a life in exchange for his soul. A tiny voice was telling him to say no. He was sure the young man would vanish as soon as he said it. However, a louder voice, and voice that drowned out the tiny voice, yelled at him to say yes. He deserved better. He had worked hard all his life. He had been dealt a bad hand, and this could be his chance to change things around. He could be celebrating with Sofia on the phone in less than a day if it was true. If it wasn't, if this was only stress and booze making him see and feel things, then no harm done.

"Yes," said Pablo.

The man vanished. The hands around his face and throat were no longer there. Pablo lifted his hands and rubbed his face and neck. Then, without warning, laughter came. He was stressed out and probably a little drunk. He needed to sleep.

A phone call woke him up the next day. A job he had applied for almost six months before was available again and the person who'd interviewed him and then turned him down had held on to his resume. A few hours later, Pablo was in her office signing a new contract that seemed pulled from a dream. Later, in the parking lot and still reeling from the call, meeting, and new contract, he called Sofia. Her tears of joy were one of a handful of memories Pablo treasured above all others.

A few years can feel like a very a long time if you spend them hungry or struggling, but they go by quickly if you're happy. Pablo hadn't forgotten his encounter at the bar, but he started doubting it'd actually happened. If it had, then he wasn't sure what it meant or when, if ever, he'd have to pay up and turn his soul over to the young man. The months that followed the start of his new job were great and he managed to convince himself that he had actually earned all his success. After all, the job he'd gotten was one he'd applied for before his encounter. He became convinced God had blessed him with a second chance and everything was going to be okay. That went away when they started seeing things. Then he knew it had all been true, and the realization felt like a cancerous tumor buried somewhere inside his happiness. The awful, desperate things we do in the middle of the night morph into manageable little mistakes under the light of day. Unfortunately, every time night came around again, Pablo found himself looking at the windows and expecting to see impossibly black faces there, their silence the most eloquent threat he'd ever received.

With his morning coffee in hand, Pablo watched Mandy play with her cereal. He'd take the day off—personal reasons—and figure out what to do.

He couldn't move. He couldn't send Sofia to Puerto Rico or Florida and spend time away from the new house to see if that worked. No, he was a haunted man and he had to figure out a way to fix it. Maybe he could visit a bar and wait for a strange young man to approach him...

The day came and went. Sofia was convinced he'd taken the day off to spend it with her and the baby, so she planned a trip to the zoo and then showed him a place online where she wanted to go pick strawberries on Saturday. When Sofia and the baby took a nap together, Pablo sat in the living room and thought about a way out. Why were those things after him while he was alive? Weren't they supposed to come collect his soul when he died? Did their presence mean his death was close? If Sofia could see them and they had pulled her leg that night, could they hurt her in order to get to him? Pablo usually thought about his predicament like someone who looks at something for a second before turning away, and he found that now, tackling it head-on, he had a lot of questions and no answers. When Sofia came down with Mandy in her arms, Pablo knew his thinking session was over, and he had no idea how to fix things.

Pablo's nights started blending together. He couldn't sleep and his days at work were spent trying to catch up and taking naps while sitting on the toilet. Every night he stayed up and every night he saw something. Shadows moved around him as soon as the sun went down. Figures with black faces came up to his windows every night. He saw them through the small kitchen window, the two large windows in the living room, and once outside Mandy's window, which was on the second floor. Pablo felt that the dark figures were closing in on him and he walked out of his house ready to fight them more than once, but they were always gone when he got to where he thought the figures had been.

Sofia knew something was wrong, but after asking a few times, she gave up. The tension between them grew.

"I'm taking Mandy to visit the grandparents next weekend," she said one morning. Pablo looked at her. "Did you spend the night at the table again?" Her question was an accusation. Pablo said nothing.

The day went by in a blur. It was Saturday, so Pablo took naps in his bed and the sofa, trying to make up for the endless string of sleepless nights he'd suffered through in the past two weeks. When he was awake, he thought of finding a priest and asking him to come spend the night. He thought about getting a gun and shooting at the dark figures through the window as soon as they showed up at night. He thought about emptying his bank account and hitting the road with Sofia and Mandy, maybe driving to Maine or somewhere else far away, stopping at motels along the way.

Look around.

The voice was loud. Pablo opened his eyes and sat up. It took him a second to realize he had been sleeping on the living room sofa. It was dark. Night had come while he was sleeping.

Pablo looked up at the two living room windows and saw three figures standing there. Their slim, dark bodies were clearer than ever and their black faces looked like pools of ink that sucked in the light around them.

CRASH!

Pablo jumped to his feet. The sound had come from the kitchen. He ran to it and flipped the light on. Everything that had been inside their cabinets was now on the floor. There was a black figure standing in the far left corner of the kitchen, its black face almost reaching the ceiling.

"What was that?"

Sofia's voice was shaky and several decibels higher than usual. Pablo turned to her in time to see her face crumble as her eyes landed on the kitchen floor and then the figure in the corner. Then, behind Sofia, two black figures moved in the darkness toward the stairs.

Pablo felt the temperature drop around him. Fear's bony hand squeezed the back of his neck and pulled the air from his lungs. He bumped against Sofia on his way out of the kitchen. He ran up the stairs and slammed against the hallway wall when he reached the second floor.

Pablo sprinted into Mandy's room, the back of his hand flipping the light switch as he entered. Yellow light flooded the room. Pablo stopped, his breath trapped in his chest, his heart a fist pounding against his ribcage.

Sofia had read a hundred articles saying you shouldn't put stuff inside your baby's crib, so she never placed plush toys or sheets inside Mandy's crib. Since there was nothing else in there, Pablo immediately realized his daughter wasn't in her crib. Instead, he found the window in her room open, the night's slight breeze gently pushing her yellow curtains around.

Just say what you love most is mine and everything you want can be yours.

Mandy, not his stupid soul.

Sofia's scream reached Pablo's ears a fraction of a second before his knees hit the floor.

The scream that came from his throat was drowned in the sound of the universe shattering.

COUNTING TUNNELS TO BERRY

ill Carling led his young son to the train. "Big step!"

Felix hopped on. "Why only two carriages, Daddy?"

"The electric line stops here. A two-car diesel train finishes the trip to Bomaderry."

"But we're only going to Berry."

"How many stops?"

"Two! Gerringong then Berry."

"Yep. Where shall we sit?"

Felix looked seriously around, double seats on one side, triple on the other. He chose a triple halfway along and slid in. Bill sat next to him. "We gonna count the tunnels?"

"Yep!"

"How many?"

"Four!"

An old woman with a nimbus of blue hair and a wide smile looked over from the seat in front. She smelled of perfume and powder. "What's your name?"

Felix grinned and scrunched into Bill's shoulder.

"He gets shy," Bill said. "This is Felix."

His son waved.

"How old are you?"

Felix held up one hand, all fingers spread.

"Five? What a handsome boy you are!"

Another old woman, east Asian features deeply wrinkled under hair still jet black, came and sat next to the blue-haired woman. "Hello, Ava."

"Mary, this is Felix."

Felix waved again.

Two teenage boys with skateboards came aboard and sat near the front, then a tradesman in a blue and orange work shirt, cement dust on his boots. A balding businessman with a briefcase and grey suit followed him. An old Koori man with skin like roasted chestnuts, his beard roughly gathered into four or five dreads, each a couple of inches long, sat in the seat opposite Bill and Felix. He held a small sports bag. Felix waved and the old man allowed a small smile that deepened the wrinkles around his brown eyes.

With seconds to spare a young, pretty brunette with diaphanous clothes and dozens of bright bangles on one arm appeared.

"Ten people on the train," Felix said.

The station master blew his whistle and the doors slid shut.

"Maybe more in the other carriage," Bill said.

"Ten more?"

"Maybe."

The train lurched and moved out, heading south. Felix bounced onto his knees to look out the window, watched the platform slide by, then garages and warehouses of Kiama's tiny industrial corner. Houses appeared, then gave way to rolling green hills with ocean only a hundred metres or so beyond.

A soft thump of air pressure sounded and outside went instantly black. The interior lights became apparent, soft yellow. Felix stared at his reflection in the window, lips moving as he silently counted the seconds, then a dim glow appeared and daylight burst back in. "One!" he shouted.

"One," Bill agreed. "Not so loud, okay?"

The woman with the bangles glanced back from across the aisle and smiled. Bill caught her eye and she nodded, as if in approval. Her eyes glittered. The businessman sat with his briefcase on his lap, hands on top, staring into nowhere. The Koori man opposite looked out the window. The two teenagers talked fast and low, barking with occasional laughter. Ava and Mary in front of Bill chatted about knitting. The tradie sat at the far end, only the top of his head visible resting back against the seat, napping.

Another soft thump, several seconds of blackness outside, then a burst of daylight. "Two!" Felix declared, no quieter than before. Bill and the woman with the bangles exchanged a knowing look.

As the track curved the ocean came closer, sunlight scintillating from it. The fields in front deep green all the way to sharp edges where cliffs fell away, the coastline rising and falling in undulating geological waves.

"Here comes number three," Felix said, pressing his face against the glass in an attempt to see ahead.

A soft *whump* and once more they were in darkness. The rattle of the old train against the tracks louder, the overhead lights wan yellow. Bill felt a soft sense of dislocation in his gut and shifted uncomfortably on the seat. The bangle woman had a slight frown creasing the skin between her eyebrows. Bill startled slightly, and saw her jump too, as light pounded back into the carriage.

"Three!" Felix almost yelled.

Bill laughed, discomfort fleeting away, and shushed Felix gently. "Inside voice, please, buddy." He took out his phone. "Hey, Felix." The boy looked around, framed by the window, and Bill snapped a selfie with them both. "Send it to Mummy?"

"Yes!"

Bill put the photo in a text message, added a smiling emoji with love hearts for eyes, and sent it to his wife.

"Number four!" Felix said, and the carriage dropped once more into darkness.

The echo of the rattling track increased, the yellow lights glowed, everyone sat reflected in the black rectangles of the windows. The darkness continued, the rattle became a hypnotic rhythm, the train vibrated slightly. Still the blackness outside persisted, the train powered on. Bill looked across the aisle and saw the bangle woman frowning again. The old man sat up straighter, still staring out the window. The dark continued. Ava and Mary chatted away, but the teenagers had fallen silent. The businessman looked up, expression confused. The tradie slept on. The train barrelled along, if anything, faster than before. The tunnel didn't end, the darkness outside pitch, impenetrable.

"Daddy, why is the tunnel so long?"

Ava and Mary drifted into silence. The old man looked into the carriage and must have seen his concern mirrored there.

"What's happening?" one of the teenagers called out to anyone listening.

The businessman stood, briefcase held against his chest. He moved a couple of seats towards Bill and Felix, then sat again.

"Daddy?"

Bill put his arm around his son. "I don't know, mate. Seems longer than normal, huh?"

Felix's face creased with confusion and fear. Bill saw the fear rising.

The train rocked along, the darkness outside persisted. The air thickened.

"What the fuck is happening," the other teenager said, voice strident with near-panic.

"Language, please!" Ava said.

"Daddy?"

"It'll be all right, mate." He doubted his words.

Discomfort became palpable as the tunnel refused to end. The hypnotic cadence of the wheels drilled into Bill's mind, like a voice that wouldn't shut up. Felix pressed his small face against his father's upper arm.

The businessman stood again, leaving his briefcase on the seat. They had been in darkness for well over a minute, maybe two. "This can't be right," the businessman declared and strode between the seats.

People leaned to watch. He went past the vestibule where passengers got on and off and to the door at the front of the carriage, DO NOT DISTURB THE DRIVER stencilled on it. He banged with the side of his fist against the glass window in the the top half of the door. A dark blue blind on the driver's side obscured any view. "Hey!" the businessman yelled. "Hey, driver!"

No response. Still the train barrelled through darkness.

The two teenagers got up as the businessman turned and came back. They met alongside Bill's seat, Ava and Mary in front, the old man on the other side. They looked at each other, all at a loss. The tradie at the far end slept on. The woman with the bangles stood and came to the group.

"This is ridiculous," the businessman said, as if it was a personal affront. "Someone should do something."

"What exactly?" the bangled woman asked.

"Wait." The businessman pushed past her and went to the other end. A door there led into a small connecting area, DO NOT RIDE BETWEEN CARRIAGES stencilled on this one. The businessman hauled on the handle to open the door, but nothing happened. He cupped his hands to the glass. "There should be lights on in there," he said.

"What can you see?" Bill asked.

The businessman turned back. "Nothing."

The train rattled on through eternal night. Felix trembled slightly against Bill. He brushed the boy's blonde hair back and smiled. "It's okay, champ. This is a strange ride, huh?"

Bill looked up beseechingly, searching the eyes of the others, but they all looked back with fear, some close to panic.

"Okay, let's calm down," the bangled woman said.

"Calm down?" one of the teenagers asked in a high voice. He was thin and blond, his friend stockier, with copper red hair. They both had acne, braces on their teeth, and both wore matching expressions, wide-eyed and pale.

The woman nodded once. "I have a theory. My name is Sandra. I'm... psychic."

The businessman scoffed, the old man frowned. Bill thought perhaps this was the last thing they needed. The train carried on, rattle and clack.

"And?" Ava asked.

"When I got on the train today," Sandra said, "I had a distinct sensation someone here was a bad person."

Felix squeaked and Bill's anger rose. This would only make it worse. "That's enough," he said.

"We don't need your hippy shit now," the businessman said.

"Language, please," Ava said, almost automatically.

They fell into silence, nine people gathered in the middle of the carriage while the tradesman at the end slept on.

Sandra kept her mouth closed for a while, looking slowly around the group, as if trying to work something out. "How about we introduce ourselves?" she said. "As we're stuck in each other's company."

The redheaded teenager's face was scrunched up, tears rolling over his cheeks. His friend looked at him, then quickly away, as if scared he might also cry. The old man stared at his hands, shaking his head slowly.

"I'm Mary, and this is Ava." The two old women smiled from their seat.

"I'm Bill and this is Felix." His son stayed buried in his side. "We're going to Berry for the day."

"We're going to Gerringong for lunch," Ava said.

Silence hung heavy again for several seconds as the train rocked and shot onwards into nothing.

"Jacob," said the tall, sandy-haired teen. "This is Max. Going home to Berry."

"Peter," the old man said, running a hand over his dark, matted beard. "I live in Bomaderry."

"Ridiculous," the businessman said. "Shall we sing Kumbaya next?"

"Your name?" Sandra asked.

"Kevin Masters. I have a meeting in Nowra. I'll get a cab from Bomaderry."

Bill breathed deeply, tried to still the shudder in his chest. He needed to protect Felix from this above all else. They loved train rides, it was a thing they did. He feared the lad would never set foot on another train after this. Would he? He had to hope there would be an 'after this'.

"We should wake him up," said Jacob, jabbing a thumb back.

"Maybe we're all stuck in his dream!" Kevin said, as if that was the most likely explanation. "Hey! Wake up!" He pushed past and roughly shook the tradesman by his shoulder. He startled and sat up.

"What the hell?"

"Wake up, this is a nightmare."

Bill almost smiled at the absurdity of Kevin's statement, but the truth of it shook down and his mirth fled.

The tradesman stood, saw them all together. "What's happening?" He looked out the window at the blackness and frowned.

Bill was disappointed light hadn't flooded back into the train as the young man woke.

"We've been in this tunnel for several minutes," Sandra said.

"The tunnels are only short."

"Not this time," Jacob said. "There's no response from the driver and we can't see into the other carriage."

The young man turned and saw the dark square of the end window, then turned back. His face bore the same tension and fear as everyone else. "What the fuck?"

"Language..." Ava's voice petered out.

"What's your name?" Sandra asked.

"Jeremy."

Silence again, but for the rattle and clack of wheels on the track. Then a quiet sobbing rose from Felix. Bill hugged him tighter, whispered reassurances. Everyone looked around as if seeking escape. Except Peter, who stared at the bag on his lap, gathered into himself.

"Why doesn't it end?" Max said in a strained voice, and fresh tears started over his cheeks. Jacob squeezed his friend's forearm.

"Something is unnatural about this," Mary said.

"Oh, you think?" Kevin's voice held an edge of anger, his cheeks red against the white collar of his shirt. He let out a frustrated breath and turned away, slumped into a seat a little further down.

"We're stuck here because someone is carrying a burden," Sandra said.

"Please don't scare my son," Bill said.

"I don't mean to. I've often thought justice is flawed. Monsters move among us and get away with things all the time, while good people suffer for no reason. Maybe, sometimes, the scales balance, just a little bit."

"What are you talking about?" Jeremy asked. He loosened the buttons on his dusty shirt, as though he were too hot.

"I'm no Christian," Sandra said, "but do you know the idea of Purgatory?"

"What's purgastory?" Felix whispered.

"Don't worry about it," Bill said. "Just something from an old book. An idea, not a real thing."

"I think it's real," Mary said. "I believe." She raised her chin, black hair swaying back from her face.

Sandra raised both hands. "As an idea. That's all I mean. Some people say it's like a fire, but a cleansing one rather than a punitive fire like Hell."

"Is Hell real, Daddy?"

"No, son. Just a story."

"What if *this* is a kind of purgatory?" Sandra said. "Are we not trapped between two states? Is this a moment of purification?"

"You're making quite a leap there, lady," Jacob said, still holding his friend's arm gently.

"I know."

"What if you're right?" Bill asked. "What do we do about it?"

Sandra nodded, lips pursed like she had been expecting this question. Waiting for it. "If I'm right and there is someone bad on this train, maybe we're stuck until they come clean."

Silence sank over them like a shadow. The train rattled on, darkness unbroken outside. Then Felix's sobs grew louder and he shook against Bill's side. Bill gathered him up onto his lap. "It's okay, mate."

"It's... my... fault!" Felix said haltingly between sobs.

"What is?"

"I'm the... bad... person!"

"No! Definitely not."

"I drew under the table with my coloured pencils. I said it wasn't me, but it was!" He devolved into wracking sobs again.

Bill held him tight. "Oh, Felix, I know it was. Of course it was. Who else would it have been? But it's okay. That's not what Sandra means."

She leaned forward, stroked Felix's head. "Definitely not you, little man. I'm talking about grown-ups." She looked at Bill with apology in her eyes. He shook his head.

"I killed their cat," Max said, tears still rolling.

Jacob frowned at his friend. "What?"

"The Smiths next door." He scanned around with desperate eyes. "I have a cubby in the back yard, down in the trees at the bottom of the garden. The Smiths cat was always coming there and pissing, made the place stink. I kept chasing it away." He talked faster and faster, the confession pouring out of him like released dam water. "One day I went down and there was the fucking cat again. As it ran past I was so angry, I kicked it! It flipped up and bent around the edge of the doorway and kinda cracked. Something in it broke, maybe its back, I dunno. I panicked. I carried it out to the road and dropped it in the gutter. Everyone thought it had been hit by a car. I never told anyone." He ran dry of words, crying afresh.

"Jesus, dude," Jacob said, with a horrified half-smile.

Silence again for a few moments, then Sandra said, "That's pretty horrible, but also a mistake."

"How do you know we're here for *any* reason?" Jeremy demanded.

"Have you done anything bad?" Sandra asked.

Jeremy scowled, looked away. "Everyone's screwed up one way or another. No one's perfect."

"Of course not. But to what degree?"

"What are you?" Jeremy shouted. "Self-appointed judge here or something?"

Sandra said nothing, just watched the tall tradie with soft eyes.

He looked away again. "I screwed my mate's wife," he said, barely audible.

"What does screwed mean, Daddy?"

Bill looked into Felix's smooth face, eyes puffy from tears. "It's a grown-up thing."

No one else spoke for a moment, then Jeremy said. "We got caught, they broke up. It was bad."

"That's the worst thing you've ever done?" Sandra asked.

"I think so."

Sandra nodded. The train rocked and sped through the darkness.

Peter muttered something.

"What was that?" Bill asked. Kevin turned to listen.

"I said I know what I've done and some of it I'm not proud of, but it's not for you to hear."

"Bad enough to trap us here?" Sandra asked.

Peter looked up, brown eyes wet. "No worse than killing cats or messing with the wives of friends."

"It's me." Ava's voice was strong as she stood.

The group turned as one to look at her.

"You?" Sandra asked.

"You think because I'm an old lady, I can't be bad? I wasn't always this old, you know."

"What did you do?" Sandra asked.

"I killed my husband."

Mutters of astonishment rippled around. Kevin stood and came back to join them, the better to hear the story.

Ava looked from one to the next, then nodded. She stepped into the aisle. "My husband's name was Giles. He was a monster. An abusive man. When I was young, I thought it was normal. And I loved him. He could be kind and generous. But he would undermine me too, tell me I was imagining things, that he didn't say things I knew he had, did things I knew he did. That I was paranoid."

"That's gaslighting," Sandra said quietly.

"Is it? I call it abusive. Then Giles became meaner and angrier. I talked to friends and realised this wasn't something I should have to deal with. Then he became violent. He would strike me, pinch me. One day, I told him I'd had enough, he couldn't treat me this way any more. He asked what I would do about it. I said I'd divorce him. He said if I divorced him, he'd kill me."

"Oh, Ava, I don't think–"

Ava held up a hand, interrupting Sandra's reassurances. "No, this is on me. I was sixty-five, and saw another who knew how long with that miserable, abusive old bastard."

"Language, please," Mary said and the two old women looked at each other and shared a moment, smiling.

When Ava looked up again, her eyes were filled with tears. She patted her cloud of blue hair, took a deep breath. "One day he got sick. Nothing serious, but he stayed in bed, demanding and onerous as usual. So I gave him double the prescribed medication to make him sleepy, then smothered him with his pillow." She gasped in a quick breath, stifled a sob. The tears breached, ran silently, leaving tracks through the powder on her cheeks. "The doctors thought it was a heart attack. No one suspected anything."

"I'm the only one who knew," Mary said. "I told her it was justified. She was freeing herself." She looked up at Ava. "Jesus forgave you then and He forgives you still."

"I'm not sorry," Ava said, drawing herself up. "I finished him and I've had another twenty good years, free. But it catches up, I suppose."

"No," Sandra said softly. "You were justified."

"Oh, it's feminist now to commit murder?" Kevin asked.

"No, it's on me." Ava moved down the aisle towards the end of the carriage.

"What are you doing?" Sandra demanded.

Ava turned to the left and pressed the Exit button. Incredibly, the door hissed open, wind buffeting violently through, the roar of it and the rattle of the tracks loud and offensive.

"No!" Sandra yelled, running to catch up. Jeremy was behind her, Bill lifted Felix aside to stand and look.

Ava didn't pause, just stepped out.

"NO!" Sandra screamed again.

The door slid shut, the carriage fell quiet but for the rattle and clack of the wheels.

The darkness outside continued unbroken.

Mary was on her feet, hands covering her mouth.

"It wasn't her," Sandra said, voice weak. "I told her it wasn't her."

The group fell into a stunned silence.

"Where did she go?" Felix asked, wide eyes turned up to Bill.

"She got off." Bill forced a smile, put his arm around his son. "She just got off."

"Can we get off too?"

"Not yet, mate."

Felix looked back at the door. "She's not okay," he said quietly.

"We've heard from everyone else, Kevin," Sandra said, eyes hard. "What about you?"

"We haven't heard from her!" Kevin pointed at Mary.

"I've made mistakes," Mary said weakly. "When I was young, I wasn't so smart. But I found Jesus."

"You think your god protects you from monsters? Or from being a monster?" Sandra asked.

"He does."

Bill stared at Sandra and wondered for a moment if maybe gods and monsters weren't so different from each other.

Sandra shrugged. "You've been lucky, that's all." She looked back to Kevin.

His florid cheeks darkened, eyes scrunched up.

"What did you do, Kevin?" Sandra asked softly.

"Why me?" he demanded. He looked around the group. "Fuck you all!" he barked.

"He's scaring me," Felix said.

"Don't worry, mate. He won't hurt you." Bill stared daggers at Kevin. He was not a fighter, but he was fit and strong, and outweighed the businessman by twenty kilos. If it came to violence, he was sure he could put Kevin down.

Kevin's face burned red, stark under his balding pate. Anger drifted from him in waves. His mouth worked, he licked at his teeth. "What are you going to do? Throw me off too?"

"What did you do?" Sandra asked again.

"I killed her, okay?" His anger burst like a boil, spittle flew from his lips.

"Who?" Sandra asked.

"She was just a hooker."

"Sex worker," Sandra said. "Give her some dignity."

Kevin stared at her, eyes tight with rage. Bill sensed violence coming off the man like a smell. He boiled with the need to hurt. It came from deep insecurity, Bill knew that much, and he thought perhaps it had found its outlet in hatred, for women. The way he looked at Sandra now, the way he acted so entitled about everything. The fact he'd killed a woman made perfect, awful sense.

Kevin growled, a trapped-animal sound.

"What happened?"

Kevin gritted his teeth, leaning slightly towards Sandra like he wanted to hit her. "Why should I tell you? I'm not jumping into the dark like the crazy old lady!"

"You have to tell someone," Sandra said.

Kevin gasped and for a moment Bill thought he would keel over from a heart attack. Then Kevin spat, "She was just a hooker!"

Bill leaned close to Felix. "This is the bad man," he whispered. "But I promise he won't hurt you, okay? Don't listen to him. You want to play Alto on my phone?"

Felix shook his head, trembling against Bill's arm. "I just won't listen."

Bill sighed. Felix would listen. Kids always did. They saw and heard everything and it formed them like crystals growing inside a geode.

"What did you do?" Sandra's voice was hypnotic.

"An account in Brisbane went tits up. We lost a heap of money. Before I went home I wanted to fuck, so I asked where I could pick up a hooker."

"Sex worker."

"A colleague told me about a street out of town. I took a cab, found a nice blonde with big–"

"Spare us."

Kevin stared, eyes furious. "She knew a motel, walking distance. I had on a hoodie, pulled it up and hunched into it and followed her. I didn't think anyone would know me so far away, but I took no chances. We checked in, I paid cash, used a fake name. I wanted to do it but I was so angry about the account. I couldn't... I tried, she tried, it didn't... She laughed at me."

Sandra nodded. "That's what did it?"

Bill put his hands over Felix's ears and the boy looked up, affronted. Bill shook his head, held Felix close.

"I thought I would only hit her once, you know? I was so angry. But the crack of it, the feel of it. The blood bursting off her lip. The horror in her eyes. And I hit her again. And again and again and I couldn't stop."

"Fucking hell, mate," Jeremy said, stepping away from the businessman.

"I kept hitting even after I knew she was dead, until my hands hurt too much and my knuckles were torn. I panicked. I got dressed and pulled the hood up, ran away. For weeks I lived in terror, sure they'd come for me. The killing barely made the fourth page, and then only once. Perpetrator still unknown. Months passed. I realised I'd got away with it. Nothing to place me there. That was it. I stopped worrying."

"How long ago?" Jacob asked.

Kevin turned a fierce eye to the teenager, who stepped quickly back.

"Four years," Kevin said.

"You're wrong inside, mate" Jeremy said.

The carriage fell into silence. Bill uncovered Felix's ears. The train raced on through darkness, as fast as ever. The group looked around, out the windows, back at each other.

"Nothing's happening," Max said.

"What did you expect?" Kevin said acidly. "You think this... idiot knows what she's talking about?"

"Admission is not enough," Sandra said.

"Too right." Jeremy's eyes were hard and Bill saw his fists were clenched, the knuckles white. Was he ready, as was Bill himself, or did he intend Kevin harm?

Sandra nodded gently.

"I'm not jumping off!" Kevin shouted, turning to stare at each of them, challenge them.

"You're a bad man!" Felix yelled. "You should get off!"

Jeremy took a step forward. He was heavier and taller than Kevin, and younger than Bill. "Get off," he said in a low voice.

Kevin backed up. "Stay away from me!"

"Get off," Jeremy said again.

"Yeah, man," Jacob said.

"Get off!" Jacob and Max said together.

Sandra smiled.

"We can't know that'll fix this!" Bill said. Part of him wanted Kevin to suffer, to jump like the others demanded, but he had to set an example for his son. While new crystals formed inside the boy, Bill had to try to make them good ones. Morally strong. "Is it our decision? Call the police."

"How?" Jeremy asked.

Bill pulled out his phone. He saw a reply from his wife. *My lovely boys! Have fun!* and a love heart emoji, that had come in right after he'd sent the selfie. Now the phone showed no reception. He looked up and saw the teenagers checking their phones, and Jeremy. They all shook their heads.

"So that's not an option," Jeremy said, advancing on Kevin again. "Off!"

"I'm not jumping!"

Jeremy struck out, punching Kevin across the side of his face. His fist made a dull *thwack* and Kevin cried out, staggered as his knees buckled. He caught a seat back and pulled himself up and away. Jeremy followed, swung again, the blow glancing off the top of Kevin's head, but it was enough to stagger him. Jacob and Max joined in and the three of them rained blows down as Kevin fell to the floor.

"Stop it!" Bill shouted. "There has to be another way! How does this make us any better than him?"

Mary had her head bowed, praying rapidly. Peter still stared at his hands. Sandra watched, impassive.

Bill stood into the aisle, looked to her. "Stop them!"

"Enough!" Sandra shouted, her voice like a slap.

Kevin curled on the floor, hands wrapped around his head, sobbing. The three young men stepped back. The train sped on through darkness.

"Time," Sandra said quietly.

"No!" Desperation made Bill's voice tight.

Sandra looked from Bill to Felix, who stared back wide-eyed. "Perhaps this is what he needs to learn," she said.

"It can't be," Bill said.

"No, no, no!" Kevin wailed, and Bill turned to see him being carried. Jeremy had him under the armpits and the teenagers each had a leg. Kevin thrashed and squirmed, but was weak from the beating and the three strong young men manhandled him easily.

Bill started down the aisle. "There has to be another answer!"

"Daddy, he's a bad man!" Felix said, kneeling up on the seat to watch.

Jeremy elbowed the Exit button and the door hissed as it slid aside. Wind and noise rushed in, and darkness seemed to curl in with it.

Bill stopped, frozen with horror. Kevin screamed incoherently, thrashing ever harder. The teenage boys' faces were grimaces of effort, then Jeremy said, "Swing once and let go!"

"It was just a hooker!" Kevin screamed. "Just a dirty street whore!"

They hefted Kevin back into the carriage, then swung him out the door and released their grip. The businessman vanished into darkness, his scream high and terrified, becoming a screech of metal wheels on track and the doors hissed closed.

With a *whump* of sound, the train burst into bright sunshine. Jeremy, Jacob, and Max staggered back, scrunching their eyes against sudden brightness. They came back along the carriage, gasping to catch their breath from the struggle. Sandra smiled darkly, reached out and gathered them all into a hug.

Mary and Peter muttered into their laps.

Bill scooped Felix into a hug.

"Is he died, Daddy?"

"He's just gone, buddy."

"Like the nice lady?"

"Shall we get off at Gerringong? Call Mummy to pick us up?"

Felix looked into his father's eyes, his soft skin glowing with youth, innocence. "Maybe still go to Berry? I want fish and chips."

Bill laughed softly. "Wow. Okay. Sure, mate. Let's still go to Berry."

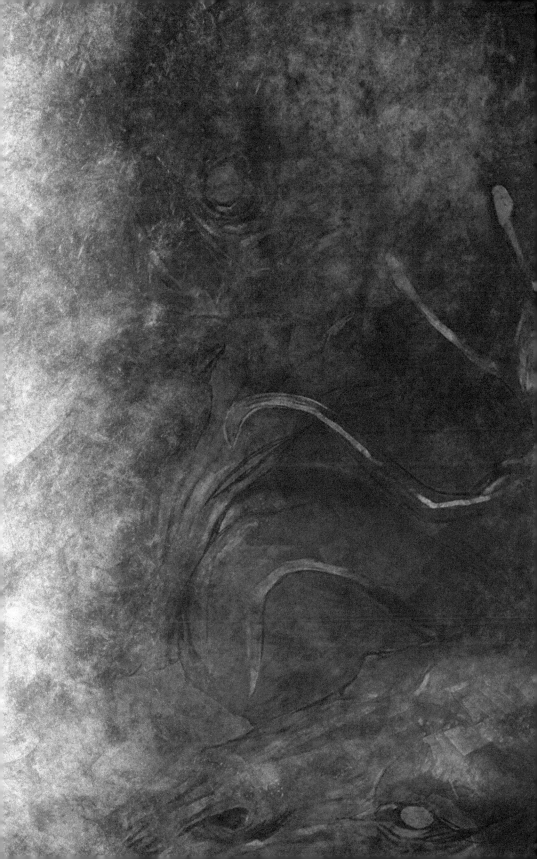

ANNIE'S HEART IS A HAUNTED HOUSE

Sheila was the next to go. Before her, Tobias and Jenny.

Now there was only Rich and me, standing in the foyer and staring at the shredded remains of our fellow inmate. Half a torso and one leg. Some of her insides were scattered across the floor, and the whole foyer was a skating rink coated in her blood. There was no mistaking it. The House Master had been here, and it had treated Sheila like a grisly piñata.

"We were only gone for a couple of minutes..." Rich turned to me, his cheeks slick with tears, and held out his hands in defeat. I stood at his side and looked at the dead girl. She'd survived longer than I expected.

How many days had it been now? Sheila was the one who kept count, scratching a thin line in the upstairs hallway for every sleep cycle. With the windows bricked up, we had no idea if time even existed here, but it kept Sheila busy, gave her a purpose.

"She was gonna be my girlfriend," Rich said, and dropped the fire iron at his side. "We just...last night..." He turned to the stairs, in the direction of our sleeping host. "You crazy bitch!"

His knees buckled, and I watched him sink to the floor in despair. I reached out to comfort him but thought better of it. There's no point now.

We made a rule in the beginning: Never go anywhere alone. It was a rule we learned the hard way. Rich had wandered away from us in search of a bathroom while we bickered among ourselves, confused, disoriented. Scared.

"This doesn't make sense, man." Tobias tugged on the chains barring the entry doors. Four chains, the heavy-duty kind with thick links, and bound by multiple locks. Defeated, he paced the foyer and mumbled to himself. "I went to bed. In *my* bed. How the fuck did I end up here? How did any of us?"

Sheila was a crying mess. Jenny held her, tried comforting her friend, but it was no use. She was equally frightened, and for good reason. We'd each gone to sleep in our own beds, in homes scattered across town, and woken up together in this massive house. A mansion, by the look of it. Everything was ornate and immaculate, not a speck of dust or sign of clutter, with dual chandeliers above and a large fountain at the far end. Mounted animal heads above the doorway—one moose and a boar on either side. Red walls. White crown moulding. Polished hardwood floors.

It was something right out of a magazine. Picture-perfect and untouched. Someone's idea of bourgeois living.

And then we heard Rich screaming for help.

We found him at the end of a long hallway. He clung to the edge of a hole in the floor, dangling above a hazy red void. Tobias took hold of Rich's hand and pulled him to safety.

"How'd you miss a giant hole in the floor? Dumbass."

"No," Rich whimpered, "it wasn't like that. I was walking and the floor just gave out beneath me—"

A square flap of flooring unfolded by itself and sealed the hole. The trapdoor's outline was barely visible in the glow of gaslights adorning the hallway walls. No wonder Rich hadn't seen it.

Sheila found her voice between sobs and asked, "What is this place?"

"Shh, it's okay." Jenny looked to me, and then to Rich. Her face slowly drained of color as realization took hold. "Could've been any one of us."

"Are we gonna die here, Jen?"

She put her arm around Sheila, gave her a squeeze. "Shh. No, Sheila, no. Right, guys?"

Silence slipped between us. We were all thinking the same thing, and were too afraid to say it.

Three days passed before we saw the House Master for the first time. We were tired, strung out, panicking because we hadn't felt hunger or the need to relieve ourselves. Everything had stopped. We were trapped in a prison of *Better Homes and Gardens,* and at first it seemed like everything was over, the world had come to an end.

God, we were so wrong, and I only wish we had remained ignorant. But then that's the nature of our punishment, isn't it?

"I don't have time for this reality TV bullshit!" Tobias raged to no one, screaming until his voice fried and he exhausted himself. He looked to me and Rich, and then to the girls. "I can't be here…I've got a game tomorrow. Or was that yesterday?" He collapsed on the floor, chest heaving, chin quivering. I saw a tear slip from his eye.

Tobias's forlorn proclamation echoed our quiet sentiment. We were seventeen, in our last year of high school—we had final exams and games and parties. Well, most of us. The others were so popular. At the top of our social pyramid, Tobias was a linebacker for the football team and had a full university scholarship waiting for him in the fall. Jenny ran track and was the president of both the National Honor Society and the Drama Club. Sheila was the homecoming queen and captain of the dance team. Rich was the class president and an active member of the Future Business Leaders of America.

And then, at the very bottom, there was me. I was the odd man out in our imprisoned group. An art nerd. President of the National Art Honor

Society. Spent most of my spare time in the art room. No scholarship, no real friends, and no place among my peers. Even I didn't understand my presence in this place.

"Please stop yelling," Sheila said. It was the first thing she'd spoken in more than a day. "It isn't getting us anywhere." She paused, shook her head in disappointment. "We all had things going on this weekend."

Tobias snorted. "Whatever, Sheila. Nothing important, I'm sure."

"Fuck you, Tobias."

"Guys, please don't fight." Rich shot a look to me for support, but I shrugged in reply. What could I say that would make them calm down or even listen? He scoffed, annoyed by my silence, and raised his voice. "Seriously, stop the arguing. It isn't getting us anywhere."

"You wanna come over here and make me, tough guy?" Tobias shot to his feet, popped his neck, and glared. Rich shrank back, played off his panic with a shrug, like the 220 lb. brick of muscle wasn't worth his time. "Yeah," Tobias said, grinning. "That's what I thought." And then, to the girls: "I don't see you two doing anything about getting us out of here."

"All I see is you whining about your fucking football game." Jenny had finally had enough. "Who gives a shit, Tobias? You whine about homework. You whine about Sheila not giving you the time of day. All you do is whine. Why don't you actually do something about it instead of crying like a little bitch?"

I really thought he would hit her. He opened his mouth, closed it, and shook his head. "Nah," he said, "fuck this, and fuck all y'all, too."

He left us and took the stairs two at a time, his heavy footfalls rattling the whole house. Rich implored him to wait, but Tobias had said his piece, and there was no stopping that freight train. We looked at one another, listening to the guy's footsteps upstairs, and held our breath when the pounding started.

Tobias kicked in every door he found in the upstairs hallway. He'd already worked his way to the far end by the time we reached the second floor. Tobias stared at us, the trunk of his torso heaving with deep breaths and his face bright red. He had a runner's stance, was about to charge straight for us. Rich gasped. Jenny and Sheila held hands, shaking. Me, I readied myself for the impact—

The jagged end of a broken wooden beam exploded from the ceiling and pierced Tobias's stomach. He gasped in shock, tried to scream, but all he managed was a slow mewling groan. Another piece of wood, this one finely sharpened into a stake, shot from above and impaled him through his chest, pinning him in place. The others cried out in terror, but I was too shocked to make a sound; instead, I could only stare and try to make sense of what I was seeing. The two wooden pieces were still attached to the ceiling, protruding from a cracked hole directly above Tobias, and I thought he'd fallen into another one of the traps.

Pieces of plaster and crown moulding broke away from the walls and merged together. Wires snaked through the cracks and wound their way around the two jutting timbers. Tobias was long dead at this point, a merciful end in retrospect—he never had to experience the truth of what killed him.

We forgot our places in the social scheme and huddled together in fear. We whimpered as the House Master assembled itself.

We watched.

Bits of drywall coated the floor and filled the air with so much dust. The gas lamps along the hallway formed eerie halos in the cloud, silhouetting a thing composed from pieces of the house. The creature's body was the size of a refrigerator, and its multiple arms of wood and rebar scraped the walls and creaked as they bent at the joints. It descended, examined its prey, and lifted Tobias's limp corpse. A makeshift door swung open from its chest, and in went the remains of our school's star linebacker. Satisfied with the kill, the House Master walked to the nearby wall, and merged with the structure. The whole upper level trembled with the creature's force, and within seconds, it was gone.

A beat later, Rich said, "What the fuck was that?"

Exploring upstairs was Rich's idea. You'd think Rich's own near-death experience would've dampened his courage, or even Tobias's demise, but no. There was a void to fill in our little group. Someone had to be step into Tobias's shoes and "be the man," or the "alpha." The FBLA had enriched his go-to attitude, nurtured the concept of *carpe diem*, and gave him just enough confidence to be annoyingly optimistic.

After Jenny and Sheila retreated back to the foyer, Rich pulled me aside and spoke in whispers like we'd been friends for years. "Listen, Adam. If we're gonna survive, we need to scope out this place."

"With that thing in the walls? Are you out of your mind?"

"Exactly my point, man. We need to defend ourselves from..." He trailed off, searching for a noun that might accurately define what was in this house with us.

"The House Master," I said. A spur of the moment title, I admit, but one which felt apt.

Rich stared for a moment, thinking it over, looking at me with the sort of expression I was used to. I could see the wheels turning in his head as he wondered what a weirdo I am. Adam, the odd loner art nerd. Voted most likely to become a serial killer in a joke poll taken by the school newspaper.

"Right..." He cleared his throat. "House Master or whatever. Anyway, I say we split up, each take a side of the hallway, explore the rooms. See if we can find anything useful."

A voice in the back of my head screamed for me to walk away, leave him, and return to my tiny bubble of isolation. "You're crazy, Rich. What if that thing decides Tobias wasn't enough, huh? What then?"

"At least if we try, we *might* be able to defend ourselves if it comes back."

He had me there. Our odds of surviving this place had diminished greatly in the last ten minutes. We needed every advantage we could find.

That's how we ended up exploring the upper floor. Jenny and Sheila insisted on joining us—"No fucking way you're leaving us here by ourselves," Jenny said—and together we slowly took inventory of the rooms. Four bedrooms, two bathrooms, all lavishly furnished. Rich claimed a fire iron from one of the fireplaces, and Sheila found a decorative sword mounted on a bedroom wall. Jenny and I came up empty-handed. The chest of drawers in the rooms were empty, as were the wardrobes, and like the rest of the house, everything was completely spotless.

There were more traps, of course. Sheila narrowly avoided a wall of spikes when she claimed the sword. They shot out of the adjacent wall, *Indiana Jones*-style, and after her initial panic she refused to explore further. One of the bathrooms opened into a bottomless pit, and I nearly fell in. After I caught myself on the doorframe and gave my heart time to steady itself, I took one of the decorative glass sconces from the hallway and tossed it into the void. Nothing shattered. For all I know the sconce is still falling.

The whole time we searched, we panicked at every creak and pop of the floor, thinking it was the foundation, or maybe the House Master lurking in the walls. I can't speak for the others, but my imagination ran wild, and I startled at the faintest movement from the corner of my eye. Tricks of the mind, maybe, but after all these years, I've learned not to trust what I see in this place.

The House Master remained absent during our search. Perhaps it was merciful enough to grant us this head start. When we finished, we met back in the hallway, and looked at the only door Tobias hadn't kicked in during his tirade. It was larger than the rest, with a bas relief depicting twin winged creatures serenading a young girl to sleep. They were too strange to be angels or demons. Too angular. Barely humanoid.

Jenny raised her hand. "I'll check this one."

We watched her twist the knob and held our breath as the latch clicked. She pushed the door inward and then jumped back, expecting another trap to be triggered by the opening. Instead of spikes or trapdoors, we were greeted by a warm glow of candlelight and a massive black canopy bed at the opposite end of what we discovered was the master bedroom.

That's when we found her. The real reason for our imprisonment in this nightmare. We stared across the room in disbelief. Sheila broke the silence. "Is that...oh, gross. It is."

A figure slept peacefully in the bed's center, surrounded by fluffy white pillows, and covered by a crimson duvet pulled up to her chin. Annie, a girl we all recognized from school.

She smiled in her sleep, seemingly pleased with the dream she was having, and why wouldn't she?

There was a note on the nightstand. A clean sheet of paper. Typed.

```
I DREAMT I BUILT A HOUSE
 INSIDE MY BROKEN HEART
  FOR YOU ALL TO REPAIR
   IN THE SWEETEST WAYS
    BEFORE MY WAKING
           —A
```

Jenny read the note aloud. When she finished, Sheila laughed and said, "What bullshit is that?" And then to our sleeping host, "Wake up, psycho bitch!"

Annie didn't stir, but something shuddered in the walls. Rich took hold of Sheila's arm and hissed. "You want to alert that thing out there? Don't be an idiot."

She pulled free of his grip and pushed him away. "Don't touch me, asshole. If this trash is why we're here, I'm gonna—"

"If you wake her, we'll die." They all turned to me, startled by the sound of my voice.

Jenny snorted. "How do you figure that?"

"Whatever, Adam. Go draw a picture or something." Sheila tugged on Annie's arm. "Get up, dammit."

"Read her note again," I said. "We have to take that at face value. She built this place in her dream."

"So?"

"So she's still asleep, and we're here physically." I knocked softly on the nightstand. "What happens to us when she wakes up?"

Rich shook his head. "That's crazy, man. This is all so fucking crazy."

"Any crazier than the monster that killed Tobias?"

He didn't have a dismissive retort this time. Sheila paused, thought about what I said, and slowly stepped back from the bed. They all did.

Tears filled Sheila's eyes. She leaned toward me and said, "What now, smart guy? What happens to us if we don't wake her up? Are we stuck here forever?"

I shrugged. "Maybe."

"Don't listen to him," Jenny said. "He's just trying to scare us. Fucking weirdo."

"I'm just saying—"

"Stop," Rich said. "No one gives a shit what you're saying. Come on, girls."

They left me standing at Annie's bedside, muttering reassurances to themselves as they walked to the door. I looked down at Annie's face, wondering if I was wrong, wondering if we'd brought this on ourselves. Her note implied as much. Were we the cause for her broken heart? And what kind of sweet repairs could we possibly perform in this place? The mansion seemed untouched, perfect in every sense, except for what Tobias—

Yes. I understood then. His end should've been a warning.

The traps we'd encountered should've been a warning.

The others were convinced this was all a bad dream we were somehow sharing. Any time now, they said, we'd all wake up in our own beds, in our own homes, and life could continue.

The funny thing is, they were half right.

Jenny, Rich, and Sheila avoided me for the most part over the ensuing days. I was fine with it, to be honest. We'd never had much to say to one another to begin with, so suffering their company in silence wasn't all that different from our days in school. The rule of staying together, however, remained in place, no matter how much they wanted to avoid me. Discussing our predicament in relation to our slumbering host upstairs wasn't welcomed, but any time the House Master made its rounds, the four of us had no choice. We banded together to survive.

Annie's pet didn't have a pattern, no discernible "schedule" for its appearances. It roamed the rooms and halls like a feral animal, always on the hunt for us, drawn by our noise, maybe even our scent. We didn't see it again for several days after it killed Tobias, but we heard it in the walls, its movement filling our ears with the creaks of timber and the shrill whine of scraping metal.

What's worse, I think, was the vibration of its approach. Room by room, an ongoing quake rattled windows and bones, and with it a slow bulge in the walls. Plaster and drywall cracked, flaked paint and dust in a kind of trail, and often the rooms were left in considerable disarray. The lavish mansion and its finer details were destroyed one piece at a time.

The House Master didn't care. It *was* the house. A piece here, a piece there, a living machination born from wood, wire, steel, and the nightmarish imagination of a teenage girl. And it wanted us. That was its only purpose: to kill us, consume us. Absorb us.

So why didn't it come right out and end us?

I didn't understand that part for some time, but as I came to terms with our reasons for being here in the first place, I began to realize the creature's intent.

Annie trapped us here in the prison of her mind, a deceptive labyrinth of fancy decoration and deadly traps, and set loose a minotaur of her own making. Not only to end us, but to punish us.

Did we deserve this? I used to think we didn't. What kind of sadistic monster would do this? We were just kids. Stupid kids, I admit, but still just *kids*. Cruelty comes so easily to us when we're at that age but without the understanding of what it truly does to others.

Now I know better.

One month. That's how long Jenny survived. Sheila had just marked our first month on the wall outside Annie's room.

We were exploring the southern wing of the mansion. Rich was certain it hadn't been there before. The rest of us couldn't remember; after all that time, the house had begun to look the same, one hallway decorated identically to another. Terminal boredom had taken hold in our minds, numbing our survival instincts, and that is perhaps what the House Master had planned for. We couldn't stay vigilant all the time. Malaise would take root eventually. And with the promise of something new to see and explore, we were more than willing to leave the relative safety of the foyer.

"This looks just like the north wing," Sheila said, holding back a yawn. "Can't we go back? I need a nap."

"We might find something useful." Jenny always said that whenever we made these short trips to other parts of the house. The possibility of change was too alluring to ignore. We never found anything useful, of course. The house wasn't built like that. Even the so-called "weapons" we'd found the day Tobias died weren't all that useful. Not really. Not against the House Master.

The illusion of safety, comfort. Another trick to throw us off our game.

In hindsight, I suppose Jenny's death was partially my fault. I was just as bored as Sheila, and in a rare moment of social interaction, I brought up Annie again.

"Enough about Sleeping Beauty back there." Jenny turned to face me, began walking backwards. "She didn't matter in school, and she doesn't matter now. She never mattered. The sooner you figure that out, the better."

"Haven't you all listened to a word I've said? God, you're all so fucking stubborn. She does matter. She's why we're here."

Jenny shrugged and spun back around. "All Annie was to me, was a mouse. Or maybe an insect." And then to Rich and Sheila: "Do you guys remember that day she tried out for *Macbeth?* When she showed up wearing those dirty clothes and her hair was all greasy and knotted? I almost felt sorry for her." She broke into a fit of laughter. "Almost."

Rich chuckled. "I remember that. She really thought she got the part of Lady Macbeth."

"God," Jenny said, "the whole 'out damn spot' scene was pure cringe. Remember what I said to her?"

Sheila perked up. "Didn't you tell her something like she'd be better off as a peasant?"

"Told her she might have a better chance as one of the witches, but she'd have to clean up for the part."

All three of them burst into laughter. Heat flushed my cheeks, and I wanted to scream at Jenny for being such a callous bitch, but I never got the chance. In their disgusting reverie and ensuing laughs, they hadn't noticed the floor ahead slowly bulging upward. Jenny was the closest, might've seen the emerging creature in time, but she was facing her friends. By the time any of them felt the vibrations stirring beneath our feet, the House Master was halfway out of its hiding place.

For a while I told myself I didn't have a chance to warn her, that I was too shocked to find my voice—which was sort of true. I was stunned by the House Master's appearance, and what it had done with Tobias's remains. Pieces of his body were wrapped around the creature's limbs like wet towels wrung tight. Shreds of his clothes hung from the thing's chest and legs. Tobias's head was tethered to its torso, the cords of his bloody neck stretched tight and tied off, his dead eyes open and a purple swollen tongue hanging from a gaping mouth.

Sure, I was frightened. I was surprised. But after all this time, I also know I could've said something, made a sound, gotten their attention somehow. Yet I didn't. Because I knew Jenny deserved what was about to happen.

She spun around, found herself standing mere feet from the hulking beast, and screamed. Rich and Sheila were already backpedaling, worried more about saving themselves, while I remained where I stood. Watching. Fascinated.

Pleased.

Jenny tried to turn, attempted to run, but the creature was faster. A flash of movement and one of Jenny's eyes shot from its socket as the House Master's limb pierced the back of her skull. Followed by another sharp limb straight through her gut. Wooden pieces groaned against metal, almost like a cry of victory, and in one swift motion, the House Master ripped Jenny's body in half. Some of her blood splashed my face. Thick. Warm.

I didn't linger. I'd seen what I needed to see, and soon I was chasing after Rich and Sheila. There may have been a bounce in my step.

Annie. Where to begin.

Every school has one, I guess. One person who's so low on the pyramid of popularity they're basically buried beneath it.

In our school, Annie's sin was her presence. She exuded the kind of "different" that most found repulsive for one reason or another. Different clothes, different attitude, different everything—doesn't matter. "Something different" is like blood in the water, and popular kids are the sharks.

Annie, the odd child in elementary school who danced by herself on the playground. The girl in junior high who still talked to an imaginary friend. And in high school, the weird book nerd who liked to draw bizarre creatures in the margins of her homework. Symbols, sometimes. A few she carved into her arms with a paperclip. The lone girl in high school who went into a witchy phase and never left, who always smelled of incense and sweat. The poor kid who wore dirty clothes, often for multiple days in a row. Everyone knew she came from a poor family, another sin for which she'd never be forgiven, but Annie thrived despite her circumstances. She didn't let it hold her back or stop her from trying to fit in. The popular kids hated her for that, and let her know it at every opportunity, but poor little Annie kept her chin up, held her smile in place, and kept trying.

Jenny's fatal anecdote of that day in Drama was only one example. For dance team, there was Sheila, who called Annie white trash in front of the entire team. For FBLA, there's Rich, who looked her in the eye and said it didn't matter how much she learned about business, she'd always be too poor to afford the necessary attire, and who'd take trash like her seriously anyway? And then there was Tobias, the worst bully of them all. Who, for three weeks straight, sought her out in between classes and shoulder-checked her so she dropped her things, scattering papers and notebooks everywhere.

And then, the day before we all woke up here, she dropped her ratty old purse in the cafeteria and small glass jars rolled across the floor. Wasn't long before the rumor that Annie had drugs spread to the principal, and she had to face the humiliation of having her locker and other possessions searched. It wasn't weed, it was other herbs and incense. She claimed it was for religious reasons, and they let her off with a warning, but the damage was done. Annie was yet again the laughingstock of the school. This time she was a drug dealer and devil worshiper. I wasn't there to see it, but I heard she left school early that day in tears.

Annie was different.

Annie was bold.

But everyone has their breaking point.

Days and weeks, a wall's worth of scratches.

Being the only two "normal" kids left in the house, Sheila and Rich bonded. Fell in love, or whatever they thought love was. We kept our distance from one another, but in a house this empty, sound carries. Night after night, I heard the primal grunts of their incessant fucking, and my resentment grew. I feared she would get pregnant and bring a kid into this nightmare. A little Sheila or a little Rich. Another asshole too many.

But that never happened. Just like we never grew older and never starved. Annie wanted to prolong this torture for eternity, or at least for the duration of her dreaming, however long that may be. Absolute stasis. No change, except for death.

The House Master bided its time. Maybe it was waiting for the right moment, or maybe it was waiting for me. After weeks of suffering their mundane banter and dirty looks, I decided I couldn't deal with being around them anymore. I broke our rule, started taking walks to get away from my companions, hoping I'd run into the thing living inside the walls. I'd let it take me, I decided. Sweet release was preferable to an eternity here. The riddle of my place here with the others had proven to be too much. The others, they'd all made Annie's life a living hell, but not me. What the hell had I done to piss her off? We didn't have any classes together. We never talked.

One night I was so caught up in my thoughts that I didn't see the trapdoor open. I gasped as gravity took hold, flailed my arms in panic, and gripped the edge at the last moment. A dark void beckoned to me from below. I wanted to fight my instincts and just let go, let myself be free of this prison, but the House Master—and Annie—had other plans. Those familiar tremors shook the world around me, and a breath later, I saw the beast looking at me from the ceiling. Pieces of Jenny's entrails decorated the hodgepodge figure, and when it reached down with one of its spindly appendages, I saw it had impaled her arm with the sharpened tip.

Jenny's hand—I recognized the purple nail polish—hovered in front of my face. I was confused, yes, but mostly elated and terrified. In the end, my instincts won out, and I took hold of the disembodied hand. The House Master lifted me to safety. Once I was back on my feet, the creature simply retracted itself back into the ceiling. I was alone again, but the odd encounter had set off a light in my mind.

It wanted me alive. *Annie* wanted me alive.

I didn't understand it then, but I wasn't about to question my luck. I'd been set aside, given a different purpose than the others, and maybe this was Annie's way of commiserating with a fellow loser and outcast. *Help me,* she was saying. *Let's get rid of them together, so they can't hurt us anymore.*

Finally, I understood. This was my way out. It had to be.

That's why I waited until Sheila was asleep. It's why I woke Rich and told him he needed to see something. "It's important," I said. "Let Sheila sleep. This won't take long."

And I led him through the first floor, toward the back of the house. I told him there was a break in the wall, that I could see light streaming through it, but of course that was a lie. There was no hole in the wall, and after we'd reached the far kitchen, I shrugged and said, "Gosh, the rooms must've changed again."

Annoyed, he said, "You weird asshole," and began his journey back to the foyer. We were halfway there when Sheila screamed, and she was mostly gone when we arrived. Just half her torso was left. That and one leg, surrounded by bits of her entrails and so much blood.

I let Rich have his moment of mourning, and while he cried over Sheila's death, I picked up the fire iron and smiled. After he'd made such a fuss about finding a way to defend ourselves, he never got a chance to put this to use.

But I did.

Exhausted and covered in Rich's blood, I ascended the stairs and made my way toward Annie's bedroom. Nothing had changed since our first discovery of her presence. She hadn't even moved, and if I hadn't known any better, I would've thought her dead. But she was still smiling, and for once, so was I.

Until I saw the card on the nightstand.

It was small, covered in pink hearts and a frilly red bow. Handmade, by the look of it. I picked it up. Holding the card sparked something in my head, a glimpse of a memory, and I resisted the lump climbing up my throat.

I opened it. The lettering was imperfect, looked like it had been drawn by a child. The kind you'd place in a kid's card box on Valentine's Day.

From: Annie

To: Adam

Will you be mine, Valentine?

Yes or No

Another image flashed in my mind. A young girl in a dirty pink dress. Unwashed hair and a bit of smeared chocolate on her cheek. Standing in front of my desk, blushing and grinning and saying, "I made this just for you."

And there's young me, already nestled at the bottom of the social pyramid, scrunching up my face like she's given me a bag of dog shit. Stupid me, saying "Ew, gross!" as I take the card and toss it on the floor. Cue laughter from our entire class. Cue little repugnant me trying to make myself as small as possible in my chair.

Cue Annie's heartbroken tears.

My whole body went numb. I dropped the card and looked at Annie's peaceful face. A single tear slid down her cheek.

The room trembled, and I'd barely uttered "No" before the House Master emerged from the wall and drew me into itself.

There was no death. No sweet release. Only the heat of my shame and stupidity.

Years have passed. I've lost count. Annie still sleeps. I'm a part of this place now, roaming its halls in an endless labyrinth of blood and memories and regret. My presence here the sweetest repair of all.

Annie's heart is a haunted house, and I am its ghost.

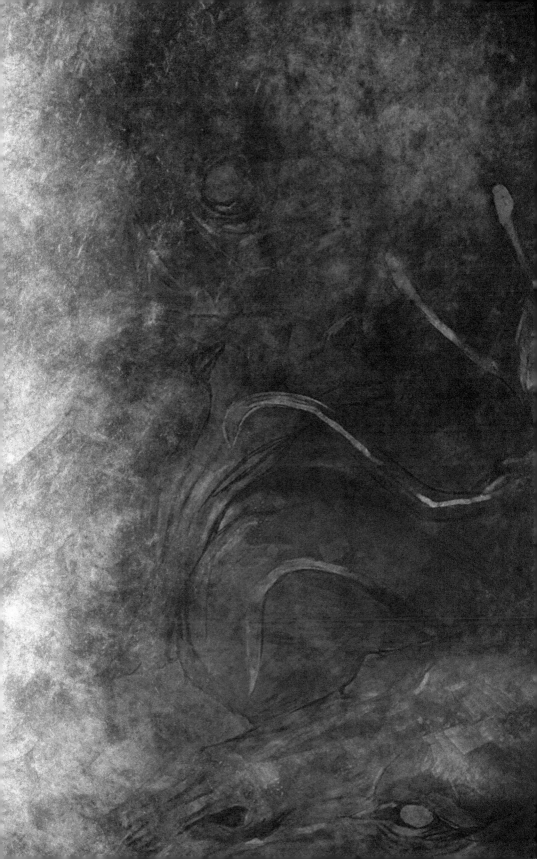

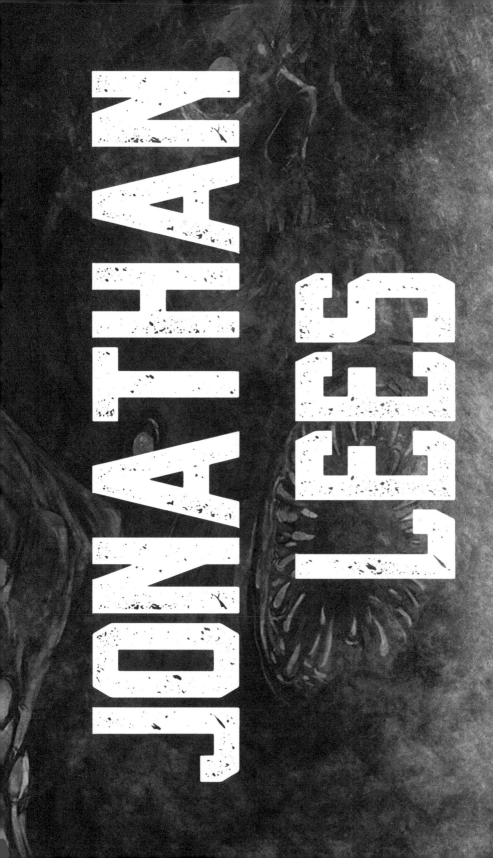

THEY ARE
STILL OUT
THERE, YOU
JUST CAN'T
SEE THEM
ANYMORE

They can never be comfortable.
They cannot escape what always surrounds them.

I can't breathe until I breach the city limits and, even then, there is a struggle.

The windows do not slide down fast enough for me to welcome the screaming autumn air. I pull over on the desolate street, kill the motor, cancelling everything until, outside, the night speaks, untranslated. A conversation between the most beautiful and hideous of creatures, all in different languages. Their actions do not concern what has been done but what must be done now.

I choose a small town upstate. One with a decent main street, a place where people can endure with the comforts of long walks and polite conversations, a community on the mend, according to the articles. One where you might explore side streets for thirty minutes without seeing another body or, better yet, hear anyone's voice.

Endless fields pass by, plagued with rusting farm silos and rows of barren lots, punctuated by houses with bruised faces and jaundiced lawns. Slouching foundations so broken they are basically leaning on each other for support. Hand-painted signs and stump posters jut out of their orifices like stuck needles telling me everything I need to know about who exists there.

Arriving as a pasty sun hides itself from the approaching night, I pull onto the stretch of road where the hotel appears with its fresh sheen of white paint reflecting in the mist, glowing. The sky is leeched of its vibrance and despite being a beacon of light on the shuttered street, the hotel is silent and the outdoor patio looks desolate. In other words, perfect.

The man at the front desk appears dead. Might as well be, considering the liveliness of his surroundings. I approach slowly and do a little finger tap dance on the poorly polished wood top. His eyes wince tight, then open quick as if escaping a dream he wanted no part of. He welcomes me with an extended yawn, taut skin rippling as if the motion might rip his jaw open. He makes sure to state that because of my arrival time, the restaurant is closed, and the fact that it's a weekday mostly everything else around is already shut down. My stomach tells him to fuck off before I can.

After checking out my room, a simple affair with grim art on the cum-stain walls, a tight, uncomfortable looking bed, and accents of natural wood furniture for appearances of a rustic vibe, I drop my bags and step out with just my wallet and keys, leaving my panicking, blinking phone on the dresser.

The town has the slick spit sheen of being recently refreshed, a crayon box of colored townhouses, renovations that preserve original details and others choosing more modern masks. A monumental effort either by determined locals bolstered by the trappings of seaside tourism, or glossed over by enterprising city dwellers looking for a place to corral their demonic offspring, creating the face it's displaying today; the surgery is apparent and the decay sticks out even more.

Most of these vacationer destinations wear the same makeup. Boutiques that sell a chaotic assortment of goods that seem to service no one. Antiques shops with prices that only the weekenders could afford. Ethnic restaurants with a twist. The twist usually being that the owners are white. Galleries with paintings by artists that had resigned their craft to replicating sun-dappled landscapes to dazzle drop-jawed tourists. I usually skip straight to the used bookstores. Humble affairs not trying to impress anyone. It calms me to scrutinize the well-loved titles, obscured by heavy creasing in the colorful spines, slowing time down enough to steady my heart rate. I pull on the door handle of a shop called *Bright Ideas* and it just shudders in my hand. Even though I can see lights illuminating the rows of books and a shadow pass beyond the register, the door remains locked. I put my hand up to the cold glass and press my face against it trying to look past my own reflection but, once my eyes adjust, the shadow is gone.

After finding one ale house remaining open for myself and a couple locals staring into their half-empty glasses, I clutch my stomach full of fried, heavily salted seafood, and with no more than a couple words exchanged with the overly chirpy waiter, I waddle back to my room and hear the insistent vibrating of the phone on the nightstand. Someone is trying to tell me something. They always are.

Once locked into a strange room, I'm never quite sure what to do. My bags are packed with books I'll barely glance at, notebooks I'll casually scribble into, layers of clothes it's still too warm for me to wear. The bed feels hard and my back whines a bit. I can feel individual bones separating, scraping together and locking up in protest. I ruminate on what I could do tomorrow to distract myself and also wonder how long I can continue to do so before everything catches up to me. Shutting my eyes and trying to force every lingering thought out of my stupid skull is a good start, instead I pick up the phone, unlock it, and go straight to the timeline where my world is exploding.

At first, the consistent pounding is just my heart hammering on overdrive after a particularly upsetting dream whose tendrils leap from wet, endless mouths.

The analog clock on the nightstand says it's 4:13 AM.

The noise and its pacing sound rhythmic and deliberate at first.

Bam. Bap. Bam. Bap. Bam. Bap.

As it gets closer, it becomes textural, sand scraping soles, and the rhythm chaotic.

Bam. Bam. Bap. Shhhhk. Bam. Bam. Bam. Bap. Shhhhk. Bam. Bap. Bap.

Was it... feet? Running? It sounded slower than that. Marching? Who the fuck?

I get up and put on my glasses and stumble over to the open window and press against the screen hard enough I feel it bow to a breaking point. From my vantage, there is only a sole lamplight shining down on the street, no movement around it but it sounds as if any moment, out of the darkness, hundreds of people will round the bend. Pulling my phone out, ignoring the cascading notifications and open the camera, slide to video and start recording when, as if they shifted direction immediately, the tremors become distant, fainter, the longer I stare at the single cone of light on the street waiting for anything to appear out of the darkness. Nothing does. I climb back into the stiff bed and realign myself in hopes to disappear again, even for a moment.

Waking late with my tongue throbbing and weighted as if a salted cod lay on it, the pummeling on the pavement is still evident only in echoes.

I stand in the scalding shower way longer than at home, using extra soap even though it smells of synthetic almond. In the pulse of the water, as it strikes my skin, in between the hissing droplets, I can hear *them* still.

Bam. Bap. Shhhhk.

I step out in a release of steam and see my phone alight again flashing in the corner of the room like a fucking dance floor. Wiping my pruned hand on the towel and grabbing the device against my better judgement, I am greeted with:

Kill urself.

Even the Lord won't save you.

Call me when you're dead.

I could have turned off the notifications, deactivated my account, deleted the app but I needed to know it was all still happening, still a conversation that is creating more characters in the chaos.

I throw the phone down and get dressed, hoping to lose myself in the tight alleyways and cluttered stores. Main Street is quiet. Most of the shops are closed due to it being a Tuesday. Another hint that it's all a facade for the visitors, not for the locals. Fine by me. I know I couldn't be up here with a weekend crowd. There's never anywhere to hide, to think.

After sitting for a light brunch in a sunny cafe that boasts only organic, locally sourced and sustainable foods, a plate of overcooked eggs arrives with damp chives and some globs of white stuff. Two bites in and my teeth hit a texture not in the ingredient list. I quickly spit into my napkin. In the gummy, masticated yolk is a wrinkled sticker that I pull apart while looking around to see if anyone has noticed. They're all locked into intense conversations and don't even so much as glance at me. Had I not done that article about false promises from the farming industry it might have been lost on me. The sticker says "Product of Kazakhstan". Organic and local, my ass. I look up from my plate and quickly avert my eyes down again after, I swear, for a second, instead of words from their yammering mouths, I only hear the tremors of something hitting the pavement.

The one knick-knack shop that is open chokes me with the heavy musk of incense coating my throat and nostrils. I gasp a little too loudly when a large pale woman, has to be over six feet tall, clops out of the back room and I immediately mew a hello.

Her face, a rugged landscape of scarred skin, each divot deep as a canyon, clashes with the cavalcade of glazed grins painted on ceramic figurines. She runs her withering hands over cases of jewelry that hadn't graced a limb in decades as I approach through the racks of hand-me-down garments that could have costumed a down-and-out cabaret singer.

She asks if she can help me find something out of the ordinary. I knew there was nothing in here for me, but out of politeness, I continue to peek around the stuffed shelves and state that I am just browsing. She keeps prodding and I deflect every coo and caw with a yup or a no ma'am. The type of woman who would continue a conversation even if you were convulsing.

Running my fingers along the tarnished leather of a beaten satchel, over the rusted zippers, and tracing the claw marks on its tanned hide, I feel the scars of its past life still apparent.

I stare into the glass eyes of a doll and wait for it to start talking.

The oak desks, stained glass lamps, and stuffed animal heads with lightless eyes give little room to move so I start thumbing through racks of vintage magazines but there's nothing of interest, just old powder puff gossip confessionals and soap opera digests, the scent releasing from each of the yellowed pages instantly calms me down, calmer still now that the giant retreats to the back, her boots clomping as heavy as her sighs. About to give up, my stomach in protest from the lack of any nourishment, I notice something else. An old book with its withered mouth cracked open. Within are five glass vials and miniature drawers where pages should be. On the inside cover is an illustration of two skeletons joining hands over a disembodied skull and below in script:

STATUT UM EST
HOMINIBUS
SEMEL MORI

Pulling open the first drawer with handwritten lettering: *Teufelsschlinge*, I extract a thin leaflet with vivid, wavy text set in a cover of flames shouting *GO TO HELL*.

I feel flushed, the proclamation is a little too close to the messages still accruing on my timeline.

The leaves of paper brittle and cracking, feeling like they will disintegrate if I flip through any faster. There are more pamphlets in each compartment:

Tricked by the Devil!

Perverts Among Us!

Are Your Children Next?!

Can You Escape the Burning Hell?

These palm-sized illustrated booklets I recognize instantly from my research on the history of lurid tracts for my article on "Coercion and Christianity". Each boldly exclaims that its pages contain the answers we seek, minuscule manifestos on how to correct our path. I can't help thinking of all the effort it takes to design and distribute these flip books only to end up forgotten in places like this, when now, people can just log in to their portal of choice letting loose any opinions, allowing the madness of crowds to sweep their message further than ever before, replicating it long enough it presents as fact. I look around to make sure the woman is still gone, shoving the false volume deeper into the shadows of the shelves, pushing random objects up against it and blocking it with a stack of magazines.

For some reason I get the chills when the bell above the door tinkles, announcing my exit.

After deciding to leave the main drag and start down one of the side streets, I immediately begin to notice aberrations. Unadorned buildings with uneven slats of wood silencing the mouths of houses, shuttered community buildings with wheat-paste art shouting RESIST, a tattered, hand-painted poster stating GET OFF OUR NECKS lay in dead grass amidst broken bottles. The color bleeds out of the woodwork the further away from Main until I come upon a park and stare at three men sleeping on stained mattresses under old vinyl shopping bags ripped open and tied down to create makeshift tents. All just a couple blocks from where a roasted duck plate costs fifty bucks. I watch one of the men suck his thumb and, for a second, the creases on his face disappear, I see the child he once was and I wonder how life stepped on him to the point that he could never get back up.

My appetite gone, I head back to the hotel and push my head into the scratchy pillow forcing my eyes to close, turning toward the incessant lights brightening the face of my phone, praying I have the resolve to not succumb to it.

The pitch of cicadas rubbing their wings have the anxiety of a city street, reaching deafening proportions, so it is within the lull of that sound that wakes me. A sudden interruption, a quiet, to make room for something approaching. The pulse of something hitting solid ground. Boots? At first in conjunction, rhythm, then faster and sporadic. Chaotic.

Bum. Bum. Bum. Ba.Dum.Bum.

Bum. Bum. Bum. Ba.Dum.Bum.

Bum. Bum. Bum. Ba.Dum.Bum.

I pull the covers over my head as everything in the room shudders. Outside, a madness of limbs slap the earth. Even though I am on the second floor, I predict a dizzying blur of faces will pass my window, some stopping to glare at me before being swept back into the watercolors of extreme speed. They will overtake the hotel and the door to my room will bulge before bursting open and they will flood this small space until I am smothered with arms, legs, and mouths. That image keeps me pressed in bed, each muscle stitched to the fabric, for fear they could hear even the slightest shift of my skin. One shout, curse, or scream to make this seem part of the natural world never comes, only a deafening swell, a sound louder than no other, shaking every limp board and loose drawer, and then it all fades out until the cicadas get the nerve to sing once again.

I walk to the window, rubbing my swollen eyes, sore from hours spent scrolling through the blinding blur of my timeline. On the faded crosswalk below, in the pool of light, someone crouches, staring at me.

What. The. Fuck?

I shiver and squint.

It is unmoving with its head turned up towards me but there is no face left.

My chest tightens.

Its form is corrupted. The body is in puzzling order, pushed into positions I believe would only be possible if it had fallen twenty stories onto the pavement.

What am I looking at?

A succession of images, in impossible close-ups, a bone shard puncturing reddening denim, a black t-shirt ripped open, a hole of pale skin mottled with a spray of blood, and its face is...

I vomit immediately, intensely, ejecting a viscous, pink liquid.

...its face is caved in from the brow to cheek but so distorted that I don't recognize it at first. It is the man I witnessed sleeping in the park not only hours before, now discarded in the most disrespectful fashion.

What transpired from the time I passed out last night I will never know. When I wake, there is no body outside. Not even a stain. Erased. A long-haired couple in suede hats, alpaca throws, and leather pants let their dog piss where the man's body lay hours before.

I am now in *A Slice of Heaven* trying to force a square of "Nonna's" pizza into my mouth but the sauce tastes like tomato-flavored water and the cheese gristles are the texture of tough grubs of skin.

And I just keep seeing his face, one eye opens wide, the stomping sounding more like the rhythm of drums. I picture their phantom boots, scuffed leather scraping his jawbone, rubber soles punching his forehead.

At the counter, a floral-frocked woman, a castaway from a jam band's tour bus, is speaking softly to the squat man whose mustache jumps around his lips at the end of each word.

The whole room smells of something burning.

I'm pretty sure the woman says: *He deserved it.*

I think the mustache says something to the effect of: *You can't feed a man who wants to starve.*

As I walk out the door, a VOTE for MAYOR poster hangs above the frame. It's outdated. I almost don't recognize him with the foolish grin and bright eyes. The last time I saw this smile didn't exist and his eyes no longer contained any light.

My stomach tumbles.

Bright Ideas is open today, filled with distractions to push the image of the crushed man away from the dark space it currently occupies where his stuck eyes pop open.

The proprietor is conducting an inventory of sodden boxes filled with vintage romance and thriller paperbacks. I tell him there's nothing specific I want and plan on losing myself in the shelves and this brings light to his eyes. Or is he winking at me?

The shop is empty of people yet stuffed with their remnants and a semblance of peace sets in as I glance at familiar friends, authors who I have spent long evenings with, their words just waiting for a new set of eyes. I know people like these writers still exist out there, I just never seem lucky enough to encounter them, instead always forced to face the desperate many who use words to get what they want or what they need to hear and for no other reason.

The silence is respectful, reverential. Each shelf speaks my language, begs for my attention, yet as I lurk about the entire store and still can't locate any section on politics or social sciences. Religion and history are noticeably absent. Psychology or sociology as well. Odd for a shop named Bright Ideas that the only ones contained within it would be fiction.

I'm about to ask the clerk for help when I notice he's watching me from the register. His arm is quivering from whatever his hand is doing below the counter.

I turn and walk up a flight of creaky steps and recoil as the store's cat hisses at me and darts into the shadows of a coffin-shaped shelf on the far end of the attic that is bursting with disorder. That intrigues me enough to investigate the unique nook, even knowing my ankles will be exposed to the claws beneath it.

After pushing aside tall books on large-game hunting, out-of-date almanacs and fat volumes of illustrated war vehicles, my fingers brush against a stuck panel lodged open just enough that a slim volume peeks through. It is a history of queer iconography, and behind it, deeper into the clandestine space, a dusty encyclopedia of pagan symbols, protest manifestos, and a couple diaries from radical scientists. Sweat springs from my fingers, clinging to the laminate covers as I swipe the remainders aside to see what else is obscured within, while the beast beneath me begins to yowl.

Behind every smile that greets me, I see phantom hands pulling the folds of flesh of their lips and cheeks back.

Behind every black pupil, imperceptible spiders spin webs.

Each shop window reflects a ghost of my own image, one with a panicked face, and behind the mirrored image of my own eyes there is always someone watching. The doors stay shut, the locks bolted, the conversations have ceased.

"You look familiar."

The voice is behind me is shocking and unwelcome. I turn and the woman approaching me looks different than most I've encountered here. There's less artifice to her appearance. Her feet are squeezing out of shoes two sizes too small. The clothes are just enough to cover what's underneath and nothing more. Her hands have swollen, reddened knuckles with no adornments. Her face wears her intention as makeup, painted thick with downturned brows and a sunken scowl.

"Yes, I know who you are," she states.

I turn and walk faster. "You must have me confused with someone else."

"*That* voice. I know that *voice.*"

Shutting my eyes and clamping my lips tight, I begin humming loudly to drown her out though I can still hear some of the sharper words stab through.

I freeze, brain buzzing in sync with the phone in my pocket, I turn, and notice the light is bleeding out around me. The shadows are taking over.

Bum. Bum. Bum.

"It is *you*."

"It isn't," I insist.

I can hear her running and then she's in front of me again waving her phone as if her arm were on fire.

"Who do you think you are?" she shouts.

A couple stares at us from across the street, their bodies cut in half by a tight line of hedges. I look up to the church and notice a figure peering from the belfry.

Bam. Bap. Bam.

"Get away from me," I try and wave her off but she moves quicker than I assume, any direction I turn she is there, her mouth wide open and what comes out is guttural, illogical, thick with phlegm and venom.

I notice more silhouettes in windows, across lawns.

Bam. Bam. Bap. Shhhhk.

The pavement begins to shake and the tree branches are panicking, frantic as my knees.

She blocks me again and rushes forward, her arms outstretched, her mouth obscene, her hands slamming against my chest, gripping, squeezing. I scream but I have no voice.

The bag of books drops and spills on the pavement, their spines crack, bodies splayed open to reveal nothing but blank pages.

Beating, battering, bashing, the uproar deafens and fills the streets until it is everywhere.

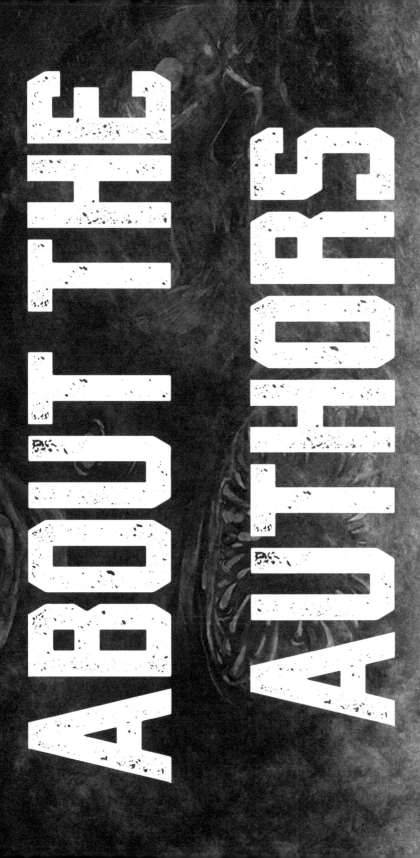

ABOUT THE AUTHORS

IN ORDER OF APPEARANCE

JOSH RUBEN is an award-winning actor, writer, and director whose debut feature film *Scare Me* premiered at the 2020 Sundance Film Festival. His second feature film, the horror comedy *Werewolves Within*, was an official selection of the 2021 Tribeca Film Festival and is now available on-demand. One of the founding members of CollegeHumor's "Originals" team, Josh has directed and/or starred in thousands of shorts, amassing views well into the billions. He has also directed sketches for *The Late Late Show*, episodes of Tru TV's *Adam Ruins Everything*, as well as a myriad of commercials for clients from Geico to Lucky Charms.

ANNIE NEUGEBAUER is a novelist, blogger, nationally award-winning poet, and two-time Bram Stoker Award-nominated short story author with work appearing in more than a hundred publications, including *Cemetery Dance*, *Apex*, *Black Static*, and *Year's Best Hardcore Horror* volumes 3, 4, and 5. She's a columnist and writing instructor for LitReactor. She's represented by Alec Shane of Writers House. You can visit her at www.AnnieNeugebauer.com.

SARAH READ's stories can be found in various places, including Ellen Datlow's Best Horror of the Year vols 10 and 12. Her collection *Out of Water* is available from Trepidatio Publishing, as is her debut novel *The Bone*

Weaver's Orchard, both nominated for the Bram Stoker, This is Horror, and Ladies of Horror Fiction Awards. *Orchard* won the Stoker and the This Is Horror Award, and is available in Spanish as *El Jardin del Tallador de Huesos*, published by Dilatando Mentes, where it was nominated for the Guillermo de Baskerville Award. You can find her @inkwellmonster or at www. inkwellmonster.wordpress.com.

HAILEY PIPER is the author of *The Worm and His Kings*, *Queen of Teeth*, *Unfortunate Elements of My Anatomy*, and *Benny Rose the Cannibal King*. She is an active member of the Horror Writers Association, with over seventy short stories appearing in Vastarien, Pseudopod, Daily Science Fiction, Cast of Wonders, Dark Matter Magazine, Flash Fiction Online, and other publications. She lives with her wife in Maryland, where their paranormal research is classified. Find Hailey at www.haileypiper.com or on Twitter via @HaileyPiperSays.

ZOJE STAGE is the *USA Today* and internationally bestselling author of *Baby Teeth, Wonderland,* and *Getaway*. A former filmmaker with a penchant for the dark and suspenseful, she lives in Pittsburgh.

ANDY DAVIDSON is the Bram Stoker Award nominated author of *In the Valley of the Sun* and *The Boatman's Daughter*. *The Boatman's Daughter* was listed among NPR's Best Books of 2020, the New York Public Library's Best Adult Books of the Year, and *Library Journal*'s Best Horror of 2020. Born and raised in Arkansas, Andy makes his home in Georgia with his wife and a bunch of cats.

JOHN F.D. TAFF is a multiple Bram Stoker Award®-nominated author with more than 30 years in the horror genre, 125-plus short stories and five novels in print. Ain't It Cool News called his novel *The Bell Witch* "A compelling and frightening read." Jack Ketchum called his novella collection, *The End in All Beginnings*, "one of the best novella collections I've read," and it was a finalist for a Stoker Award in 2014. A short story from his latest collection *Little Black Spots*, "A Winter's Tale," was a finalist for a Stoker in 2019. His serial novel *The Fearing* released in 2019 to critical and reader acclaim. Robert R. McCammon called it "A powerful and epic trip into the land of feardom!" Look for more of his work in anthologies such as *Dark Stars, Gutted: Beautiful Horror Stories, Shadows Over Main Street 2* and *Behold: Oddities, Curiosities and Undefinable Wonders.* Taff lives in the wilds of Illinois with two pugs, one cat and one long-suffering wife.

LEE MURRAY is a multi-award-winning writer and editor of science fiction, fantasy, and horror from Aotearoa-New Zealand. Winner of the Sir Julius Vogel, Australian Shadows, and Shirley Jackson Awards, Lee is a four-time Bram Stoker Award® winner. Read more at https://www.leemurray.info/.

JOSH MALERMAN is a New York Times bestselling, Bram Stoker Award-winning author and one of two singer-songwriters for the rock band The High Strung. His debut novel Bird Box is the inspiration for the hit Netflix film of the same name. His other books include Unbury Carol, Inspection, Pearl, and Goblin. He lives in Michigan with his fiancé, the artist/musician Allison Laako.

SARA TANTLINGER is the author of the Bram Stoker Award-winning *The Devil's Dreamland: Poetry Inspired by H.H. Holmes,* and the Stoker-nominated works *To Be Devoured, Cradleland of Parasites,* and *Not All Monsters.* Along with being a mentor for the HWA Mentorship Program, she is also a co-organizer for the HWA Pittsburgh Chapter. She embraces all things macabre and can be found lurking in graveyards or on Twitter @SaraTantlinger, at saratantlinger.com and on Instagram @inkychaotics

JO KAPLAN is a Los Angeles based writer also known as Joanna Parypinski. She is the author of the novels *It Will Just Be Us* and *When the Night Bells Ring.* Her work has appeared in Fireside Quarterly, Black Static, Nightmare

Magazine, Vastarien, *Haunted Nights* edited by Ellen Datlow and Lisa Morton, and Bram Stoker Award nominated anthology *Miscreations: Gods, Monstrosities & Other Horrors*. She teaches English and creative writing at Glendale Community College.

CYNTHIA PELAYO is a two-time Bram Stoker Award nominated poet and author. Her modern day horror retelling of the Pied Piper fairy tale, *Children of Chicago*, is an International Latino Book Award winner for Best Mystery. She lives in Chicago with her family.

RICHARD THOMAS is the award-winning author of eight books— *Disintegration* and *Breaker* (Penguin Random House Alibi), *Transubstantiate, Herniated Roots, Staring Into the Abyss, Tribulations, Spontaneous Human Combustion* (Turner Publishing), and *The Soul Standard* (Dzanc Books). He has been nominated for the Bram Stoker, Shirley Jackson, Thriller, and Audie awards. His over 165 stories in print include *The Best Horror of the Year* (Volume Eleven), *Behold!: Oddities, Curiosities and Undefinable Wonders* (Bram Stoker winner), *Cemetery Dance* (twice), *PANK, storySouth, Gargoyle, Weird Fiction Review, Shallow Creek, The Seven Deadliest, Gutted: Beautiful Horror Stories, Qualia Nous, Chiral Mad* (numbers 2-4), *PRISMS,* and *Shivers VI*. Visit www.whatdoesnotkillme.com for more information.

GABINO IGLESIAS is a writer, professor, book reviewer, editor, and translator living in Austin, TX. He is the author of *Zero Saints* and *Coyote Songs* and the editor of *Both Sides*. His work has been translated into five languages, optioned for film, nominated to the Bram Stoker Award and the Locus Award and won the Wonderland Book Award for Best Novel in 2019. His reviews appear regularly in places like *NPR*, the *Los Angeles Review of Books*, the *San Francisco Chronicle, Vol. 1 Brooklyn, Criminal Element, Mystery Tribune*, and other venues. He's been a juror for the Shirley Jackson Awards twice, the Newfound Prose Prize, the Splatterpunk Awards, and *PANK Magazine's* Big Book Contest. He teaches creative writing at SNHU's online MFA program and runs a series of low-cost writing workshops.

ALAN BAXTER is a British-Australian multi-award-winning author of horror, supernatural thrillers, and dark fantasy. He's also a martial arts expert, a whisky-soaked swear monkey, and dog lover. He creates dark, weird stories among dairy paddocks on the beautiful south coast of NSW, Australia, where he lives with his wife, son, hound and other creatures. The author of more than twenty books including novels, novellas, and three short story collections (so far) you can find him online at www.alanbaxter.com.au or find him on Twitter @AlanBaxter and Facebook. Feel free to tell him what you think. About anything.

TODD KEISLING is a writer and designer of the horrific and strange. His books include *Scanlines, The Final Reconciliation, The Monochrome Trilogy,* and *Devil's Creek,* a 2020 Bram Stoker Award finalist for Superior Achievement in a Novel. In 2021, he was the recipient of This Is Horror's Award for Cover Art of the Year for his cover design of *Arterial Bloom.* A former Kentucky resident, he now lives somewhere in the wilds of Pennsylvania with his wife, son, and quartet of unruly cats. Share his dread online at www.toddkeisling.com or Twitter: @todd_keisling.

JONATHAN LEES originally hails from a shuttered mill town in New England and now can often be spotted lurking in the alleys of New York or within the barrens of New Jersey. In addition to fifteen years of creating strategies and video series for outlets ranging from *Complex Media* to *TIDAL,* he has also spent decades championing independent filmmakers through his work with the *New York Underground Film Festival, Anthology Film Archives* and more. He has been writing for as long as he can remember and, now, has finally found the guts to finish what he started. His first published story, "The Ritual Remains," debuted in the NECON anthology, *Now I Lay Me Down To Sleep* and he is looking forward to seeing you in the dark.

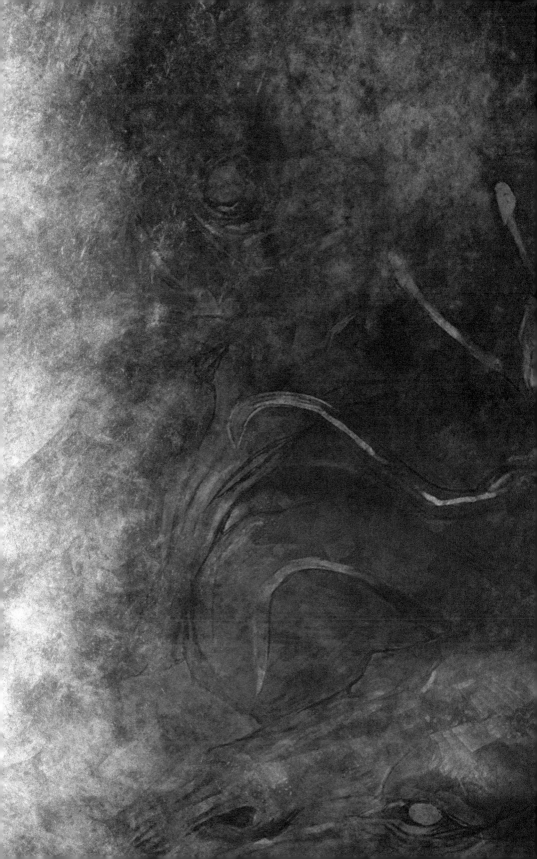

ABOUT THE

EDITOR

DOUG MURANO is the Bram Stoker Award-winning, Shirley Jackson Award-nominated editor of a number of critically-acclaimed anthologies, including *Gutted: Beautiful Horror Stories* (with D. Alexander Ward), *Behold! Oddities, Curiosities & Undefinable Wonders*, and *Miscreations: Gods, Monstrosities & Other Horrors* (with Michael Bailey). He lives somewhere on the Great Plains of South Dakota with his wife and their four children.

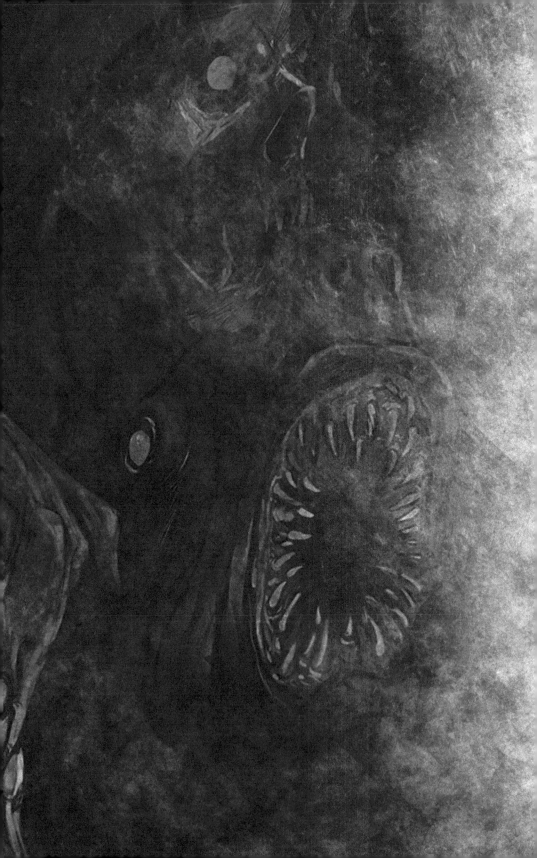

CPSIA information can be obtained
at www.ICGtesting.com
Printed in the USA
LVHW071214240722
724267LV00010B/337